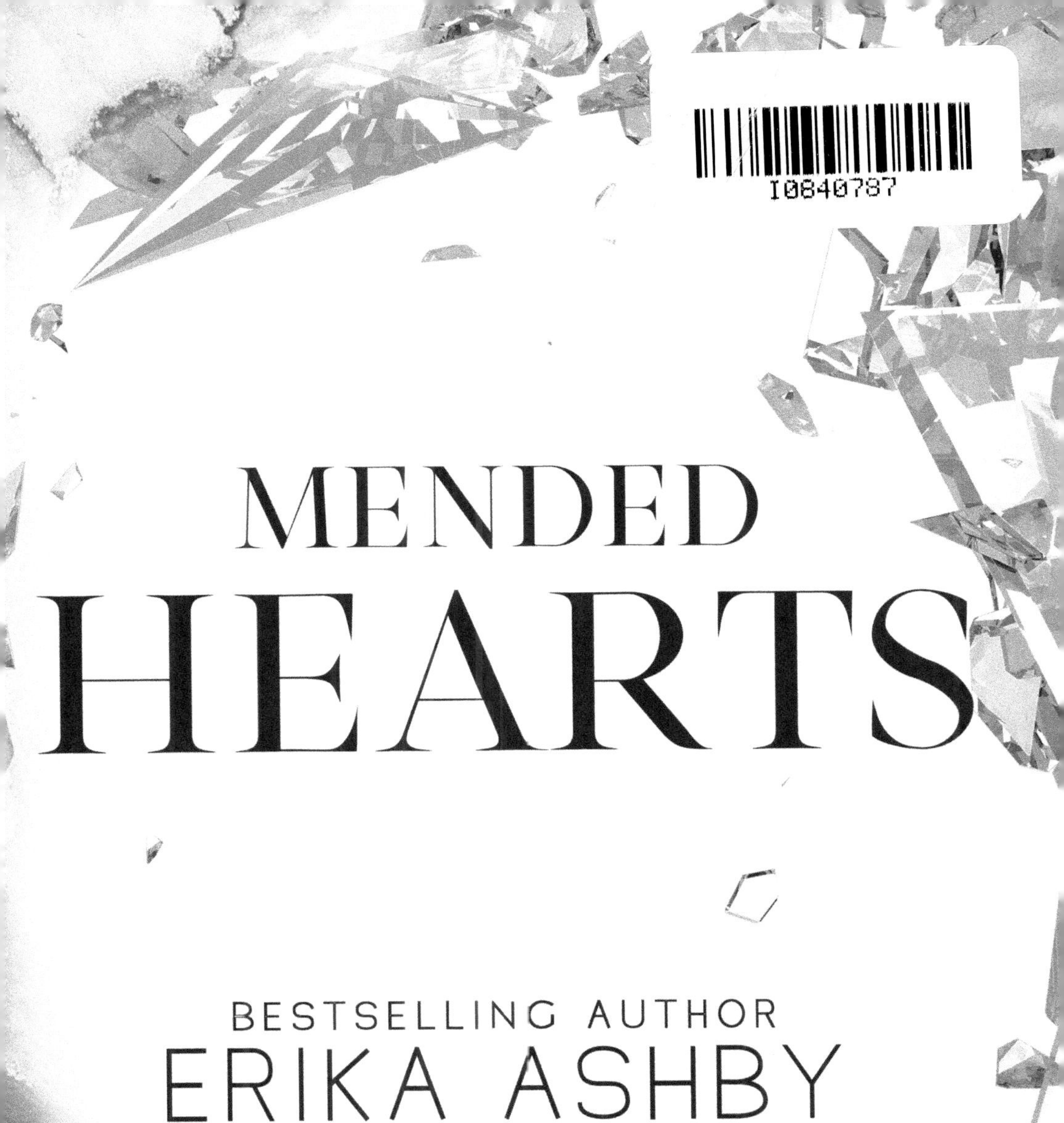

MENDED HEARTS

BESTSELLING AUTHOR

ERIKA ASHBY

Mended Hearts
Broken & Mended Series, Book 2
Copyright © 2024 Erika Ashby
Stock Image from Adobe Stock
Cover Design by Sommer Stein at Perfect Pear Creative Covers
Interior Formatting by Devin McCain at Studio 5 Twenty-Five
Developmental Editing by Megan Hand at Story Girl Editing
Copy/Line Editing & Proofreading by Emily Lawrence at Lawrence Editing
ISBN: 979-8-9902492-2-6 All rights reserved.

Foreword

A Note From Erika:

Nine years ago, I wrote Brokenness, a Broken Wings companion novel. If you read it, I'm sorry. It was a hot mess.

Nine years later, I gutted it, retitled it and recovered it. Some might say Mended Hearts is a completely new book.

So, if you read Brokenness, I hope you're willing to read Mended Hearts. I promise you I gave the characters the story they deserved this time around.

And, as always, thank you for giving me and my books a chance.

"And in the end, we were all just humans...drunk on the idea that love, only love, could heal our brokenness."
F. Scott Fitzgerald

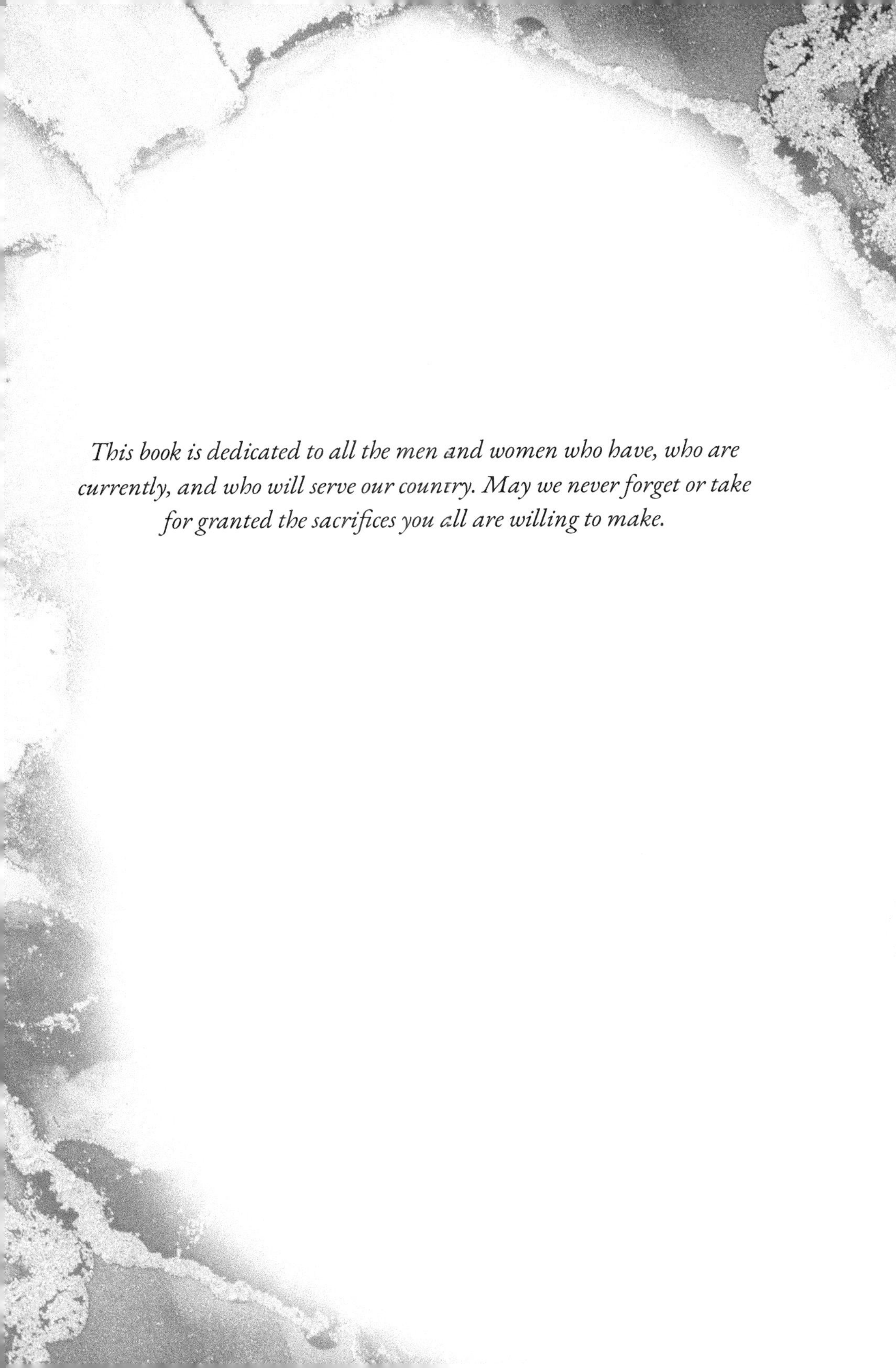

This book is dedicated to all the men and women who have, who are currently, and who will serve our country. May we never forget or take for granted the sacrifices you all are willing to make.

There are brief encounters of war, PTSD, domestic violence, and attempted suicide.
If you or someone you know suffers from any or all of these, please reach out to the resources below:

<u>Suicide Prevention</u>
Call or Text 988 - https://988lifeline.org/

<u>PTSD</u>
Call 866-903-3787 - https://mentalhealthhotline.org/ptsd-hotline/

Call 866-955-4035 https://veterans.warriorsheart.com/

Call 800-273-8255 https://www.woundedwarriorproject.org/

<u>Domestic Violence</u>
Call 800-799-SAFE (7233) or Text START to 88788
https://www.thehotline.org/

Prologue

DUSTIN

May 2014

It's been a long time since I've had a reason to wear anything other than fatigues. I think my brother being honored with an award tonight is just the right reason to do so. Being transferred to a different unit before getting sent back overseas for another tour gives me a very small window of opportunity to make this surprise happen. Soooo small that my mother couldn't grasp the idea of why I needed her to bring my dress suit here instead of me flying home first and making the five-hour car ride with them.

Because that sounds delightful. The thought alone causes me to shudder.

I've been avoiding my hometown like the plague since I left thirteen years ago. I've also been avoiding my parents and anyone else who reminds me of that godforsaken town. Including Dax—the one person I regret pushing away. But the truth is, if I could go back in time and redirect my trajectory, I wouldn't. My distance is safer for the few people I care for. Truth be told, I shut my heart off a long time ago… because it's safer for me that way. Self-preservation at its finest.

Droplets of water cascade down my body as I stand at the counter, examining my face in the mirror as I contemplate shaving off the scruff. My better judgment gets the best of me, and I decide to keep the light stubble shading my face. No need to pretty myself up just to get dumped in a sandy land far, far away in a few days. A knock on the hotel door causes my body to tense. My feet instantly feel heavy with dread. I groan, walking toward the door. I already regret being here. The idea to sneak out the window crosses my mind, but I remind myself I'm doing this for Dax…and I'm on the third floor. I let out an exasperated breath that borderlines a growl and grab for the handle. The door swings open and I tighten my jaw as my mother barrels in with zero care for one's personal space. She tosses my freshly pressed dress suit to the side and misses the bed, stretching her arms wide for a hug.

"My suit." I narrow my eyes and snap, pivoting away from her embrace. I know she has no regard for the Army and loathes that I joined it, but damn, a little respect would be nice. I walk over to the open closet and drape the hook of the hanger over the top so my suit rests flush with the door. She begins to stammer as if she can't collect the right words to form her thoughts, and I glance back toward her. My stomach drops with regret, and I'm reminded why I keep my feelings turned to nonexistent. All of a sudden, I'm a teenager again, wanting to console my mother. But I don't. Thirteen years of residual anger have a way of keeping one callous.

"So many scars," she whispers, staring at me with a mix of horror and sadness. I grasp where my towel connects around my waist, wishing I had thrown a shirt on. I didn't sign up for a pity party.

"It's not that bad, Ma," I admit, knowing she can't see the biggest scar of all—the one she had a part in.

She glances up with a hint of a smile. "You haven't called me Ma in so long." And just like that, all traces of a smile fade, covered with sadness. Enough of this jog down memory lane. I need to get ready and flip her mood around. I refuse to show up to Dax's award ceremony with this sour puss in tow.

I close the distance between us and grasp her shoulder, causing her to look up at me. "Remember why we're here." I slightly tighten my grip to reassure her and drive my point in simultaneously.

"Dax."

"Yes, Dax," I repeat. "Now let me get dressed." I offer a weak smile before placing a quick kiss on her forehead. I'm not above offering a sacrifice every now and again.

She regains her composure—as if nothing happened—just like she has all my life, and says, "I'll go wait in the car with your dad."

I lock the door behind her for safe measure and walk to the closet, then pull the plastic covering my suit. I take in the deep blue jacket and all its adornments that don't mean squat to me. I don't do what I do for badges or for show. I quit caring about participation awards after the last one I got my senior year in high school. But damn if I don't take pride in it or give respect to the other men and women proudly wearing them.

A knock at the door shakes me out of my stupor, and I cautiously walk over and peek out the peephole. Flipping the lock, I open the door halfway.

"Your mother forgot to bring up your shoes." My dad offers, holding my shoes out. "I even looked up how to shine them for you." He lets out a chuckle, brushing his hand through his hair, and I take in how weathered he looks.

In what feels like forever, I genuinely smile. "Thanks, Dad," I say, inspecting my pristine black dress shoes. Impressed is an understatement.

A hand clamps on my bare shoulder and my smile falters as I peek up, barely meeting my dad's gaze. A gaze that feels so distant with mere inches between us. A lump forms in my throat, and I slowly push it down, trying not to make it visible. I'm responsible for the distance.

"It's good to see you, son." My dad nods, holding my view. His fingers curl into my shoulder in the same manner mine had just done to my mom, and I nod back in agreement and understanding.

THE DRIVE STARTS abnormally quiet. So quiet I wish Dax were riding back here with me like when we were younger. There's no way the ride would be silent if he were with us. I'm not sure if that word exists in his vocabulary. My mom finally starts talking, my dad nods, and I stare out my window. Just like old times. I keep my fly-on-the-wall stance and listen. Okay, well, listened. Once she began complaining about my brother's current situation and seeming to insinuate Lincoln's widow is holding him back from the life he's destined to live, I began tuning her out.

After all these years, she still hasn't changed. *News flash, Ma... I have.*

Ten minutes later, we pull in, and I thank God. Then take it back, knowing there's nothing to thank him for. He left me high and dry when I needed him the most. Instead, I thank myself for not losing my shit on my mom during the short car ride here. Stepping out of the car, I breathe out a sigh of relief as if I were holding my breath the entire drive. I'm used to the heat, but right now, I'm feeling overheated. I rub the back of my neck, checking for sweat, relieved when my hand returns dry.

Nerves, it must be nerves. But why? To see my brother? The one I walked out on and never turned back even for a second glance? Yeah, that one. And yes, definitely nerves.

"Shit," I mumble, rolling my shoulders back, trying to gain my composure—something I typically never lose. I glance over and catch my father's eyes watching me intently. I see the worry in his brow, but thankfully, he doesn't say anything. It's a little too late for those kinds of talks. Thirteen years, to be exact. I bend over, double-checking my shoelaces, and grab the penny partially sticking out from under the car. It's on heads.

We begin walking across the parking lot, and I fall behind, following my parents. I don't want to lead, nor do I want to present a united front. Through the years, my mom has been good at keeping me informed about Dax, something I've always appreciated. Despite what she may believe, I've read all the letters she's sent me. There have even been times I've sat down to write a reply, but the words remained tethered, never leaving the tip of my pen.

Five steps up, and we're walking through the double doors. There are more people here than I was expecting, but I can't take my eyes off the huge fountain directly in front of us. I walk to it, leaving my parents at the registration table while I examine the foliage-covered stone. A lone quarter in the middle of the water beckons me.

"Why not," I mutter, reaching in my pocket for the penny I just found, and flip it in.

"Dustin, this is not a wishing well," my mom chastises as she sidles up next to me.

I shrug. "I beg to differ. There was already a coin in it." I point.

I can sense her eyes rolling. Sometimes I wonder how hers haven't completely flipped upside down from the number of times I caused that action growing up.

"Come on." She tugs my arm. "Your brother is down here."

Again, I fall behind, following. As we approach, Dax's back is to us, and he's laughing with others around him. I stop short and use the time to take in my baby brother, who is far from a baby now. Seeing him in his dress suit, same as mine, ignites a sense of pride within me. I want to run up and tackle him. Hell, run up and give him an old-fashioned bear hug. But he has to be a head taller than me now. I'm the one who'd be shaken around like a rag doll, not him.

I patiently stand and wait. I shove my hand in my pocket and rub the back of my neck. Nerves are still rampant, now accompanied by excitement, and the patience I was trying to channel has dissipated.

Okay, okay, I've waited long enough. We all know I'm who he really wants to see but will never be expecting to. That thought has the taste of regret and guilt all over it.

"Ahem." I clear my throat and take a step closer. Dax's eyes shift to mine, and I swear I see every emotion pass through them. The same emotions I feel but keep tightly hidden. He shakes his head, shaking the shock away. His pretty boy smile illuminates his face, and I can't contain the one spreading across mine.

Commence bear hug. Dax's long legs and quick strides have him hugging me in no time. Out of reflex, my body stiffens. Embracing is foreign to me, but Dax's embrace tightens, and the reserve I've managed to keep up falters. This is my brother. My brother who could've died. The thought alone constricts my airways. I swallow hard, pushing the emotion threatening my eyes back down with it. I'm not going to think about the 'could haves.'

"Man, you've sure grown up." I keep a hand on his shoulder, fully taking him in, seeing what all has changed. His facial features are sharper, more defined. Bright hazel eyes still filled with wonder and dark golden hair, truly embodying the Golden Boy term of endearment. No more towhead. He's grown and it makes me want to pinch his cheek and ruffle his hair. But I'd have to reach up to do that.

"Take a picture. It lasts longer." Dax snickers and I laugh at him using one of his key phrases from our childhood. "But on a serious note," he starts, placing his hands on my shoulders, almost like he's fusing me to the ground to keep me from taking off again. "You don't know how much you being here means to me." He looks away, pausing. "It means more to me than this award." His bottom lip quivers slightly, and I nod in agreement.

"I'm being reassigned and didn't plan on making any pit stops," I admit. "But when Mom got ahold of me and told me about this award..." I look away for a moment, trying to hide the emotion within. "I couldn't miss it."

He smiles. "I love you, too."

"I'm really sorry about Lincoln. I know how close you both were." I hate that I couldn't be here for him during that time. He nods, accepting the condolence.

"I have someone I need to introduce you to." Dax turns around and pulls a woman to his side when he turns back. "This is Lynsie Fox." And now, the conversation my mother was having with herself on the car ride makes sense.

"It's nice to meet you, Dustin." She smiles, sticking her hand out to shake mine.

I quickly glance at my brother for answers but know this isn't the time or place I'll get any. I close my hand around hers and give her a genuine smile. "It's nice to meet you too, Lynsie."

With Lynsie attached to his side, I catch up with my brother for a moment. I mainly stand and listen to them as I soak this all in. The distraction is something I've needed. I've denied myself the interactions and communication with those who know me best; those who love me. I like to say I didn't choose the life of solitude, it chose me, but I'm beginning to second-guess that idea.

People start to make their way into the room where the ceremony is being held, and we slowly meander in that direction.

"Lynsie," I hear coming our way, causing Dax and Lynsie to swing around. They chat with the new posse member, and I stand, deep in thought. So many thoughts. I look around, giving curt smiles and nods as people walk by, feeling awkward standing here.

"You look gorgeous, girl." I hear who I presume to be Lynsie's friend say and something about the voice feels familiar. I pull my gaze back, right in time for Lynsie and Dax to slightly part from one another, revealing who's on the other side.

I stop in my tracks, and my body instantly tenses. The idea that I've died and gone to heaven truly crosses my mind, but I'm snapped back to reality. Dax turns my way, eyeing me. I close my eyes tight and shake my head. I feel like I'm seeing a mirage—something I want to be real but isn't. I mean, she can't be. There's no way, after so long, we'd finally cross paths.

Nope, not a ghost or a figment of my imagination. I run my hand through my hair, resting it at the crook of my neck. It's ridiculously hot, and the nerves I felt earlier are child's play compared to the ones flowing through me now. She hasn't seen me yet, and I contemplate making a run for it. It's been thirteen years, and I feel as lost as I did when I realized she was gone. How is that possible?

I can see the questions in Dax's eyes, much like the ones I have for him, but her attention is now on him. I listen and watch intently.

"Look at you, Dax. You sure clean up nice." She playfully smacks his cheek. Happiness and jealousy envelop me at once. I clinch my fists together, unsure of what to do with them or these feelings.

"You don't look so bad yourself, Echo," Dax replies, glancing back my way.

With a wide smile, she starts to reply, but then her eyes dart past Dax, falling straight on me, and her smile vanishes. My shoulders slightly fall, hating that I caused it. We stare at each other in silence for what feels like forever—a lifetime. I don't want it to ever end.

"Dustin," Echo whispers with a hint of disbelief as if she's now the one seeing a ghost. And I've never wanted to equally die and live in the same breath as I do right now.

I unclench my fists, roll my shoulders back, and stare, unable to take my eyes off her. My God, she's even more beautiful than I remember. And my memory is impeccable. How do you forget every single feature of someone when you dream of them every night of your life? You don't, and I haven't. I shove one hand in my pocket and run the other over my face and inwardly curse. I should have shaved. She looks back and forth between Dax and me, piecing it together.

"So y'all are brothers." It comes out as more of a statement than a question as her voice slightly cracks.

I nod. He nods. We both nod.

"How do you and Dustin know each other?" Lynsie asks, watching Echo carefully. Uncertainty fills her expression like a sucker punch. She looks at the ground and begins fidgeting with her hands. Quirks of hers I'm all too familiar with. I envision closing the distance between us and taking her into my arms to comfort her like I did many times before.

She begins to stammer with indecision.

I clear my throat. "We went to high school together." Stabbing pain sears my chest, and I make the mistake of looking at Echo. Her beautiful face is trained on me, and for a heartbeat, the same pain I feel consumes her brown eyes. I just belittled what we had—what she was to me.

Dax keeps looking back and forth between us, trying to place her. But with the shitty situation she and I had, he's not going to be able to. I keep my eyes on her, wishing we could shut everyone around us out. Wishing she could read my thoughts. Wishing I could announce what she meant to me...what she still means to me.

Dax mumbles, "Oh shit." Like he just had an epiphany.

I take a step forward and open my mouth, needing to expand on my words. She cuts her eyes in my direction, stopping me dead in my tracks. I finally pull my eyes away from her, refocusing my vision on our surroundings. That's when I watch my new platoon sergeant walk up and put his arm around Echo.

"I see you've met my platoon leader," he states before placing a kiss on her cheek.

She musters a smile, not daring to look away from me. "Seems so."

My heart drops and my hand twitches at my side, begging to be fisted.

For a second, my belief in the universe and God had reappeared, making a glimmer of hope break through within me. But the reality of the situation quickly snuffs out all hope, making me remember why I quit believing in all the fluffy shit so long ago. All hope does is inflict hurt.

I suppress the maniacal laugh reverberating within my ribs. I know firsthand how cruel the world can be...but boy did it just one-up the hell out of me. In this moment, I know the world has it out for me. I'm hated by the stars that were supposed to align for me and Echo.

Stupid stars, and universes, and constellations. Stupid astrology. It's all bullshit.

13 YEARS AGO

Chapter One

ECHO

July 2000

Being the new girl always sucks, but besides being the pastor's daughter, the new girl is who I've always been. I'm not sure which is worse, as they both seem to come with their own set of cons. As the pastor's daughter, there's a certain stigma that's expected and must be maintained. I've always felt that I've been manicured to be this perfect person because if I wasn't, I'd reflect negatively on my father. And his image seems to be something he's rather proud of. Rightfully so, as he's made a good name for himself and his mission.

For me, being the pastor's daughter has meant lots of moving. There have been times when my father did evangelism and we were constantly on the road like a traveling circus. During our circus days, I was always homeschooled. It just seemed to be more convenient. I think my dad would also agree it was a form of protection. As I got older, I started resenting our lifestyle and at times, even my parents. I know they love me, want the best for me, and for me to live God's will, but I'm beginning to think that sheltering me and essentially taking away my free will isn't the way. I consider myself a social butterfly, and I don't like feeling like my wings are taped down.

As Ariel said it best, *"I want to be where the people are,"* dang it. When I was younger, I was able to go to elementary school, but as soon as puberty hit, homeschooling began. I never really complained. I had sports. My dad made sure I was always on a softball team no matter where we lived. Albeit, it hasn't always been easy joining a new team each season. The older I got, the more I had to prove my worth and skill each time to make sure I'd get a shot at playing. So while being the new girl in general can be a drag, being the new girl wanting to come in and take your spot on the softball field hasn't made me an instant favorite with fellow team members. But now that I'm older, I need more than sports. I need experiences and I yearn for a sense of stability —and friends.

Definitely friends.

The move to Georgia hasn't been as big of a culture shock as I thought it would. Maybe it's because we settled in a small town, and I'm used to those back home. Well, the only place I consider home since it's the one place we seem to gravitate back to. Even though it's situated on the Bible Belt like a perfectly aligned star on a constellation, I don't mind Oklahoma. The perks of living a nomadic life are also the things I crave. When you aren't in one place long enough to form relationships with others, you don't miss them when you leave. But there is one person I will miss from our gypsy days in Oklahoma— Brian. We have a common denominator that seemed to forge our union—he's a preacher kid. Our bond didn't happen instantly as he's known for being a little rough around the edges. Still to this day. But with some persistence, he eventually sweetened up to me. From day one, he's been the epitome of the preacher's kid stereotype. Mouth like a sailor, roughing up the other boys on the playground, and all by fourth grade when we first met. Even though I was a grade below him, we still had the same recess and lunch. I was lucky enough to have a couple girls who befriended me on my first day at the new school, but I quickly found out that the boys weren't so nice.

"Echo. Echo. Echo. Echo," the redheaded boy yelled, lowering the pitch each time to mimic an echo. I turned around as he looked back at his group of friends, laughing. "What a stupid name!"

My fists curled unexpectedly and without much thought, I was going to make my way over to that mean group of boys. And do what? I didn't really know. A hand curled around my bicep, stopping me in my tracks.

"Echo, don't." Brian was staring at the group of boys, then looked at me. "I'll take care of it later," he said, nodding. And that boy kept his word. That day at lunch, Brian sent that boy and his tray of food sliding across the cafeteria floor by placing his foot in the right place at the right time. He tried to play it off by saying, "Whoops," but he still ended up with detention.

Ever since then, he's had my back. Not sure what made him take such a liking to me, but he became the brother I never had, and he was the one person I was always sad to leave behind.

We moved here a month ago, and I still don't feel settled in. Maybe I subconsciously worry that as soon as I get comfortable, I'll just have to pack up. Part of me wonders if it's all too good to be true. Like why now? The other part of me knows I don't have to be in a hurry to unpack since we're finally planting ourselves somewhere. The former pastor of the church passed away a couple years ago, leaving his house to whomever succeeded him at the church he'd founded. A win-win, if you ask me.

Planting roots here goes deeper than us getting a home. It means we will no longer be a traveling show any longer. My dad's putting his own roots down, something I've always wondered if he was capable of doing. The local Pentecostal church here has been desperately looking for a new pastor the last two years. They had been filling the services with missionaries for the time being. One might say the timing of it all is a God thing. That's what my mom says, anyways, but she says that about everything. Even though ministry is my dad's calling and job, it always seems to be a family event—just one I don't get paid for. I know my routine and where I fit into our trio. My father preaches, my mother sits in the front row like the doting preacher's wife, and I, well, I'm the prized singer with the killer vocal cords. My mother's words, not mine. I'm somewhat more modest than that. Modest, not shy. Far from shy. The singing skills I inherited from my mother. I initially started off singing side by side with her for fun. A way for them to show off their daughter's God-given talent. Then one day, it was just me in the spotlight. I'm not sure why my mom no longer wanted to sing. I think it was their way of grounding me more in the church. Hoping and praying it'll keep me from ever straying. Performing in front of people has never bothered me. I'm a pro at blocking out all my surroundings. There's only one other place where I feel that same sense of comfort. The pitcher's mound. Softball is more than a hobby for me. It's my passion. Something else my dad made sure to instill in me.

Chapter Two

DUSTIN

August 2000

"Dustin, hurry up! We're going to be late," my mom yells from downstairs. I trip over my tennis shoes, stubbing my toe on my dresser in the process.

"Shit!" Perfect way to start out Sunday morning as I'm getting ready for church. A church we haven't been to in months. But since the new pastor arrived in town, my parents want to give it another shot. "Let's see how many weeks it'll last this time." I snicker as I tighten my belt. I bend over and grab my shoes, the damn sneakers that nearly caused the demise of my big toe, and plant my ass on the edge of my bed to slide them on.

I run into the bathroom to brush my teeth. In the past, I never cared about my appearance when we went to church. It's not like I'm going there to pick up chicks or make any sort of impression. But as I glance at my appearance in the mirror, I figure it can't hurt to make myself look a bit more presentable. I turn the water back on, not even allowing it to warm up before wetting my hands and shoving them through my disheveled hair to dampen it. I open the tube of gel and squeeze some in my hand before rubbing my hands together. I focus on the top part, giving it that spikey, pushed-forward look girls seem to appreciate. I quickly wash my hands off and grab my Lucky cologne, giving my shirt a few spritzes before I head downstairs.

My parents and brother are waiting impatiently by the front door, staring at me as I jog down, hopping off the fourth to last step.

"Sorry," I mutter as my feet smack the hardwood floor.

"Next Sunday, we better not be waiting for you," my mom warns as we make our way out the door like ducks in a row.

"If there even is a next Sunday," I mumble under my breath.

The short drive to church is filled with Dax bugging our dad about some airplane exhibit that is coming through town. I stare out the window, listening to him as he names off the different types of planes that'll be putting on the show. Although I'd never admit it, it's quite impressive. For some reason, Dax and his best friend Lincoln are obsessed with all things planes. I thought once he hit middle school, he'd find a new obsession, but that has yet to happen. In fact, they're both so over the top with it they plan to become pilots together after graduation. It's gotten so far out of hand that they have everyone refer to them as Maverick and Goose.

The gravel parking lot is jam-packed. My mom glares at me, pinning the blame for our late arrival solely on me. As we reach the front doors, my mother cuts her eyes my way as the sound of praise and worship music bellows out the older orangish brick building. I shrug my shoulders, walking through the doors. She should be thanking me. I got us out of the whole "before we begin, turn to your neighbor and tell them you're happy they're here," awkwardness.

My dad spots a section near the back with enough room for us to quietly slide in. I shift to the side, allowing Dax in ahead of me so I can sit at the end of the pew. As he squeezes by me, I notice how much he's grown. Before I know it, he'll be taller than me. The top of his head reaches my nose. We have a four-year age difference between us. I can't have him catching up to me or he'll think he can overpower me, and that will never happen. I resist the urge to ruffle his hair as he passes by. That would surely piss the parentals off. I take that minuscule moment to study his features. The full cheeks he once had are no longer there and definition resides where they had been. His boyish features are slowly dissipating, and I've never taken the time to notice. He's still more of a toe-head in comparison to me. I wonder if it'll darken more like mine, or if he'll stay a blondie for life.

"Bro, take a picture. It'll last longer," he whispers with a chuckle. I shake my head and pat him on the shoulder. In this moment, I'm feeling like a proud brother. I want to take the time to soak it up. Any given second, he'll be back to annoying me and this moment will pass as if it never happened.

While I sit, they stand and clap along as if they know all the words to the songs. Every so often, my mom shifts her focus on me, giving me a look of disapproval. What's new. I just go about my business, letting my fingers drum across my thighs, keeping up with the tempo of the songs as I scope out the congregation. Even though the lighting is dim, I can make out a few familiar faces. But one in particular catches my attention as I fixate my eyes on the stage.

This must be the new girl in town—standing up on stage, singing with the rest of the band. The tapping of my fingers subsides as I straighten in my seat, shifting my body forward. I look around, seeing everyone just as captivated as me. Well, those whose eyes are still open. The rest are captivated by Jesus, praising him with their hands up. I hear Dax chuckling at my side, and I smack his leg.

"Oww." He fakes a whine, knowing damn well it didn't hurt.

I can feel my mother's eyes burning into me. I don't even have to look to know it's there. I'm all too familiar with it. In fact, I think she reserves that facial feature just for me. I also don't look because I don't want to take my eyes off the stage.

I could get used to this whole church thing.

I listen to her soft yet strong voice flowing through the speakers. I don't even notice the pastor walking onto the stage until he starts talking. My shoulders slump as the praise and worship team begins to walk off the stage. Service seems to fly by. Crazy how that can happen when your attention is elsewhere. Mine is practically focused on the back of the new girl's head, praying she turns around and makes eye contact with me. That's about as good as I get when it comes to praying. After service, I make my way outside to wait by the car while my parents play Good Samaritan with the new preacher and a few church elders. Everyone else seems to have gotten the hell outta Dodge. Most likely hitting up the Shoney's buffet.

"I'd like to be hitting up a buffet," I mumble aloud as my stomach growls. I silently thank the man upstairs that my body didn't betray me during service, waiting until I was in the deserted parking lot alone to do so. I lean against our black sedan, looking down at the gravel, lightly kicking it around. I hear laughing, causing me to look up. That's when I see her, walking out the front door, the wind whipping her long brown hair every which way. She bends over, flips her hair toward the ground, gathers it all in her hands, and places it in a messy bun on top of her head.

She stands back up, catching me staring. Instead of giving me the shy look I expect, she smiles and confidently walks across the street, right toward me. For reasons unknown to all of mankind, it makes me nervous. Real nervous, and I don't get nervous. I evoke it. What do I do with my hands? I mean, it's not like this is the first time the opposite sex has approached me. I've been approached by plenty of girls, plenty of very attractive ones. Something about this girl feels different, though.

As my nerves begin to lessen, I can't keep my smile from widening with each step closer she gets. I still don't know what to say. For once in my life, I'm speechless. Or so I thought. She stops in front of me and without hesitation, the cheesiest thing flies out of my mouth.

"So...you come here often?" I ask, cocking a brow for effect.

She stops in her tracks. In mocking fashion, she cocks a brow back and gives me a once-over before covering her mouth and laughing. I let out my breath, relaxing my shoulders, feeling like I'm wound up tighter than a Jack-n-Box. I silently thank Jesus for her not running off. Every ounce of stupidity I feel for being such a cheeseball leaves as soon as that sweet sound erupts through her full lips. The twinkle that fills her brown eyes and the perfect smile on her face are added perks.

"Just every Sunday and Wednesday," she replies through more giggles.

So far, I gather three very important facts about her: she isn't shy, she has an amazing voice, and she has a sense of humor. Now all I want to know is where I need to sign to make her mine.

"Dustin," I say, extending my hand out to her. My fingers clasp around her slender hand as we shake.

"Good to know," she replies with an ornery smile.

We look over, seeing my parents coming out the front door, along with what's left of the congregation. I groan, and as I look back her way, her carefree demeanor falters momentarily. I follow her gaze directly to her father, who is staring in our direction, no longer smiling himself. Just as quickly as her smile fades, it reappears as she turns back toward me and starts walking backward, almost as if in defiance of her apparently disapproving father.

"What's your name?" I ask as she continues backward.

"Echo." She gives me a full-blown grin before turning around and jogging back across the street. I run my hand through my hair, letting out an audible *hmm* before grabbing the door handle and falling into the car. This must be what they call love at first sight. Or voodoo.

Definitely voodoo. Because this girl has put a spell on me. I just don't know if it's love or magic. Whichever it is, I have to get to know her. Here and now, I make the decision.

I'll be right here every Sunday, Wednesday, and any other day these church doors are open.

Chapter Three

ECHO

Starting school tomorrow has my nerves all over the place. I'm supposed to be working on my room, emptying the rest of my boxes, but instead, I fall onto my bed and let the afternoon sunshine warm my face. I think about Dustin and how cute he is. I spotted him when I was singing on stage, a boy I haven't seen this whole month we've been here. I haven't really seen any kids my age yet. That's why I was so eager when I saw him. While everyone was watching me, I only took notice of his eyes on me. Leaning forward, he was intently watching me with fixated eyes. It made me feel something I hadn't felt since I first started singing on stage—butterflies.

"Ugh," I groan. "Knock it off, Echo," I tell myself as I roll onto my stomach. "The last thing you need is to start getting boy crazy. That'll have your dad pulling the plug on everything." I remind myself. I don't need to step into the danger zone from the get-go.

But on the other side, I've been hoping to make at least one new friend at church who could help me not feel like such an outsider the first week of school. At least, I finally made conversation with someone who looks close to my age the day before school starts. A cute someone, that is. While he seemed nice and funny, he's merely just an acquaintance at this point. An acquaintance that surely won't take me under his wing and show me the ropes. I'll be going in blind. Going into unknown territory where I know no one, but they all at least know who I am. Not to mention, there's usually a stigma that comes from being the preacher's daughter. I will either be instantly classified as a goody-goody or a rebel in disguise. I've learned that small towns usually have their cliques set in place since grade school. Heck, since their parents were in grade school. It's like a pact they're all born into.

Trying to squeeze into one of those this late in the game can be almost as impossible as trying to beat Timmy Tyler at Red Rover back in fourth grade. All I can say is I gave it my all. As in, my left incisor that had been holding on for dear life was finally defeated when I did a flip over his arm and landed face-first on the ground. Despite that, Timmy still didn't loosen the death grip he had with his teammate Alex. The teacher literally had to say game over for that to happen. At least the Tooth Fairy took pity on me and left me five dollars under my pillow. Who's the real winner now, Timmy? I wonder where Timmy would be if he had taken scholastics as seriously as he did Red Rover. I mean, he was already rocking his second year of fourth grade. He had to excel at something. Being a human brick wall, it was.

At least I'll have softball. I think as I roll out of bed. I have to start practicing soon. It'll be my escape.

A much-needed escape from my overbearing father.

THE AROMA OF dinner fills my room and summons me to the kitchen. I walk in just as my mom sits the pan of pork chops on the stovetop and shuts the oven door with her foot.

"Do you need any help?" I ask, moving quickly her way to assist.

"Everything is done in here. Could you set the table?" She gestures to the plates and utensils she has sitting out on the kitchen island.

I grab the items and walk through the archway that leads to the dining room. The area is naturally bright with the curtains to the double windows pulled to the side. I begin humming as I set the table, taking the extra time to place everything just right. Although I'm nervous about this new beginning tomorrow, I'm also excited. I've learned over the years that it's all about your mindset. I know I have a perma-grin plastered on my face, but it's hard not to be giddy when everything seems to finally be lining up for me.

My mom sets the last item on the table. "I think we're ready. Honey," she hollers, "dinner's done."

"Yeah, honey." I snicker as my dad rounds the corner. He looks my way, a smile barely crossing his face. "It's okay to smile, Dad. I'm pretty sure the Lord would approve," I say as I pull my chair out, knowing I just poked the bear.

I try to keep my thoughts to myself because they never get perceived correctly, but as I get older, it's getting harder to remain tight-lipped. I glance at him and regret it. While the Lord might approve, my dad does not. Sometimes I wonder what made him become such a stick in the mud. Thankfully, he doesn't voice his disapproval. He takes his seat at the far end of the table and blesses the food. My mom then gets up and fixes his plate like she does for every meal before sitting back down to make hers.

"Why are you in such a cheerful mood?" my dad asks, seeming to imply that I'm not usually cheerful.

"School, softball, new beginnings. Life in general. You know, the things I'm usually happy about." I shrug to play off my annoyance at his question.

"I'm sure it has nothing to do with that handsome boy who was at church this morning. I saw you two talking after service." My mother snickers, giving me a quick wink. I wish I could kick her foot under the table without getting reprimanded for it.

"Better not have anything to do with some boy," my father warns, adding, "And don't be encouraging that, Donna."

I glance at my dad, watching him take a bite out of his roll. Wrinkles are beginning to fill in around his mouth. His once dark brown hair has lightened over the years. It's even thinned out some. His brown eyes dart my way, catching me studying him.

Caught off guard, I stammer. "It doesn't. Okay?" I push around my green beans with my fork, no longer hungry.

"Oh now, Eric," my mother chides.

My eyes focus on her perfectly manicured nails as she cuts her green beans. *Who cuts green beans?*

"It's perfectly natural for teenagers to have crushes."

I sigh quietly. My mother is always trying to smooth things over, but she can try all she wants. We all know her say is never the final one.

"You know how kids are these days, Donna. They just can't be trusted," Dad says matter-of-factly around his mouthful of food.

I drop my fork. The metal hitting my glass plate gains their attention.

"Oh, so now I can't be trusted."

My dad swiftly angles his head in my direction, and I unrelentingly hold his stare. His eyes are filled with disdain, lacking the compassion I long for.

"Don't take my words out of context, Echo Dian." He shakes his head, dismissing the tension, and goes back to cutting his pork chop. Unbothered as always. I could argue and point out how I didn't take his words out of context, but it would be useless. I'll always be wrong, and he'll always be right. Seems to be the ongoing theme. Sometimes I just wish he'd be quiet. Listen to absorb, not listen to reply. He's so used to people going to him for answers that he forgets to be a safe harbor for his own family. I've become rather observant being an only child. My mom is loving as can be, but sometimes I wish she'd toss the

June Cleaver act and say what she's really thinking. She might be fine with being a pushover, but that's something I'll never be.

"Can I be excused?" I drop my napkin onto my plate and scoot my seat back. The wooden chair legs squeak, sliding across the linoleum flooring.

"Sure, honey," my mother answers, giving me an understanding nod.

"You haven't even touched your food." My dad motions, pointing his fork at my plate.

"I'm not hungry. I think it's first-day nerves."

My dad shrugs and I take the gesture as a small win as I head to the kitchen.

I sit my pork chop to the side on a napkin before scraping the rest of my plate in the trash can. I wash my dishes, wrap my pork chop up in the napkin, and head to my room. I lied when I said I wasn't hungry.

Unlike me, my mom has wasted no time unpacking. The hallway is filled with family photos—mostly of me. The places we lived in before were fully furnished, and when we lived in an RV, there wasn't space for much. I never took into consideration what all my mom has been giving up this entire time as well. Selfishly, I've been too focused on what I've been missing out on. I slow down, fully examining each picture. I look happy in them. My mom looks happy, too. My dad... well, my dad looks constipated.

Starting from the beginning to the end of the hall, it's almost like a moving photo album. Mom and Dad's wedding pictures—happy. Dad and baby Echo—happy. Dad and toddler Echo holding a plastic bat— happy. But as I grow, his smile fades. It's almost like watching reality sink in over time. He now looks as if he has the weight of the world on his shoulders. I wonder if my dad enjoyed his life growing up. I wonder if my dad enjoys his life now. Sometimes I feel like he's just on autopilot, going through the motions. It's a sad thought and the main reason I can never stay mad at him. His heart is always in the right place. I just wish he'd show it more.

I let my door lightly shut behind me and rest my back against it. The sun is still out, filling my room with its warmth. I'm thankful it hasn't set yet. It brightens the light-yellow walls I'm surrounded by. This is all so new to me. I've never had my own room before. I don't know how to decorate it or make it mine. I'm just thankful to have my own bed. I walk forward, climb onto my bed, and sit Indian style on it. I'm facing the window, looking into our fully fenced back yard. There's a big willow oak in the middle out back. I notice the remnants of rope dangling from the lowest thick branch. I imagine a tire swing full of kids laughing; carefree. Part of me wishes I could go back to those days and experience them all over again. Back when my dad was more carefree.

I HAVE THE worst case of first-day jitters as I walk through the school's double doors. *You've done this more than a dozen times. You're a pro.* I keep trying to remind myself. But the fact that I tried on my entire closest this morning before settling with a simple pair of jeans, Switchfoot T-shirt, and my new shell-toe Adidas sneakers has me questioning my *'pro-ness.'* I do almost look like a skater chick, though. Brian would be proud.

But none of my mental mantra or ego boosting is calming my nerves. I'm nervous as hell. *Yeah, Dad, I said hell. And not in the biblical sense.*

Thankfully, my parents and I did a full walk-through, so I know the basic layout and the direction I need to go. But doing that walk-through in real time with the halls filled with kids is kind of distorting my memory. I spot a sign on the brick wall and follow the directions that lead to the office. Being a late enroller postponed the availability of my schedule, meaning I have no clue what classes I have.

"Can I help you?" the older lady with short blond hair asks as I step up to the desk.

"Yes, ma'am. I need to pick up my schedule. My name is Echo Price."

"Just one second, please." She begins typing into her computer before getting up and walking to the back of the office.

I turn around and walk over to the announcement board. All kinds of sports-related news fill it, along with fundraisers and future upgrades the school has planned.

"Echo." I turn around to see a man in gym shorts and a school T-shirt.

"Yes." I grab the hand he has extended.

"I'm Coach Fields. I heard you tell Mrs. Carter your name and wanted to introduce myself," he explains.

"Nice to meet you, Coach." I smile, hoping to make a good first impression, although I know the only impression to make is on the field. "I met your father, and I'm glad to finally meet the girl he's been bragging about." He raises his coffee cup to his mouth and takes a slow sip of the steaming brew.

My cheeks heat with embarrassment. "I really wish he hadn't done that," I say, looking down at the ground. I know my dad thinks I'm the best, but it doesn't mean everyone will agree with him. Plus, it just puts even more pressure on me.

"Ahh." He waves off what I said. "Us parents only want what's best for our kids." I nod in response before he continues, "Anyways, I'm going to tell you the same thing I told him. Our starting pitcher graduated this past school year. So now we are basically having tryouts for the position. But don't let that discourage you. Even if you don't get picked for the pitcher's mound, I'm sure we can find somewhere to fit ya." He smiles with a nod, and I do the same, hoping mine doesn't look as fake as it felt. Not that proving myself is something new, but playing another position on the field surely would be. It's just more motivation for me to put in the necessary work. Now that I'm finally in school and my senior year, this is my last chance to get noticed by scouts. I can't screw it up.

"Ms. Price." I turn back to the front desk where the secretary is standing. "Here's your schedule, dear." She smiles, holding out the paper.

"It was nice meeting you, Coach Fields," I finish before grabbing my schedule and hurrying out. The last thing I need is to be late on my first day of class.

Reading the numbers on the lockers, I continue walking down the hall, trying to find mine. I want to put my backpack up and make my way to first period. I round the corner and see a group of guys in ball hats with a few girls in the mix. Typical jocks with their little groupies. Besides me initially noticing them, I pay no further attention as I continue my journey.

"Echo," I hear, stopping me in my tracks. An uncontrollable smile creeps upon me and butterflies consume my abdomen. Again. I turn around, tilt my head to the side, and purposefully ogle Dustin as he makes his way to me.

"Did he just say Echo?" A thin blonde with too much blue eyeshadow snickers.

A couple of the guys laugh, and I roll my eyes. I don't know about them, but I'm in high school, not elementary. And the last time someone made fun of my name, they ended up eating their lunch off the cafeteria floor. Pick something better to laugh about. I know I'm supposed to be the example, be the bigger person, but sometimes turning the other cheek is hard. I keep my smile planted and my eyes on Dustin as he makes his way toward me. He stops right in front of me, big grin and all.

"What kind of name is that?" The overly tan brunette laughs. I almost expect her to twirl her gum around her finger all valley girl like.

Like, totally!

"We can't all have boring names like Kelly and Jamie," Dustin hollers, looking back over his shoulder. The girls scoff and I put my hand over my mouth to stifle my laugh. He looks back my way, flashing me that golden boy smile of his. "Sorry about that."

"It's cool. I've heard it before. I just expected high schoolers to be a little more mature." I say the last part louder than necessary.

"Were the kids at your former school civilized?" He raises his eyebrows with a look of confusion.

"Oh no. I was homeschooled before we moved here," I reply, remembering he doesn't know anything about my past.

"You poor, sheltered girl." He laughs, patting my shoulder. "And now you're being released into the wild." He teases before saying, "Guess I'll just have to watch over you."

I want to retort that I haven't been sheltered. I went to school until middle school. I'm always around people. I can take care of myself. But the idea of him watching over me sounds too appealing to refute.

"Schedule?" he asks, pointing to the paper in my hand.

"Yeah." I bite my lip, unable to stop grinning at him.

"Let me see," he says, reaching for my schedule. Dustin quickly glances over it, and I wonder if we have any classes together. "Looks like you have Mrs. Whiteman for English first up. She's right down this hall." He gestures. "Now let's go get you situated." He holds his arm out for me.

"Let's," I reply, looping my arm into his. I can't help but have high hopes this year is going to be one of the best.

I WALK THROUGH the front door and drop my key on the entryway table. "Mom," I holler, making my way back to my room.

She replies, "In the kitchen."

I toss my backpack on my bed, kick my shoes off, and shimmy out of my jeans. I grab my oversized shorts out of my drawer and slide them up, then put my sneakers on. Yanking the scrunchie off my wrist, I begin to loosely braid my hair as I walk to the kitchen.

"How was your first day?" my mom asks with a smile as I lean against the counter. Her eyes glance up momentarily before darting back down at whatever her hands are mixing together in the bowl. Meatloaf, maybe? She blows at the piece of bang that keeps falling in her line of sight and I take in her Suzy Homemaker demeanor as she fixes dinner in a dress and heels. Obviously, with an apron covering her attire. She looks up again, pausing her meat mashing. "Echo?" Her eyebrows knit with worry as she waits for my reply.

"Oh, I'm sorry." I shake my head and smile. I put my hand on my hip, thinking back on my day. "It was really good." I begin a slow nod, hoping the excitement from my day isn't evident.

"That's great." She lets out an audible sigh as if she's been holding her breath, expecting the worst. "Can you grab about ten of those crackers and crush them into my bowl?" She nods to the other side of the counter where the unopened package lies.

I wipe the residual cracker crumbs off on my shorts and give my mom a quick peck on the cheek. "I'm going to go outside and practice." I throw a cracker in my mouth and head for the back door.

It's hot. While I'm used to heat, the humidity is what's going to take time adjusting to. Thankfully, my dad perched my makeshift pitching mound under the big willow oak. A couple rectangular hay bales stacked on top of each other, showcasing a bull's-eye, lean against the privacy fence. I wince at the splotches of white powder that stick out like a sore thumb on the fence before spraying it off with the hose. It's just one of the ways my dad tests how good I'm getting when he's not here to catch for me. The thing that sucks about his process is the powder doesn't really show on the actual target. Therefore, only showing the times I miss, not the accuracy of my pitches. But knowing that the wall gets cleaned fresh each time, and I practice throwing my filled bucket of ten softballs at least five times, he has a good idea of how well I'm pitching. While I enjoy the alone time, or him not breathing down my neck if I don't throw with precision and speed every single time... I'd love to have someone catch for me so I'm not having to track down all the balls just to do it all over again times five.

Four buckets down and I hear the back door close. I keep my focus, holding my hands together outstretched in front of me, and slide my foot as soon as my arm winds then releases, snapping as the ball hits close to the center mark. I continue with the rest of the balls as my dad just watches and assesses. He follows me as I walk to the target and start gathering the balls. He tosses me a couple and then eyes the fencing.

"Looks like you only had a few strays this round." His brow rises, and he nods in approval. I wish I could get this rise out of him more often.

I sit the filled bucket down and sit on it. "I met Coach Fields today. Guess you can say I'm determined to make starting pitcher," I admit. With my hand, I shield the sun from my eyes and tilt my head up in his direction. He looks off as if he's in deep thought, but I can still see a sense of pride in his eyes.

"Just stay focused and stay away from all distractions." His voice is curt. Heaven forbid he give me a *'thatta girl.'* I inwardly roll my eyes and let out a low sigh. "Come on, dinner's ready." He turns to the house, and I watch momentarily, missing the days when I was younger. My stomach growls and I stand, grab my bucket and glove, and head for the house.

Chapter Four

DUSTIN

September 2000

It's been a month since Echo came into my life, and for the most part, we've been inseparable. Whatever this pull is between us, it feels natural. I've enjoyed getting to know her yet feel as if I've known her my whole life. I'm having to put real effort into not rushing this thing between us. I don't want to chance scaring her off or getting on her dad's bad side.

The bell rings, and I dart out of class in hopes of catching Echo before she takes off for practice. I wouldn't say she's kissing the coach's ass by going above and beyond anyone else on the team, but she definitely wants to be noticed. The girls' team only plays spring ball, but her coach has a knack for offering an alternative practice in the fall for those who don't play other sports. Echo is taking full advantage of it. I have a slight feeling the pressure she receives at home brings out the overachiever in her. I can't even imagine being a preacher's offspring. It's hard enough being the offspring of normal people.

"Whatcha got going on today after practice?" I sidle up to her, resisting the urge to pull her into my arms.

She slams her locker door and huffs. "A youth rally."

"You sound angry about it." I would laugh, but I can tell by her tight facial features and the way she shoves her book into her backpack that Echo is annoyed. I don't want to add to it.

She flings her backpack over her shoulder and stands silent, looking off to the side like she's deep in thought.

"It's just..." She pauses, and I grab her hands, encouraging her to continue. I want her to feel safe with me—to be able to tell me anything and everything. "Have you ever felt like nothing you do is good enough? And just get tired of trying to be this person everyone around you expects you to be?"

"Yeah, I do." I cup her chin, forcing her to hold my gaze. Staring into her chocolate eyes damn near puts me in a trance. And the way she looks into mine—like she can see right through me and the bullshit walls I've been known to put up—has me shaking my head to regain my thoughts. "Not trying to downplay what you're feeling, but I believe a lot of us suffer what you're going through. And it's going to get worse before it gets better. They only have until we graduate to ingrain their values into us."

Echo snickers. "I just don't feel like they're leaving my life choices up for option. It's never been 'here you go, decide what would be best.' No, it's always been laid out with no choice whatsoever. I want me to be my own person, but they want me to be this Jesus-praising robot."

"I have a proposition for you," I request, sparking instant interest in Echo's eyes. They sparkle with curiosity, and I love that I provoke it. My heart thumps harder against my chest, and I chance glancing at her lips. Her pouty, pink lips look incredibly soft and kissable. I look forward to the day when I finally feel them against mine.

"When you are with me, be one hundred percent you."

"I am," she starts.

"I know we both have our own issues at home, and I don't want us to use each other as an escape, but I think the beauty about us is how real we've been with one another since day one."

Echo nods, biting her lip, making me want to taste it even more.

"We only have a good seven months left before we can blow this joint. The possibilities will be endless. We can make all the mistakes we want."

Her smile falters, and she lifts her brow, questioning me.

"Fine. Not intentional mistakes." I laugh. "Is that better?"

She grins and shrugs her shoulders.

"My point is, do what you gotta do to keep the parentals happy. And then"—I place my hand against her cheek and rub my thumb along her cheekbone—"come to me, and I'll do whatever I need to do to make you happy." I slide my hand down to her neck and lightly wrap my fingers around the back of it, pulling her face into mine. So close I can feel her breaths dance across my lips as they escape her mouth. I lean my forehead against hers and take in that feeling longer than I should. "Deal?" I ask as I peel my eyes away from her lips.

She looks up at me, and I see an adoration I've never seen before. She nods, repeating, "Deal."

"Good. Now let's get our asses to practice."

"Shit!" Echo shrieks.

I laugh because I'm pretty sure that's the first time I've heard her cuss. I pull her bag off her shoulder and toss it over mine.

I expect Echo to drop me like a hot potato as soon as we make it to the girls' locker room. But she doesn't. She slowly pulls her bag off my arm. As she watches the bag; I watch her.

"What do you have going on after practice?" she inquires.

"No plans. Why, what's up?"

"Any chance you'd do me a favor?" she asks, looking down at the ground, kicking at the grass.

"Will I be spending time with you?"

Her head snaps back up, and a shy grin tugs at the corner of her mouth. Her answer doesn't determine mine. The truth is, no matter what it is, I'll do it.

"Of course." She nods, giving me a full smile that makes my heart stop and I vow to do whatever she asks if it earns me that beautiful smile of hers.

"Then it wouldn't be a favor. It'd be an honor." I fake bow.

She laughs and calls me dumb before rushing into the locker room.

Yeah, she likes me.

* * *

I HAVE NEVER been to a youth rally before, but I'd use any and every excuse to hang out with Echo outside of school. Her parents don't make it easy. It's not like I'm a bad kid or one they should be wary of, but I have a feeling I could be the president's son, and I still wouldn't be good enough for their daughter.

There aren't very many kids in the youth group as is, so we only have to take one church van to the rally. Dave, the youth pastor, has Echo and me wait until the other kids fill in the back first. I roll my eyes at the fact that we can't even choose where we sit for the forty-five-minute ride.

Echo steps in close to me, presses her mouth near my ear, and says, "Sorry."

I glance at her while grabbing her hand and give it a reassuring squeeze before releasing it. This isn't her fault. I don't want her to feel bad about something she can't control. Thankfully, after we climb in, Jacob shows up. He's more on the hefty side, so when he scoots in next to Echo, he pushes her tightly into my side. I inwardly smile, enjoying the closeness.

When we arrive at the church, I'm amazed at how packed the parking lot is with vans and buses from other churches. Do kids really hang out at church on a Friday night? This concept is foreign to me, but I'm curious to see why. I mean, I know my reasoning behind it, but it's not Jesus. We walk in and the place seems electric. I can feel the excitement as I watch all the different kids mingle, laughing and smiling, full of absolute happiness. We make our way into the sanctuary and sit in the mid-section of the pews. It starts with a singer on stage, getting everyone hyped up as the music begins to play.

"We want everyone on their feet," they yell. "Now jump." And on command, everyone around me starts jumping.

"Come on." Echo urges as she smiles, jumping up and down with the crowd. I finally let go of all my reserves and join in. I don't know the song, but I can clap to the beat of the music. Three songs in and my legs are slightly sore, and my arms are over me clapping. I didn't know I was going to get a second workout. They slow the music down, urging us to praise our Lord. I watch as those around me do. I've yet to really form a relationship with God, so I'm unsure how all of this works. So instead of standing and praising with raised hands, I sit down and bow my head. I decide this is a good time to talk to God; something I've never done before.

They close out the service with prayer, asking if anyone would like to make Jesus their Lord and Savior. Prompted by a tug in my heart and a feeling I can't explain, I step out of the pew and make my way down the aisle. There are young adults waiting near the stage for anyone needing prayer. I walk toward the short, dark-skinned male closest to me, still unsure of what I'm doing or supposed to do. The man steps in closer, and leans in near my ear, asking me for my name.

"All right, Dustin. Are you ready to accept Jesus as your personal Lord and Savior and ask Him to come live in your heart?"

I'm unsure of what any of it means, but I tell him yes. His voice is deep but full of kindness. He keeps his hands on my arms as he begins praying, lifting me up. He then recites the sinner's prayer, having me repeat after him. I open my eyes and smile at the gentlemen standing in front of me. His eyes are bright, and his smile is wide. He clasps my hand and then brings himself in, giving me a bro hug.

"Thanks, man," I say as we pull apart, feeling lighter.

I make my way back to the pew where Echo is gushing at me. She pulls me in, giving me a tight hug. "I'm so happy for you," she whispers in my ear before pulling away. Surprise washes over me as she grabs my hand, holding it for whoever to see. And by whoever, I mean her youth pastor who takes notice of it. We make our way back to the van, and thankfully, the seating arrangement remains the same for the ride home. Except this time, since it's dark, Echo and I hold hands the entire time.

Once we arrive back, Dave pulls us to the side. "Listen," he says with one hand on his hip, the other hand rubbing over his short brown hair. "I'm in a peculiar situation." He eyes us, mainly Echo, looking for understanding. "More like under strict orders." He sighs.

"My dad," Echo mumbles, looking down in defeat.

"Yeah," he admits. "I don't make the rules, and I also don't want to get fired. So just make sure you watch the closeness when in my vicinity."

"Do you have any advice?" I ask, not wanting to accept the obvious.

"Umm." Dave blows out a breath. "Maybe a formal introduction with Pastor Price. Maybe if you were to introduce Dustin to your father, it'd allow him to let some of his defenses down." He offers.

"Yeah, right." Echo laughs, looking my way. I slowly shrug and hold her gaze, pleading with her. "But at this point, I'm willing to try anything."

"Also, what do you think about playing drums for the youth worship team?" Dave asks, directing his attention to me. I scrunch my brows, confused about why he'd even ask. He continues, "Don't think I haven't noticed you drumming your fingers on everything." He raises a brow, then adds, "And maybe it'll help win the pops over." His eyes dart to Echo, meeting her big eyes as if he's just had the best idea ever.

"Yes, that would be perfect." She turns to me, grabs my hands, and intently holds my gaze, her eyes pleading with me to give in. The gesture is unnecessary. I will never have the power to tell her no. Plus, if this helps get on her father's good side, I'd be stupid not to do it.

"I'm in," I say.

Echo jumps with excitement and gives me a hug. The things I'd do for this girl. I'm starting to believe I'd go to the end of the world for her.

Chapter Five

ECHO

October 2000

Introducing Dustin to my parents, mainly my father, isn't something I ever wanted to do. The fact that my dad is the new pastor in town and small towns usually consist of gossipers, I know he'll inevitably hear about it. And I can't risk him hearing about it from someone besides me. If I keep it a secret, he'll think I'm hiding something, making it look more suspicious, and give him a reason to question it—even more than he already will. I want to believe that being open and honest with him will help gain his trust. Although I have a nagging sensation it will do the opposite.

"You want to do what exactly?" My dad folds the newspaper and crosses his legs, giving me his undivided attention. I hate it. I want him to stay distracted while I bring up the boy topic. I'm not a fan of the one-on-one time with the man.

"I want to go to the dinner down the street with my friend Dustin. He also plays drums for the youth now," I add for good measure.

"And what's the point in you doing this?" he questions. I think he does so in hopes that I'll just back down altogether instead of facing his judgmental ways.

"Uh, to grab a bite to eat and hang out." I want to add a "duh," but that won't be beneficial whatsoever. I cringe once I realize I labeled Dustin a friend. Technically, he is just a friend, but he's one that I like. A lot. But I can't tell my dad that. Apparently, I have no balls when it comes to him.

"Just a friend, you say?" He raises his brows.

"Ahh." I look past him to where my mom is standing. I don't want to lie because I want my parents to trust me, but then my mom does the most unexpected thing ever and nods. She's standing behind my dad, so I know exactly what she's doing. She wants me to tell my dad yes to shut the man up. She knows him far better than me, and for some reason, she's helping me out.

A knock on the door causes me to jump. I know it's Dustin. Suddenly, I begin to sweat. I told the boy to wait for my cue, but just like always, he doesn't listen. He's stubborn and likes to do things his way—which, for the most part, usually works out perfectly.

As I stand, I look over at my dad, who is eyeing the door. "Yes, he is a friend. One that I like. And if you give him a chance, you'll like him too."

The closer I get to the door, the stronger the butterflies in my stomach become. It's amazing that my excitement to see Dustin overpowers my nerves about him meeting my father.

"Good afternoon, Echo," Dustin says with a huge grin and a wink as I open the door. He knows how worried I am about introducing him, and I know he'll do everything to give the best impression.

My mother comes to my side, and Dustin instantly sticks his hand out to her. "Pleasure meeting you, Mrs. Price. I'm Dustin Adams."

This guy has manners, and man, it's hot. Not that I expected any less from him because he's always carried himself differently than most guys, but seeing that side, the *I can make anyone love me, even your overbearing parents'* side, makes me fall for him a bit more.

"Nice meeting you, Dustin. But please, call me Donna."

"Yes, ma'am," he says with that Dustin charm and Southern drawl. "If I slip up and call you Mrs. Price, please don't take offense. It's a habit my parents have instilled in me since I could talk. So I'm not sure it can be turned off."

"Completely understandable." My mother smiles, and I can see that she's impressed.

"That's a habit more parents need to teach their children." My dad walks up, making his presence known. "It's partly what's responsible for the youth in this day and age," he mumbles.

"So good to finally meet you." Dustin bypasses my mother and me and extends his hand to my father. "I really enjoyed your sermon last Sunday."

"Is that so? Well, son, what part stuck out to you the most?" There it is. My dad is testing him. He's calling bullshit without saying it.

Dustin answers without skipping a beat. "I enjoyed it all, but the part that stuck out was men being the leaders in the household. And that it's their responsibility to lead a godly lifestyle for their family to pursue. Being from a family that hasn't always been in church, I never really understood the value. So it was a true eye-opener."

I watch him intently, appreciating the sincerity in his tone and words.

And that, folks, is how you win over an overbearing pastor father—you agree with his way of thinking.

My dad eyes Dustin for a moment, contemplating what he said. I'm sure he's performing his own lie detector on him, watching for any weird twitching or some form of deceit. But the truth is that Dustin isn't lying. He isn't trying to get on my dad's good side by making stuff up or putting on a facade. He's being genuine, and when my dad's stance goes from being on guard to relaxing, I can tell he sees it, too.

My dad crosses his arms, and his stoic features settle back in. "Then I'm sure you'll enjoy this Sunday's. It's titled, *Dating the Pastor's daughter*." His voice is deep, with no sign of humor.

There's a slight pause. My dad eyes Dustin and then me. Then he smiles and lets out a laugh. We all follow suit, and before it gets more awkward, Dustin, being the smooth guy he is, shakes my dad's hand one last time, saying, "I'll make sure to be there."

"All right, see y'all later," I said, practically yanking Dustin out behind me.

"It wasn't that bad," he says, taking my hand in his. I look back, making sure we're in the clear. Dustin looks back, then tightens his grip, stopping us in the middle of the sidewalk. He stands in front of me, lets go of my hand, and places his hands on my face. His light green eyes hold my vision in a vise. I could stare at them for the rest of my life. "I know you're worried. I get it. I'll never do anything to jeopardize this." He glances down, shaking his head, and I know he wants this just as badly as I do. "I'll do my best to smooth over anything that might come our way." His brows furrow as he glances away momentarily before looking back at me with a fierceness I've yet to see. "But I also won't cower away from your father."

"But..." I try to speak, but he silences me.

"But nothing, Echo. Everything about us is only becoming more. One day, he is going to have to accept this and who you want in your life...because I'm not going anywhere."

I see a rock-solid certainty in his eyes, and I know he means what he says. He pulls me closer, placing a kiss on my forehead.

I lift my hands, drape them over his shoulders, and let out a sigh. "Thanks. You're just the first guy I've ever liked." I hate admitting it, but I know Dustin won't revel in it.

"And your last," he emphasizes, making me smile. The idea of having Dustin forever gives me butterflies.

"Sometimes I just wonder how far my dad will go to get his way." My smile fades as that sinking feeling hits me.

"Hey, hey. Let's not think about the what-ifs. Let's live in the *what is*. And the *what is* right now is we're about to go get our grub on...in public...together." He grins, causing his perfect dimple to come into view.

He's right. There is no reason to dread what could happen—it will only keep me from enjoying the present. Somewhere in the last few weeks, he has become my voice of reason. And after that, my voice of reason and I walk hand in hand the few blocks we have left to the diner.

"Seat yourself," a middle-aged brunette says from behind the counter. "I'll be with ya in a sec."

"Back here." Dustin drags me behind him to the booth at the very back. It is deserted.

I sit down, and to my surprise, Dustin doesn't sit next to me.

"As much as I want to sit next to you, I'd rather sit across from you so I can see your beautiful face." It's as if he read my mind...or maybe my face. He seems good at doing both.

"What can I getcha to drink?" the brunette asks, dropping two flimsy menus in front of us.

"I'll have a root beer, please."

"Same," Dustin says with a smile.

"Be right back." She dashes off.

Dustin looks down at his menu, naming off each item and rating it. "I'd give their burgers a solid eight. Their chicken fried steak is subpar."

I snicker at him, causing him to look up.

"What?" he sheepishly asks, grabbing my hand that's on the table.

"Nothing." I shake my head. "You're just cute."

"Cute," he repeats, raising a brow.

My cheeks heat and I know I'm blushing. "Fine, more than cute," I admit. He shrugs, accepting my answer as the waitress returns and sits our drinks down.

"Y'all know whatcha want, or do ya need a minute?"

"I'm not really all that hungry," I admit as I shut my menu.

"Well, in that case..." Dustin gives me a wicked smile. "Let me do the honors." He grabs my menu, places it on top of his, and holds them out for the waitress. "Extra-large chocolate shake for her. And an extra-large order of fries for me," he orders.

"I'm not sure who's going to croak from a heart attack first." I laugh at the calories we're about to intake.

"I have a feeling if there's any croaking, it will be mutually timed," he retorts.

"Aw, are we going to die like Noah and Ally did in *The Notebook*?" I propose with a giggle.

"*The Notebook*." He scrunches his nose and furrows his brows.

"Never mind." I shake my head with a smile.

Our waitress returns and sits the massive chocolate shake in front of me and the fries in front of Dustin.

"We're sharing," he adds. "Fries are meant to be dipped into chocolate shakes. I'm pretty sure it's a rule somewhere. Just like peanut butter and jelly. They go hand in hand." He shrugs.

"Are you pregnant?" I ask, trying to keep my face serious but can't. I burst into a fit of laughter, and he follows suit.

"Listen," Dustin says, dipping a fry into my shake, then shoving it into his mouth, "don't knock it till you try it." He raises a brow, challenging me.

"Fine," I huff, grabbing a fry. I lightly dip it into the chocolate goodness, not wanting to fully coat it. I'm not about to go all in and it be disgusting. I hold it in front of my face and stare hesitantly. I look at Dustin, who's snickering and shaking his head.

"It's not going to kill ya."

I close my eyes and take a bite. I almost pinch my nose for safety measures. I'm not one to step outside of my box. When I know I like something, I stick with it. I don't continue trying other things to add to my palate. Maybe I'm uncultured. The cold chocolate hits my taste buds first, followed by the salty warmth from the fry. I quickly push the bite down my throat and take a long sip of my chocolate shake to get the taste out.

"You're nasty, Dustin. I can't even believe I like you," I tease, taking another slurp of my shake. "The only thing that should ever go with French fries is ketchup. Or ranch. Because ranch goes with everything." I huff.

"Now you're the one who's nasty," Dustin says as he shivers with disgust.

"Take it back." I stand and move to his side of the booth. "Take it back, Dustin." I start tickling him. "If this is ever going to be more, you need to take it back." I laugh as I continue tickling him.

"You can't tickle me into submission." He laughs, acting like he's trying to get away. But I know better. He likes the closeness, even if it's just us being silly.

HAND IN HAND, Dustin walks me back home. A block away, he stops and kisses me on the cheek.

"I had a good time," he says as we stop in front of my house.

"I did, too." I smile back. He walks backward a few steps before turning away and walking in the direction toward his home. I stand on the porch, watching for longer than I should. I know without a doubt I'm being watched. Hell, I wouldn't be surprised if we were followed from the get-go.

I sigh and brace myself for the persecution I'm sure to receive. The smell of garlic hits my nose as I open the door, and I know my mom's making her signature chicken alfredo with my favorite garlic sticks.

I inhale deeply. "I'm home," I announce as I try to head straight for my room. But that would be far too easy. My dad clears his throat, and I stop dead in my tracks, knowing exactly what it means. I walk backward a few steps and look to the right, spotting my dad sitting near the front room window.

I called that.

"I'm okay with you having friendships with boys. But it's obvious you and that young man are beyond friends," he starts the talk by pointing that out. I want to deny it, but I can't even force myself to. It would be a lie. And there is no point in doing that. "I'm just going to lay it out there. My house, my rules. No boyfriends, no dating, no nothing until you are out of this house. You have far too much going for you to let some boy screw it all up."

It takes every ounce of strength not to let the anger I'm feeling spill over. I bite the inside of my cheek to keep from spewing the words I so desperately want to. The faint taste of blood fills my mouth. I want to scream about how unfair he is. I want to huff and puff and make a big scene. But I don't. I keep my composure. If I act out, it'll only make it worse.

"Do you understand?" He holds my stare while I contemplate how to reply. Obviously, I'm going to answer yes... I just don't know if I'll do so politely or not.

"Yes, sir." The Jesus in me won that round.

"Good. Now," he says as he stands up, "I don't want you sitting by him anymore at church either. You can return to sitting up front next to your mother."

I groan. There goes my freedom. Well, all the freedom I care about.

Chapter Six

DUSTIN

The thing I typically love most about the school year is how busy I am. Between school itself, working at the local hardware store, baseball season, and conditioning (which seems to be basically year-round) I'm practically never home. I love my mom, but I'm far from a momma's boy. The woman wears me out, but I'm thankful for her dedication to me playing ball. She's never missed a game and still makes sure to bring snacks for all of us guys after every single game. They love their Mother Teresa, as they call her. You can always count on her to be sitting in her chair next to the dugout, full of school pride and screaming for her boy. Correction, boys—she considers the entire team her boys since we've grown up playing together.

I bounce down the stairs with my glove in my hand, rounding the way as I land on the tile.

"Dustin? Is that you?" my mom hollers from her sewing area in the dining room. The stitching noise comes to a halt when I reach the entryway. "Oh good. Look at the shirt I made for this season." She holds up the orange shirt with black lettering.

"Nice shirt, ma," I say, doing a quick glance, not paying much attention. She's made these types of shirts since I played T-ball.

"It's just"—she sniffles—"it's your last year." A sob erupts as she pulls the shirt to her, hugging it. Mother Teresa has never been one to be overemotional. Overbearing, yes.

"Oh, Ma." I walk over and lean down to hug her. "I'll be playing ball next year. Your shirt making days aren't over," I tease, trying to cheer her up.

"I know, but you'll be in college. You won't be here." Her voice cracks with realization.

"But I won't be far. And you'll still have Dax." I remind her.

"Not the same," she replies, gaining her composure.

"I know." I give her one more squeeze before pulling away. "He'll never be me, but second place will have to work." I grab a black sharpie off her sewing desk and slide it into the pocket of my mesh shorts.

"Hey, I heard that," Dax whines from the kitchen.

"I wouldn't expect anything less, radar ears." I swear he hears everything.

My mom neatly folds the shirt and wipes under her eyes with the back of her hand, removing the proof of her sadness. Standing, she looks at me, eyeing my glove in my hand. "Where are you going?"

"I'm heading to the school field to catch for Echo while she practices pitching. Then work." I lift my baseball hat off my head, flipping it around backward before sliding it back on.

My mom's face shifts to a disapproving stare—one that I'm all too familiar with. "Is that the preacher's daughter?" she snidely asks, placing a hand on her hip.

I roll my eyes and turn away, heading for the front door. I don't have time for her antics. I plan on making Echo mine today, and she's not going to interfere like she has in the past.

Hot on my trail, she places her hand on the door before I can open it. Annoyed, I avoid looking at her, waiting for her to be done with this dramatic burst. "Dustin." Her voice is low, almost a whisper.

I shift my gaze to her, seeing a look of desperation. The tension in my body eases without my approval.

"Don't forget about your future." She pleads with a softness I've never seen.

I want to tell her to calm down, that I'm just going to play catch, but I don't want to prolong this moment any longer than necessary.

"Okay, Ma." I nod, holding her gaze. She slowly pulls her hand away from the door and I quickly turn the knob before she tries to trap me again. "Bye, love ya," I say, getting the hell outta Dodge.

I don't look back as I jog down the concrete stairs of our porch, landing on the cracked sidewalk. I look over at my Blazer parked on the street and curse, realizing I left my keys on my dresser. My shoes begin slapping the pavement as I take off jogging toward the school. I'd much rather take the six-block journey by foot instead of going back inside and chance seeing my mom.

"COULD YA USE a catcher?" I ask, patting my glove as I take the crouching catcher's position behind home plate.

"It'd be highly appreciated," Echo replies somewhat breathlessly, making her way back to the pitcher's mound from gathering up her practice balls.

Her face fills with determination, shutting everything else out. She whips her arm around and slides her foot together in unison. The ball slaps into my glove with a loud thud, tingling my hand.

"Damn," I mutter, shaking my hand as I throw the ball back. I expect her to pop off a joke, but she quickly resumes her position, staying in the zone. We continue this back and forth for about thirty minutes.

"You're pretty badass," I admit as she makes her way toward me.

"Thanks," she replies, looking down, a light blush forming on her cheekbones.

"Ahem."

I hear the clearing of a throat. I turn around to see Echo's dad. A bubble of worry seeps in as I try reading his stoic features. He doesn't seem happy to see me, and I start to pray I didn't just get her in trouble.

"Hello, Mr. Price," I say with a wave. I want to walk up to him and properly greet him, maybe even indulge in some small talk, but the stern look across his face tells me I should think otherwise.

"Thanks for your help, Dustin." Echo smiles, trying to play cool.

"Anytime." I grin. "Oh, hey. You forgot one." I toss her the softball I had set aside when I first got here. She catches it with ease. I watch as she follows her dad, finally looking down at the ball in her hands. She glances back my way, and with a huge smile on her beautiful face, she gives me a nod.

Lord have mercy... I'm a goner.

Chapter Seven

ECHO

I hate that I'm made to feel guilty for something completely innocent. My dad most likely thinks I had this whole scheme orchestrated when I had no clue Dustin was going to show up. But no matter the ramifications, I'm thankful he did.

"What's he doing here?" my dad asks, looking back at Dustin, who stands with one hand in his shorts pocket and gives a small wave bye to the both of us. My dad nods, and I watch Dustin a little longer. Long enough for him to give me his signature grin that shows off his adorable dimple. That little indentation mixed with his pale green eyes makes my heart go pitter-patter.

"Honestly, he showed up all on his own just to spot me." My words are true. I just hope he believes them. Just because I have a crush on the boy doesn't change the status of what he is to me. I begin turning the ball in my hand. My heart goes from pitter-pattering to beating record fast. The words *Be My Girl* are scribbled across the ball. When my dad isn't looking, I glance back at an eagerly waiting Dustin and give him a quick nod as I hold the softball snug against my chest.

Excitement and dread fill my senses. My dad pops open the trunk, and I sit my bucket of softballs inside. I tuck the ball Dustin gave me in my glove, then place it in the bucket with the other balls. I close the trunk, then look at my dad, who's standing next to the open driver's side door. He's probably waiting for me to ask to drive because normally, I would. I have my license, but who knows when I'll have my own car. Probably never.

"Umm." I look down and rub my sweaty hands on the bottom of my shirt, suddenly feeling anxious. "Is it okay if I jog home?" I glance back up, chancing a look at my dad. He rests his hands on the roof of the car, looking at me and then out at the field where Dustin no longer resides.

"Is there a reason you're wanting to?" His eyes narrow, discerning my words.

"Well, I just need to start conditioning myself and think it'd be a good way to do so." I shrug, hoping it sounds believable. It's not a lie... fully. I can't tell him that my heart is overstimulated right now, and I can't sit still in the car with him. I can't tell him that the guy I just claimed to be 'a friend' is now more than 'a friend'. I can't tell him that I hate that I can't be excited about things like this and feel I have to hide it from him. How can something that feels so right feel wrong just because someone else disapproves?

"Fine," he says with a slight smile. "I'll give you a head start." He nods, urging me to take off. And I do, knowing he's going to beat me home no matter what because I plan on taking the long way. I have a lot of excitement I need to burn off before walking through the front door. I jog around town, exploring the outskirts I haven't really seen yet. Houses are a bit more spaced out, with larger yards to maintain. I come to a dead end that leads to the cemetery. I pause, taking in the rocky entrance with tall metal beams framing it. Cut-out letters spelling cemetery fill the space between the two beams, connecting them. I debate on venturing in but think better of it. I slowly walk backward before turning around and running back toward where I just came from. Having to backtrack is a disadvantage of not fully knowing the town, but I'm okay with it extending the time of my jog.

I make my way downtown to fully see what it has to offer. Passing the post office, I take notice of the pharmacy across the way. I slow myself to a walk to read the signs of the buildings that are tightly packed together. Old brick and rock forming most of the two-story shops. There's something whimsical about every small town's Main St. So much history that the town and its people seem dead set on preserving. And I see why. A flooring store, thrift store, bakery, and bar line the side I walk on. A bank, hair salon, and hardware store across from me. I stop and take in all the moving parts around me. Children laughing, cars passing by with music blaring, and car horns followed by people waving prove this small town is a lively one.

I'm about to continue my way home when a voice catches my attention. My head snaps across the street, where I see Dustin help load some items into an older woman's car. I smile, watching him sit her items inside with care before telling her to have a great day. I look both ways and jog across the street once the road is clear. I push open the glass door and the bell chimes.

"I'll be right with you," he says with his back toward me, intently scanning the shelf. "Can I help you?" he asks, stepping down from the stool, back still to me.

"Yes, I'm looking for my boyfriend. You might know him." I hold my hands behind my back, shifting my weight back and forth. That sounded way better in my head, and now I feel nervous saying it.

He spins around in my direction with a huge grin plastered on his face, taking a step toward me. "Yeah, I might know him." Two more steps and he's closed the distance between us. "He's a lucky son of a gun."

"You're right," I admit with a shrug, finally letting go of my hands as they drop to my side.

Dustin glances down and grabs one of my hands, taking it in his.

"You calling me your boyfriend sounds better than I could've imagined." He lifts his gaze, meeting mine.

Pitter-patter.

Pitter-patter.

So much for running all these feelings away.

"Ahem." I hear from behind. The joy drains from Dustin's face, replaced with annoyance. He drops my hand, crosses his arms across his chest, and leans to the side, looking past me. "You're not getting paid to flirt, pretty boy."

Dustin's jaw ticks, and his fists clench. I turn around, slightly placing myself in front of Dustin, and notice the tall, slender redhead. I'm pretty sure he's in my math class.

Peter... Patrick...ahh, Paul, his name badge appears in my view.

His cocky grin falters as soon as I begin to speak. "Hey, Paul," I start.

His face pinches together in disbelief as he fixates his gaze on me. I don't dare point out the obvious; that I only know his name because of the badge attached to his work smock.

"I stopped in for some paint samples," I lie. "Dustin saw me cradling my hand and asked to see my finger to check if it was possibly broken or just jammed," I lie again to cover up why he was holding my hand. "See," I say, holding my hand up long enough for him to look before covering it back up with my right hand.

"Mmmhmm," Paul says, narrowing his eyes at both of us. "And what was the consensus?"

"Jammed," Dustin grits out, causing a small smile to tug at the corner of my mouth.

"Well, at least it's not broken." Paul shrugs, now looking at only me. "I can help you with those paint samples, Echo." He finally smiles.

"Ahh." I glance down at my watch. "It looks like all this chitchatting has caused me to run out of time." This one isn't a lie as I do need to get home. "Maybe next time." I offer to lighten the blow.

It's a third lie as I don't need paint, nor would I want him to be the one helping me with samples. I turn toward Dustin, slowly walking backward to the door. "Thank you again, Dustin."

He finally loosens the stern face he has with Paul and waves. I wave back and add a wink for good measure. It earns me a low chuckle as he shakes his head before throwing a hand back through his hair. He keeps his eyes fixed on me until I turn around, and I know they're still on me until I'm outside the door and he can no longer see me.

I quickly make my way home, knowing my dad is going to have a conniption. I'm surprised he isn't out driving around looking for me. Ten minutes later, I'm heaving and out of breath but home nonetheless. I bend over, placing my hands on my thighs to get my breathing under control. I straighten my stance and hold my arms above my head, making my way to the front porch. My bucket of softballs is sitting next to the front door, and my heart sinks. I slowly make my way up the two steps and to the bucket. Reaching in, I grab my glove. My empty glove. Anxiety sweeps over me as my joyous mood now turns to dread.

"Looking for this?" my dad asks from the porch swing. The bushes lining the porch hid him so well. He tosses the ball to me just like Dustin did, and I catch it, reading *Be My Girl*.

Oh, shit.

Chapter Eight

DUSTIN

November 2000

I had heard the stories of love-struck fools. I had heard the stories of guys being whipped by their chicks having them wound tightly around their fingers. But I thought they were fables; something of folklore that Shakespeare wrote. So look who's now one of those love-struck, whipped fools who's wound around his girl's finger—ME! And I wouldn't have it any other way.

The guys on the team tease and call me whipped. It's all fun and games until Bryant loses his damn mind and calls me pussy whipped. That's where I draw the line. I'm in front of him faster than Speedy Gonzalez. Three of my teammates have to pull me back from demolishing his face.

How can you be whipped by something you have yet to experience?

Idiot.

"Dude, I was just joking. No need to Hulk out on me," Bryant says, rolling his shoulders and fixing his shirt where my hands had gripped it.

"Learn to watch your mouth and I won't have to," I growl, ready to really throw some fists if necessary.

"Yeah, whatever," he mumbles, leaving the locker room.

I continue shoving my dirty clothes into my bag. From the corner of my eye, I watch as our first baseman, Wes, makes his way toward me. He stops right beside me and places his hand on my shoulder, and I look up at him. "He really didn't mean any harm, you know?"

And the truth is, I do know. But just because his intentions aren't ill-willed doesn't mean they shouldn't bother me. If something bothers you, and you don't let the person responsible know, the likelihood of it happening again is high. Granted, I probably went about it all wrong. Okay, I'm sure I did.

I toss my bag over my shoulder and jog out of the weight room. While all the other guys are in a hurry to get in their cars and go to the big lake party Drew Nickols is throwing, I'm in a hurry to watch my girl and that hellacious fast ball of hers. Ball season hasn't officially started yet. We are just in the throes of practice. Her coach has been having Echo do some extra one-on-one practices with him lately.

The sun is her backdrop, and it showcases her beauty perfectly. Her brown hair sits messily on the top of her head, with a colorful headband wrapped around her hairline. All the girls seem to wear them, but for some reason, it looks best on her. Duh.

I walk up to the fence and drop my bag. Raising my hands above my head, I link my fingers with the chain-link. I want to whistle and do a bunch of obscene catcalls, but I don't want to distract her. She takes the game just as seriously as I do. Focus is written all over her face and in the way she directs her body. The catcher throws the ball back and Echo lifts her glove at the last minute, catching the ball with ease. I have the belief that she can play this game blind—play it off of hearing alone. That's how in tune she is.

She rolls the ball in her hand and stands with her right foot on the pitcher's mound. She extends both arms out straight in front of her with her glove covering her right hand. With her arms swung down, her left resting against her right leg, her right swinging behind her as she bent over. She pushes off with her right foot and seems to be flying through the air as her left foot shoots out in front of her and her arm swings around with such intense momentum. Echo lands with her feet spread apart. The right one slides up from behind as her arm comes up from underneath, releasing the fastest sailing ball I've yet to see another female duplicate.

"STRIKE!" her coach yells from behind the catcher.

"Hell yeah!" I put my fingers in my mouth, whistling. I don't think. I just act. I'm excited and proud and can't keep quiet about it.

She looks over at me, shaking her head with the biggest grin ever. She starts to head over my way, but her coach hollers for her. She mouths, "One minute," while holding up a finger. I nod and enjoy the view as she turns and runs toward her coach. Man, do the shorts she's wearing look good on those thick legs of hers. The girl has curves for days, and I can't wait until I'm able to test drive them.

She stands tall and straight with confidence in front of her coach. The nosy ass side of me wishes I were closer so I could hear what's being said. She nods a few times and then excitement takes over as she begins smiling, and her body goes from statuesque to bouncing with joy.

"Dustin!" she yells, running and jumping into my arms. Not sure if it was the momentum or the excitement, or a combination that took us to the ground.

"Sorry." She giggles.

"Mmm. Never apologize for being on top of me." I push the falling strands of hair out of her face.

She pauses momentarily, taking in what I said, then nods. "Deal. So guess what?"

"What, babe?" I ask, feeling my own excitement building—in more places than one.

"I'm starting. Coach said I've gone above and beyond and have proven myself. He's making me the starting pitcher." She squeals the last part out.

"Baby, that's amazing! I told you!" I lean in, instinctively grabbing her face with both hands. And without a second thought, I bring her lips to mine. She pulls away, touches her lips, and for a moment I worry that I overstepped. Then she drops her hand and places it against my cheek.

"You never cease to amaze me. Your faith in me knows no bounds. Thank you for that." She leans down, pressing her lips to mine. I want to slide my tongue against them, beckon them to grant me access, but not here. This is not the time or place to leave her breathless.

"I will always be your number one fan, Echo. Always." I pat my hands on her bare thighs. "But now you're gonna have to get off me, or I won't be able to walk for a while."

"Huh?" Her brows bunch together in the cutest way as she tries to make sense of my request. I grab her hips and rock mine against them a couple times, driving in my point, which only makes it worse on my end. Her eyes get big as saucers and an innocent smile plays on her mouth. She felt it. That's for sure.

Chapter Nine

ECHO

It sucks that Dustin and I can only see each other at school, on the ball fields—if the timing works out—and at church. Even though Dustin's parents quit coming three Sundays after Dustin and I initially met, he's made sure to be here every time the door is open. I know, in the beginning, he wasn't really into church, or religion, for that matter. I'm sure some of what was preached interested him, but he wasn't coming for a lifestyle change. He was coming for me. But I believe that night at the youth rally changed his motivation. I believe after that, he was coming for himself, and I was just an added perk.

"It's stupid we can't sit together," Dustin mutters, pulling his lips from mine. We found a safe hiding spot in the church's stairwell a few Sundays ago. It's only a matter of time before he gets fed up with our situation. As much as he promises and reassures me he'll never go anywhere, I always worry. One day, all the strictness and secrecy will drive him away.

It's a fear... No, more like dread. Because, deep inside, I know it's inevitable.

"I'm sorry," I whisper, looking down. "I understand if you don't want to continue this—if you don't want to be with me."

"Are you crazy?" His eyes widen, searching mine, and he tightly grabs my hands.

"Maybe," I reply seriously. I'm starting to believe I might just be crazy for believing something with him might work. It's obvious my dad is going to play the "over my dead body" card. "My dad is more than anti D plus E forever."

"That's fine and dandy, miss."

I look up and smile at the innocent look he's giving me.

"Your dad can be against us all he wants. But we have fate on our side, and what's fated cannot be undone." He brings my hand to his mouth and places a light kiss on it.

His words cause my heart to pound against my chest. Fate—he thinks fate brought us together. He feels the connection, too. He knows it isn't misplaced or temporary. Knowing this makes me fall for him even more.

Okay, a lot more.

"You really think so?" I ask, needing reassurance.

He nods. "I know so. The universe is our limit. And I'm betting we could surpass it if we wanted."

"Echo Dian Price."

Dread instantly prickles my skin. Dustin quickly steps back as we both look over, seeing my mother, who appears to be extremely pissed. Her face is piping mad as she whisper-yells, "Have you lost your mind?"

The thought of saying 'maybe' crosses my mind. Instead, I stand frozen, unable to form any words. This is it—where it all comes to a halt. There's no way the universe is letting us off unscathed.

She continues staring, her arms crossed. Her head tilts angrily and she waits for a reply—for something.

"Ma'am," Dustin speaks up. "This is all my fault. I followed her out. I had to ask her a—"

"That's enough," my mother says, raising her hand to cut him off. "This is where you need to leave. And by leave, I mean go home."

Dustin looks at me, indecision and torment on his face. He isn't keen on being told what to do—especially when it goes against what he believes.

I nod. "It's okay," I say, slightly out of breath and not looking forward to what's to come after he walks out those church doors.

I can see his frustration and second-guessing if he should abandon me to the wolves—because surely my father will be showing up next. After all, wolves run in packs. Dustin finally lets out a deep breath, and his shoulders drop. He isn't hiding his disapproval. I love him for his instinct to protect me at all costs. But there's nothing he can do, and he leaves out the back door once he realizes that.

I shudder when the door slams. I hope it didn't shake the entire church in the same way I feel my life being shaken up like a snow globe. I have a sinking feeling all things between Dustin and me will forever be altered. Surely, he's done being with me now. The thought makes me want to cry, but I stay strong. I can face whatever is coming my way.

"I'm just not even sure what to say to you right now," my mom states, pacing back and forth. She keeps glancing back toward the sanctuary, making sure no one sees us. "First off"—she stops pacing and points her finger as she takes a few steps toward me—"this sneaking around business is highly unacceptable. I mean, of all places to do it, you had to do it in the house of God." She scoffs in disbelief. "What if it had been your father who found you? Or a deacon? Or anyone else besides me?" Her hands remain at her sides, bunched up tightly. But I see a trace of something else lingering in her eyes. Indecision. She straightens her dress out, then props her hands on her petite waist and looks to the side deep in thought.

I study her with confusion. I'm absolutely dumbfounded by her words. What does she mean by anyone besides her?

Out of nowhere, compassion fills her face, and she drops her hands, taking mine into hers. "I know you think no one understands. But that's where you're wrong. I was you once. I was smitten with a boy, and I had a super strict dad who forbade it." Her right hand comes up to my face, cupping my cheek. She looks deeply into my eyes, and I see sadness. "That's exactly why I know how this is going to end. And all I want to do is protect you from getting hurt."

"What?" I pull away, shaking my head. She's not a mind reader. "Why would you say that? Dustin isn't going to hurt me."

She sighs. "Echo, you're both seventeen. Life isn't some fairy tale. Things happen and come into play that can alter everything. And the biggest thing of all is people change. That's bound to happen."

A feeling I'm all too familiar with seeps in. Determination. Except I'm determined to prove her wrong. What happened to her will not happen to me. She flips my mood from being full of worry about my father to now not caring if she tells my sins to the whole world. I've never fully experienced this feeling of defiance before. I've always poured every ounce of myself into making sure I do what I'm supposed to in order not to go against my parents. I've always cared too much about disappointing them or not having their full approval.

For the first time in my life, I don't care.

And it feels...freeing.

"I didn't want to hear it, either," my mother mumbles as she turns away from me and begins walking off. "Come on," she orders. "If your father asks...*when* your father asks," she corrects, "you were sick in the bathroom. Make it believable." She looks back at me and I nod.

She's going to lie for me. She's on my side after all. I feel like I've been throat punched, and I choke back a sob I feel reverberating in my chest. My heart softens for her, and while the idea of rebelling against my dad is still at the forefront of my mind, I don't want her to get caught in the crossfire. Her confession and actions now have me questioning everything I thought I knew.

Chapter Ten

DUSTIN

"You have a wicked arm, Striker," I say, calling her by the nickname I've given her as I wrap my arms around her from behind.

"I'm so sweaty. I wouldn't even touch me." She tries pulling away.

"Well, good thing I like you." I pull her in tighter. "I wish I could catch more of your practices. These preseason tournaments are making it impossible." Times like these, I wish we only played spring ball like the girls instead of this preseason stuff they started doing three years ago.

"Well, at least we have that in common." She turns around in my arms and faces me, lightly draping her hands around my neck.

"Oh, is that all?" I ask with a smirk.

"There might be a few other things." She reaches up and presses her lips against mine, pulling back before I can deepen it. "I'd like to think we're both good kissers."

"That might be questionable," I tease. "I need you to try that again so I can come to the same conclusion you have." I pucker up and she obliges to my request. This time, she doesn't pull back. In fact, it's her opening my mouth, granting me access first. My hands tighten around her perfect hips as I pull her body into mine.

Honking in the distance brings us both back to reality and we slowly peel ourselves from one another.

"I'd hate for one of my dad's spies to see us." She gives me a half smile, attempting to joke about it, but I know it's something she truly worries about. After telling me what her mom had said, she's lucky it was her who found us and that she didn't tell her father.

"Yeah, I need to get home too. Mom's making my favorite meal."

"And what's that?" Echo asks as we walk side by side down the student parking lot behind the school. We'll have to split ways once we make it to the front.

"Lasagna." I grin just thinking about it. My mom makes the world's best lasagna. I'm convinced of that, and I could quite possibly eat it for the rest of my life and never complain.

I kiss my girl on the lips and tell her bye, watching as she heads home. I can't help but wonder what's bothering her. I just hope she believed me when I told her I wasn't going anywhere. She's worth the pain in the ass her dad can be. I'm not going to let him dictate my future. I just pray she won't either.

"About time you got home," my mom says as soon as I walk in the door.

"I hurried," I lie. "I knew what tonight was." That part is at least true.

"Good, because you're the only reason I make it. There's a lot of work that goes into all this goodness." My mom looks up from the steaming dish she just grabbed out of the oven and smiles.

"I knew I was your favorite," I murmur. For some reason, I have a strong urge to hug her. We have our moments when we butt heads, but I can't complain. Plus, Ma has never missed a single one of my games. That takes true dedication. The same dedication my dad throws into Dax. He used to come to my games when I was younger, but now they branch off if Dax's and my schedules collide. I used to let my dad not attending all my games hurt my feelings. I'd see him and Dax going to all these airplane shows and always wanting to go check out new exhibits at the Air and Space Museum and get jealous. I was his first son—a baseball prodigy—and he'd rather look at fossils. As I've grown older, I've learned it's not necessarily that Dax is my dad's favorite, it's just the two of them both enjoy the same things. I can't blame them when they invite me to join and I always decline.

Being with Echo has opened my eyes a bit. It's easy to think negatively about your life and the people in it. Until you witness what someone else has to deal with. I will forever be grateful to my parents. They've let me spread my wild wings since day one, and never once did they try to clip them.

Suddenly, something wet and cold smacks me in the back of the neck. I turn toward my brother, who's trying to suppress a laugh with his hand over his mouth, and I glare. Way for him to ruin the moment.

"Sorry, bro. I was aiming for the sink."

"Aiming for the sink with your eyes closed apparently," I smart off, bending down to grab the rag. I lean past my mom and toss it in the sink.

"How'd you guess?" Dax replies, being completely serious. He continues setting the table and I shake my head. We definitely are complete opposites. Where I'm a sarcastic smartass, he's carefree and goofy. I can't help but chuckle as I watch him play *Duck, Duck, Goose* with the cups he's setting down. He's such a nerd.

I come up behind him and smack him on the head. "Goose."

"Hey," he whines as he starts to chase me around the dining room table. Now I feel like a carefree eighth grader again. And I revel in the lightness of it all.

THE NEXT DAY at practice is much cooler than it has been lately. November is always my favorite month of the year—the beginning of fall. It's no longer sweltering heat outside, but it's also not cold yet. This in between is my happy place. I quickly gather my things once practice ends. I know my girl will be waiting, and I can't wait to see her. It isn't like I can touch her in school. So our fields are the only semi-safe place for us to get in a little PDA, and for some reason, today I'm feeling extra frisky.

"I'm sure impressed by that wicked arm you have." Echo gives me a sexy smirk as she rounds the dugout, using my words back on me. I had just walked out from changing when I spot her. She leans against the deep-red cinderblock, propping her foot back against the concrete. She keeps her eyes focused on me as I stride toward her.

"I think you're mistaken, Striker." I drop my bag, standing right in front of her. I press my body against hers. Her breath hitches as she begins to drape her arms over my shoulders. I let my hands run down the length of her arms as I push them above us, pinning them against the dugout wall with one hand. "You're the one with the wicked arm. I'm merely just a third baseman.

"And that's where you're mistaken, Chipper." She squirms against me, a little breathless. "Who says I was even referencing baseball?"

"Mmm." I lick my lips. I press my lips to hers and she moans, her body sinking against mine.

I grab her hand, lacing our fingers together as I pull her around to the opening of the dugout. It faces out toward the wooded area behind the school. Out of view from anyone who may be lingering around the fields. We never have privacy and I'm going to take advantage of the space and time we have at the moment.

Once we're inside, I twist her so she has her back to the wall and is facing me.

"I want to test your theory," I say before kissing her. She moans into my mouth as I deepen the kiss. I can't hold back the want to please her that's taking over me. "Sit down, baby." I hold her hands as she slowly sits down on the small, wooden bench. I kneel in front of her, looking up at her curious face. She isn't scared or remotely indecisive as to what I'm about to do. I stare into her eyes, knowing this girl trusts me completely...and I'll never give her a reason not to.

"You know what I love most about these shorts you always wear?" I ask as I rub my hands up her thighs.

"Hmm?" she moans in response, never taking her heavy, heated eyes from mine.

"Easy access." I slide my hands underneath the mesh fabric, and my breath hitches once my fingers meet the material between her legs. I proceed to show her that not only is my arm wicked, but so are my fingers. Once I'm finished, she returns the favor.

"Let me take care of you."

My heart melts, and as soon as I feel her hand touch me, everything goes a bit blurry. Yet it was the clearest it's ever been all at once. I thought I was putty in her hands to begin with, but the way she handles me with such love and intensity ruins me. The feeling of desire she ignites within makes me unable to see straight or, hell, think straight. My heart knows what's taking place. In fact, it encourages it.

This woman of mine takes me to a place I've never been. I don't want to return to earth. The way she makes me feel is unbelievable. We stare at one another for what feels like an eternity. She's an absolute goddess. I offer her my hand as I stand, pulling her up with me, and hold her tightly against me.

"Thank you," I whisper in her ear, causing a shiver.

"No, thank you," she murmurs, letting out a heavy sigh of contentment.

"I'm so in love with you," I admit, no longer able to keep it in.

She pulls away from me, resting her hands on my hips, and stares at me intently. Her eyes bounce back and forth, searching for any sign of doubt. She has to know how I feel. I cup her face in my hands, holding her gaze with the same intensity. I could get lost in her dreamy eyes.

"I'm in love with you," I slowly enunciate each word.

Her shoulders drop, and the tenseness that took over her body dissipates.

Sincerity floods her eyes, and her hands dig into my hips. "I think I've been in love with you since the first day I saw you."

I crush my lips to hers, reveling in the knowledge that this girl of mine is in love with me. I'll never know what I did to deserve someone as perfect as her.

Afterward, we grab our bags and head for the parking lot. I know I'm cheesing like a fool, a love-struck one, and so is she. We're both cheesing, blushing fools. I can't help what I'm feeling. I stop, grab her hand, and pull her into me. I don't care if there are people nearby. I need to feel her lips against mine. The kiss becomes so deep and mind-numbingly amazing that I forget we're out in the open. Until I hear a loud, obnoxious throat clearing.

Echo's body instantly stiffens. But I don't. I remain calm for both of us. I can tell just by that annoying noise that her mood has changed like a light switch being flicked off.

"It's okay." I place my finger under her chin, tilting her head up, giving her my reassuring smile before lightly kissing her forehead. My feelings for her know no bounds. Most guys, ones that are smart or scared, wouldn't have taken that extra step in the public affection department. I can tell Echo is half annoyed I did. I know she's nervous about her dad, and the last thing she needs is the inevitable prolonged by more kissing in front of the overbearing man. But I'm done bowing down. I'm not going to cower away when we aren't doing anything wrong.

Chapter Eleven

ECHO

The few blocks back home are torturous. My father doesn't say a word the entire car ride. He even turns the radio off of the sermon he had been listening to. I know I'm in for it. He isn't one to ever hold his tongue about his beliefs or enforcing them upon me. What he witnessed completely rendered him speechless. Until we pull into the driveway.

"I don't want you ever seeing that boy again." My dad finally breaks the silence as he stares out the front windshield, refusing to look my way. He's clearly disgusted with me and I'm not sure how to take that. Or if I even care.

"I go to school with him," I mumble.

"Well, we can change that if it's going to be a problem," he threatens, clenching his hands around the steering wheel. "And you're grounded."

I bite my tongue, pushing the words and bile that want to spew at bay. I internally count to ten to gain my composure before finally speaking. "For how long?"

"Until I say you're no longer grounded," he barks, startling me.

My body tenses and I hold my breath, unsure of what's to come. When he opens his door, I do the same. My side is closer to the house, so I manage to beat him inside and attempt an escape back to my room.

"Hurry and wash up," my dad mutters from behind as he shuts the door. "Dinner's in ten minutes."

"I'm not hungry," I whisper as I keep walking, not even bothering to look back.

"Did I ask?" he snaps back.

I drop my bag, letting it slam to the ground, and turn to face him. "What for, Dad? So we can pretend to be some perfect family?" I know I'm asking for it, but my "give o' shit" meter is broken. I feel so defeated.

"No family is perfect," my mother whispers from behind me. Almost as a peace offering. I know she's trying to be a mediator. That she doesn't want to blatantly go against my dad, but also, she feels sympathy for me. I can see it in the little things. It almost makes me feel sorry for her and the situation she's in. But then I remind myself she's the one who chooses to stay in it.

"Then I guess we can drop the act, right?" I look back at her, catching a glimpse of sadness and understanding before cutting my eyes back to my dad. His look is anything but sadness and understanding. His closely resembles anger and disgust.

Yes, me, his pride and joy, have brought out that look. The sad thing is he should be feeling those things toward himself. I'm not saying I'm perfect and acted innocently. But if he were reasonable, things would've gone differently. They never had to go to the extent he's taken them. He caused the ridge that is now between us. He caused me to push him away and rebel. He can blame the devil all he wants, but he's the one doing his work.

God doesn't want you to shelter people and restrict them to a box. He wants you to teach them His ways and then let them have the option of how they will live. God wants people to have choice because

God is selfless. He wants people to live for Him because it's their choice to. Not because they are forced to. What my dad is doing to me is not of God. And like my father always says, *"If it's not of God, it's of the Devil."*

"Just go to your room," Mom proposes, sounding completely crushed. My dad's eyes dart past me to her with such an unfamiliar intensity.

"Gladly." I seethe, looking at my dad. I reach down and grab my bag, tossing it over my shoulder. I take a step, then glance back. "I hope you find the man you used to be before you suck the life out of all of us." The first tear makes its way down my face. I look away so he doesn't see it. "Kind of ironic how God gives us free will, yet you can't do the same." I laugh in disbelief, making my way down the hall. I hear a door slam, knowing it's the door to my dad's study.

Good. He needs to go spend some time with the Lord. I wish it consisted of him truly seeking God and praying for guidance. I wish it were him being humble and asking God to reveal what he cannot see. But I know he's in there praying for me, and probably my mother, as well. Him and those blinders. He'll never be able to see his wrongdoing if he never lifts them.

I DON'T GO to school the following day. I play sick, and my mom allows it. I want to go to school. I really, really do. I mean, it's the only place I'm going to be able to see Dustin. So logically, staying home makes no sense, but I'm emotionally drained. I know Dustin would make me feel better, but I don't want him to see me like this—wallowing in self-pity and doubt. Even though my dad isn't here, I hide out in my room most of the day. Many times, I find myself daydreaming about Dustin and me in the dugout yesterday.

Thinking about our intimate time brings a pang of guilt in my stomach. I never want to regret anything when it comes to Dustin.

How can something that feels so right, be wrong? I push the idea away, chalking it up to my dad's overbearing beliefs and how disgusted with me he'd be. I countlessly replay him telling me he's in love with me. Those words give me hope. Hope that this all hasn't been for nothing. Sometimes hope is enough for survival.

The doorbell rings at 3:20 p.m. and I know exactly who it is. Dustin is smart and sneaky. I figured he'd come up with a ninja plan to check on me. It was probably torture for him to wait until school was out. I walk up to my closed bedroom door and push my ear against it, listening carefully. If my door didn't creak, I would open it.

"Hello, Mrs. Price."

My mother doesn't offer Dustin to call her by her first name this time.

"Dustin," she replies thickly, acknowledging him. The boy has balls, I'll give him that.

"I noticed that Echo wasn't at school today." He states the obvious.

"She's sick," my mother throws out. I hate how short she's being with him.

"That's what I figured. So I went around to her classes and gathered her work. I missed two days of school once, and you'd think I had missed a month. It made me wonder if they just threw in extra work to make me suffer. I felt like I was never going to catch up." He laughs, trying to lighten the mood. Just something else I love about him. He's always trying to make the best of a situation.

"That's really thoughtful of you, Dustin," she says, a slight softening to her tone.

I can practically see his charming smile. "Anytime, ma'am."

"Well, I better get this to her. Thank you again."

"Anytime," Dustin repeats before I hear the door close.

I run back to my bed, jump in, throw my headphones on, and pick up the book I have been reading. I know my mom will be coming straight to my room, but I can't make it obvious that I'm anticipating it. I stay turned away from my door even though I hear the knocking. I stay turned away even when I hear the creaky door opening and my mother saying my name. I stay turned away until the moment I feel tapping on my shoulder.

"Ahh," I jump, surprising her. I yank my headphones off and let them fall to the floor.

"Sorry." My mom laughs, and it seems like it's been forever since I've seen her genuinely smile.

"Mmmhmm, I'm sure." I smile back. I need to have one advocate on my side. My mom has already proven she has skin in the game, but she can't be my cheerleader for its entirety. She's only able to hide on the sidelines without the coach knowing. She can't get caught. And I don't want her to. I don't want to come between her and my father. I don't want sides to be chosen, or a line drawn between the three of us. I want to ask if she's happy, if she made the right choice so long ago. Something tells me she'd lie, so I don't bother breaching the subject. Doing so won't change anything.

I sit up in my bed, and she holds out both hands with my schoolwork in them. I reach for the book and the few loose papers, giving her a questioning look.

"The boy brought this for you." She gives me a sympathetic sideways grin.

"The boy," I repeat her words. The boy has a name. "The boy we shall not speak of, I presume."

"Yeah, that one." She sighs. "You know, Echo," she starts, but I shake my head.

"No, Mom. It's all been said and done. Nothing can fix this."

She nods in understanding, then turns to walk away. When she reaches the doorway, she looks back. "I have dinner soon with some of the ladies from church. It's at Mrs. Martha's house. I'm unsure how late I will be, but your dad should be home in a few hours."

I want to say, *"Yay, lucky me."* But I just nod. "Have a good time, Mom."

"Oh yeah, a blast," my mom says sarcastically, rolling her eyes. I get the nagging feeling my mom is getting burned out living her purpose in life through my dad.

I look at the papers I have for homework. One is an English assignment. I have to write a paper. Big shocker, since that seems to be all we do in that class. The last sheet is Trig. I'm not a big fan of the mathematics department. I sit the papers to the side and then open my Trig book, where a blue Post-it note sticks out the top. I frown at it, knowing I have never put one in this book, or any book for that matter. I don't even think I own any Post-it notes.

Use this page for your homework sheet.
Now turn to page 272 for your other assignment.

I turn to page 272. Another Post-it note sticks in the center of the page.

Now go to your window.

Chapter Twelve

DUSTIN

s soon as Echo's mom shuts the front door, I run to the side of the house and open the wooden gate. I remember her complaining about how it can be a pain and get stuck, so I make sure to be swift and lift up as I push in.

I know Mrs. Price will walk straight to Echo's room to give her the work I picked up. That gives me plenty of time to sneak into the backyard while she's on the other side of the house. I also notice she's dressed up, so I'm really hoping she's about to leave. I need to talk to Echo. With her dad catching us the day before and then her not being at school today, I fear the worst. I wanted to leave at lunch when I knew without a doubt she wasn't showing up. But then this brilliant idea hit me, and I knew I'd get farther with it than trying to sneak around midday.

Her blinds are shut, and I can barely hear talking. I pull out my pocketknife and start carving into her windowsill as I wait. I don't make my masterpiece big; just big enough for her to notice it. I want it to be a reminder for her. I want the girl I love to never forget about me, no matter what happens with us. I want to make sure I implant every small thing I can to keep her mind on me. It's the little things that count. Grand gestures are nice, but it's all the small things that come around at the most unexpected times, taking your mind back to a moment, or a person. Those are the things I want to create between us —the small, meaningful things that will always keep us connected.

The old, heavy front door shuts, rattling all the windows. I hear the start of a car and know I'll be seeing Echo any second. I blow at the pieces of wood and white paint and brush the remaining dust away with my hand. I watch with anticipation as the blinds slowly lift. Inch by inch, I begin seeing my girl. I want to break the window and jump in and tackle her, but I refrain. Barely.

She smiles as soon as she sees my face, making my heart skip a beat. I'm not going to lie; I was scared shitless of how she'd react. Not seeing her today put a whole new level of doubt in me I haven't experienced before. I hate feeling her father has the power to instill doubt in both of us.

She kneels on her bed, places her hands on the glass, and pushes the window up. "Hey, handsome."

"Hey, gorgeous," I reply as I take her in. Her hair is extra messy from lying down, and I love it. I want to be the cause of the messiness. One day, I promise myself.

"Thanks for the delivery."

"No biggie." I shrug. "I had a hidden agenda."

"Oh yeah?" She giggles. "And what's that?"

I push up on the screen, releasing it, and then lower it to the ground. "Kissing my girl," I say as I lean in to claim her lips. She returns the kiss but doesn't fully give in. She's reserved and hesitant. And I hate it.

She pulls away, looking down. "We're going to get caught. Again." She pulls her bottom lip between her teeth in a worrisome manner.

"No, we won't." I grab her hand that's resting on the windowsill and pull it to my lips, placing a kiss on the soft skin.

She looks up at me, and it nearly breaks my heart. A few tears spill from her eyes and slowly roll down her face.

"We will. Somehow. Some way. It'll happen. Someone will see us and tell my dad. Or, for all I know, God himself might do the snitching." The funny thing about her last statement is I can see her father saying God revealed it to him.

"We'll just be extra careful," I assure. "We won't make the same mistakes and be so careless."

"I can't lose you." She begins to sob, making me realize just how hard this is on her and the extent that it's gone. "Next time we won't be so lucky. My father can be an extremist. I don't even want to know what he'd do if he caught us together again." She shudders at the thought.

I take her hand I'm still holding and lower it to the outside windowsill. I move it back and forth across the letters as if it's Braille. "Do you feel this? Do you see what this says?"

She glances down and tries to smile, but more tears fall instead.

"Echo," I say, urgency in my voice. She looks up at me. "This is my promise to you." She glances back down and begins tracing the D+E 4ever. "Scooch back for a minute." As soon as she moves, I hop in, landing on her bed. I don't care if I'm going against everyone and their dog's wishes—or commands. My girl needs me and I'm going to hold her. She doesn't argue or urge me to get out like I half expect. I need to calm her down and reassure her everything will be okay...with time. Things might seem impossible at first, but if both people want them bad enough, anything is possible.

"It won't be easy, but it'll be worth it," I say as I hold her against me.

"Promise?" she whispers.

"Hell yeah, I promise it'll be worth it."

"No, promise you won't leave me." Her voice cracks a bit.

"Never. I'm never leaving you," I vow. The thought of losing her inflicts a palpable pain in my chest. The sensation brings tears to my eyes.

"I believe you." She breathes against the crook of my neck.

We sit quietly, just taking each other in for what feels like forever. I don't want to let her go, knowing she's filled with such grief and doubt. I want to comfort her and erase all those feelings, but I know I can only do so much. She has to trust what I feel and have faith in us. However, I fear with her father hovering over her, those feelings might remain until we graduate.

Just seven more months to go.

"You better go," Echo says, sitting up quickly. "My dad will be home soon." She starts having a mini freak-out.

"Hey, hey." I grab her hand. "You gotta stop. Freaking out won't help anything. The only thing it'll do is make you look guilty. Okay?"

She nods, breathing in and out, calming herself down.

"Okay. We got this."

We stand together and I wrap my arms tightly around her. I want her to feel secure and to know she's safe with me. She lets out a sigh, and her body relaxes against mine. I love it.

"How are you able to handle this so well? Why haven't you run in the other direction?" she asks as we both look at each other.

"Because I don't throw away something that's valuable. And I see value in you and what we have together." I give her the short answer. We don't have enough time on this earth for me to list all the reasons.

She looks at me with such astonishment, like I hung the moon. I will hang the moon for her every night of my life if that's what she wants.

Chapter Thirteen

ECHO

December 2000

Dustin and I have been keeping our distance from one another in public. I feel as if I'm slowly starting to lose myself to this situation. Maybe that's what my dad was worried about—that I'd catch a case of puppy love and lose who I was to keep the boy. It's crazy the opposite is what is causing it. Not being able to freely have the boy and the puppy love wears me down, changing me in ways I never thought possible. I hate it. I want me back.

The realization of it all finally hit me, and determination has since taken over. I'm not going to be ruined by this. I already walk on eggshells with my dad. Why does the rest have to feel like an impossible tight rope to balance as well? I start hanging out at Dave's on the weekends with the rest of the youth, trying to find a semblance of my old self. But doing it makes me miss Dustin and his presence even more. His humor, the jam sessions they'd have, the play wrestling matches the boys would have…it's just not the same without him there.

To everyone around us, Dustin and I are single. We made the tough decision to cut the world off from what we have going on. Denying his existence when I see him in the hall is one of the hardest things to do when my entire being feels pulled toward him. But it's necessary and seems to loosen the vice my dad has on me. All I have to do is make him believe he's won. Surely, we can keep the charade going long enough.

Tonight, my parents are gone to a Christmas party, and I just can't pass up the opportunity to see my guy. Sometimes the risk is worth the outcome.

"I got a surprise for you," Dustin says as he jumps in through my bedroom window.

"A surprise for me?" I ask as I walk up, pulling him in for a hug. "What for?" I hold him tightly, never wanting to let go.

"Do I need a reason?" he breathes against my ear, causing my body to shiver.

He pulls back and hands me a bag. I eagerly pull the handles apart to see what he got me. I giggle as I pull out the package. He found me a glow-in-the-dark Orion's Belt to place on my ceiling.

"Oh my gosh. I can't believe you found this. It's perfect. I love it. I love you," I say, throwing my arms around his neck.

"I love you, too," he says against my skin, causing a ripple of goose bumps. He laughs at the effect he has on me as he pulls back. "So"—he glances up at my ceiling—"where ya wanting to put it?"

I climb on my bed, standing up. "Right above me so it's the last thing I see before I go to sleep and first thing I see when I awake." I extend my hand for him to join me. We stand on my bed and place the glow-in-the-dark constellation on the ceiling, right above my pillow.

"Did you know that Orion's Belt is also called Three Kings?" he asks, rolling the sticky putty into a ball before squishing it to the back of the piece he's holding.

"Yes, and it's an asterism or a pattern of stars in the constellation Orion." I've always had an unnatural love for astronomy. It's so hard for me to grasp how vast and beautiful the universe is. I can't understand how some people don't believe there's a God who created it all.

"For some reason, I always thought Orion's Belt was the actual constellation. I never knew it was basically just a cluster of stars within one," Dustin admits with a sense of astonishment. I stretch as far as I can without falling over. I hear him slightly snicker. He knows better than to offer to do it for my stubborn self.

"I think most people assume that." I grunt from the unsuccessful stretch, then begin bouncing, determined to get the last piece up. Five jumps up and I nail it, hearing a sharp snap when I land. "Whoa!" I shriek as we both start to wobble as my bed buckles beneath us.

We collapse together onto the plush mattress as the foot of my bed crumbles to the ground, leaving it at a slant. My body starts shaking with laughter. Dustin lets out a laugh as well and I can't help but take in how amazing it feels to just...be ourselves. It makes me wonder how amazing this could be if it was allowed to blossom on its own instead of being snuffed out like a controlled fire that's run its course. I don't know when I'll have another moment like this with him. I don't want to waste the few and far between times we are able to sneak in.

I roll on top of Dustin, and his laugh instantly fades, replaced with something else. I watch as his eyes turn from bright with amusement to dark with desire. He feels it, too. I push one hand through his hair as the fingertips from my other trace over his facial features, wanting to embed every inch of him into my memory.

His hands move to my back, rubbing them up and down in a reassuring way. I can feel his slight hesitation as if he's holding back. I understand it because I feel the same, but I also don't want the opportunity to slide through my fingertips.

"I love you, Dustin. I'm not sure of a lot of things in my life, but my love for you is certain." I hold his gaze, feeling the same amazement I do about the stars.

"God, I love you," he whispers, swallowing hard. His fingers graze my cheek before tucking a piece of hair behind my ear. I watch the movement of his hand and see a glimpse of all the emotion he's trying to avert.

I grasp his face between my hands, causing his arms to tighten their grip around me. Bending down to his ear, I let my words dance across his skin. "Please don't hide your feelings from me. I want you to feel everything with me. I want to be your first and your last." I keep my lips pressed against his skin, wrapping my arms underneath his neck, fully embracing him. I never want to let him go.

"Are you sure?" He pants as if he's been holding his breath for an eternity.

I even my face with his, desperate for him to see how I feel. "I've never been more sure of anything." His hands lock onto my hips, holding me tightly against him.

The front door shuts and we freeze momentarily. Then panic sets in and I swing myself off him, almost rolling off the broken bed. Dustin grabs me in the nick of time, keeping me from falling to the floor with a thud. I muster up a small smile as a thanks offering. I hear the keys hit the entryway table and my mom begins hollering my name.

Shit. Shit. Shit.

Like a ninja, Dustin flips over and scales the incline of my bed. Careful not to break it further. With swift precision, he lifts the window and slides out with it half open. I climb up my bed and give him a quick peck before he turns to his escape route. Quietly, I push the window back down into place and yank my curtains shut right as my bedroom door swings open.

I flip around breathlessly as if I've been caught red-handed.

"What in God's name happened in here?" my mom questions, eyeing my broken bed. "And why do you seem out of breath?"

My dad walks in behind her, closing the distance between them. His eyes go wide as they inspect my room, narrowing as he sets his gaze on me. When he doesn't give me his own set of questions, I answer the ones my mom asked.

"Well," I start, letting out a nervous laugh. "I was putting up my constellation." I glance up, pointing to the ceiling. Their eyes follow mine. "And my bed kind of gave out beneath me."

While my mom's stance eases as her shoulders drop, believing my story, my dad's posture remains stiff. "Why does your curtain look out of place?" He eyes Dustin's escape route.

"Welllll," I say again, letting it drag out longer this time. "I'm sure my flailing arms caught it as my bed broke." I want to sneer, shake my head, and say, *Duh*, but I also want him to believe me. I mean, ninety-five percent of the story is true.

His eyes stay affixed five beats longer than they should on my window while he plays out what I just said, seeing if there're any holes in my story. He doesn't say anything before turning away and walking out of my room.

Love you, too, Dad.

My mom walks over to me, assessing the damage. "The bed was kind of old." She shrugs. "But doesn't mean you should've been jumping on it. You're not a kid anymore." Her brow rises, and the corner of her lip pulls upward into a slight smile.

I let out a heavy sigh. "I'm still a kid at heart, Mom." I smile, finally letting my body relax.

"Yes, I know." She bends down and places a kiss on my forehead. "I hope you know how much I love you." I think I do.

"Love you, Mom."

My mom turns and walks out of my room, closing the door behind her. I can't help but have a dreadful sense that I won't be left at home alone anymore.

Chapter Fourteen

DUSTIN

Infuriation runs through my veins. "He said what?" I bellow, not believing what I'm hearing.

"Dustin, I'm sorry. I'm not happy about this, either, but what can I do? I'm just the youth pastor." Dave looks at me, trying to put a reassuring hand on my shoulder, but I yank away before he can. I see him wince at my action, but I can't help it.

"Well, you could have some balls, for starters." It's obvious no one has any when it comes to this man. Myself included. I pace back and forth, not knowing what to do with these feelings that are consuming me. I finally found my niche outside of baseball. And now it's being yanked away from me.

Exasperated, Dave sighs. "I wish it were that simple."

I stop pacing and look at him, seeing the fight in his eyes. He simply looks defeated and now I feel remorse for having put him in this position. "This isn't your fault. I hate that you have to be the middleman. I just don't know what to do," I admit, feeling as if I'm at my wits' end, but knowing I'll never give Echo up.

"Pray about it." He suggests and I scoff. I was just told by the youth pastor I'm no longer allowed to play drums for the youth group. I already had to give up hanging at his house with the rest of the youth, and now this—the final straw. I'm being stripped of the things that keep me rooted in this church. This is now stretching beyond my relationship with his daughter, and it pisses me off.

"Thanks for the heads-up, Dave." I extend my hand to shake his. He's truly a great guy, which is why this whole thing stings even more.

He holds my stare, eyes full of sympathy. "If you need anything, please don't hesitate to reach out. I'm always here to talk." I push down the laugh threatening to bubble out. It's not that I don't believe his words, but they are just pointless.

I nod and then walk out the doors to the youth building, knowing I'll never enter them or that entire church ever again. I hop into my Blazer with a bone to pick. It's time for me to put my money where my mouth is and let my balls out. I've held back and been pleasant long enough. I'm not scared of the pastor, and I'm done playing nice with someone who doesn't play by the rulebook.

I come to a skid as my tires catch on some loose gravel in front of their house. I might have also done so on purpose, intent on making my presence known. Leaving my door open, I head up to the front door. I don't plan on taking long to make my point. I make quick strides, taking the two steps onto the porch in one swift hop. I lift my hand to bang on the front door until someone opens it.

"I figured you'd bless us with your presence," Echo's dad announces from the porch swing to my left, completely catching me off guard. I drop my hand, wondering where my balls went before turning toward him.

"How'd you know?" I stammer, realizing how cowardice my words sound. I quickly regain my composure, remembering who the hell I am and my purpose for being here. He drops his chin, narrowing his eyes at me. "Oh, dream killer Dave." I laugh. "Oh, wait, that's you." I narrow my eyes back at him and cross my arms.

"Listen, kid." He pushes off the swing and stands. "I don't know what mission you're on or why you think you need to drag my daughter along with you, but it's not going to happen. So end this game now before you really hurt her."

I drop my hands and ball them at my side, taking a step closer. "You're the only one who's going to hurt her." I seethe, digging my nails into my skin to keep myself from decking the guy.

"No, I'm saving her." He steps closer to me, putting a good foot between us.

"You. Aren't. God," I enunciate every word slowly, spewing them through my lips. A flash of anger crosses his face, and I know I just struck a nerve. Good. I like nerves. "I love your daughter," I admit even though he doesn't deserve to hear it. His shoulders sag a little as he backs up to sit back down on the swing. He lets out a deep sigh, picks his glasses back up, slides them up the bridge of his nose, and grabs a newspaper he has sitting beside him.

"It's just puppy love, boy." He chuckles. "Easily replaceable." Opening his newspaper, he doesn't even bother to look up at me. The idea of ripping it out of his hands and shredding it in his face crosses my mind, but I think better of it.

"No one will ever replace Echo," I proclaim, unclenching my fists as I retreat backward. I glance at the door and see Echo watching in horror, tears streaming down her face. Her mother is close behind, holding her in place.

Mr. Price looks up over the top of his newspaper. "Pull the Band-Aid off, boy, and save you both the grief. You won't like the outcome if y'all keep this up," he warns, and I know he means it. I want to retort and yell back that nothing he can do will keep us apart, but a part of me fears the lengths he's willing to go to. I turn to walk down the step, and he stops me. "Oh, and no more sneaking through my daughter's window." My skin prickles at the thought of him knowing I had and I pray he hasn't unleashed his wrath on Echo for it.

I jump the steps and all but run to my Blazer. I hear the screen door slam and Echo yelling for me.

But I don't look back. Seeing her hurt twists something within me. I have to get away and regain control of this anger that is coursing through me. Or maybe it's pain. Whatever it is, it's something I'm not familiar with.

Chapter Fifteen

ECHO

January 2001

I haven't seen Dustin since the night he stormed off my front porch. The feeling that my dad has finally won pushes me over the edge I had been teetering on. I'm a shell of who I used to be. It's not like my dad has spoken much to me since that night. I'm sure it has a lot to do with me screaming *'I hate you'* at the top of my lungs. He winced. My mom chastised. And I meant it with every fiber of my being. I wanted him to hurt. To feel a sliver of the pain he had instilled in me. You can't purposely inflict pain and suffer no repercussions.

I know hate is a strong word. But in that moment, it's what I felt coursing through my veins as I watched the boy I love retreat from our house...from me. I still feel a tinge of that feeling when I hear him talking to my mom or see him in passing, but it's most prevalent when I sit in the front pew, watching him preach. I have to constantly push the taste of bile down my throat during each service. I'd have to be eating for something more to come up. Maybe I'll apologize one day. You know, be the bigger person. But since I'm just a child who's incapable of making her own decisions, being the bigger person doesn't apply to me.

I spend Christmas break holed up in my room, refusing to interact with the ones who are dead set on ruining my life. I feel like a prisoner for the most part. I've tried hanging out with girls from the team, but then my dad would ask a hundred questions because he didn't believe me. I got tired of answering them or dealing with him period, so I just quit trying to hang out with anyone. It's evident he doesn't approve of me having a life outside of our house, church, and the field. And even the last two are questionable. It's not like I can fully enjoy them when he watches me like a hawk. I get that I broke his trust, but damn. He's suffocating me.

On top of our father/daughter relationship being completely obliterated, I also refuse to continue being paraded in his church circus. I'm no longer stepping into the role of his prized possession, angel daughter he throws in the limelight. The energy I used to feel on stage when I'd sing had disappeared. I got tired of scanning the audience in hopes of spotting Dustin, only to be disappointed. I was trying hard to keep from becoming depressed, but it was impossible. My dad can fake it all he wants, but I was done.

Holiday break is finally over, and I've never been more excited to go back to school. To be quite honest, I half expected my dad to pull me and have my mother homeschool me for the remainder of the year. I'm up earlier than normal so I can leave earlier than normal to make the walk to school. I put my jeans on, throw the new green sweater I got for Christmas over my head, and slide my Doc Marten boots on, then tie them with a double knot. I put on some mascara and leave my hair straight and down just like Dustin likes it.

A feeling I haven't felt in so long has fixated itself within me. Excitement. I am so damn excited to see Dustin. And so damn nervous. Dread that he might be done with us, with me, sits nagging in the back of my mind. I want to stay positive, to hold tightly to his words, but the way he looked that night—completely defeated—still causes twinges of pain in my chest when I think about it. I'm not so certain he still thinks I'm worth the trouble. He deserves more. I want more for him. Hell, I want more for me. But that's not going to happen while I share the same roof as Preacher Man.

I grab my backpack, jacket, and beanie in one swoop, leaving my room in haste. "Bye," I yell, closing in on the front door. So close I can taste it.

"Are you not having your mom take you?" my dad grumbles from his study.

I pause for half a second, grabbing the door handle. The idea of ignoring him crosses my mind, but I'm not a complete brat, so I give him something. "Nope, walking." A very short and to the point something. I'm sure he watches me as I leave, making sure I don't jump in someone's car. Hell, he'll probably get in his car and trail me from a distance. The idea causes me to shiver. How did we end up here? I want to ask him *who hurt you* to make you this way? But, again, I'm just the child in this situation.

Chapter Sixteen

DUSTIN

February 2001

Not seeing Echo is torturous. Not being able to talk to her about what happened hurts even more. Stupid Vo-Tech keeps me from getting to see her at school, and the unknown keeps me from seeking her out other ways. This living in a town where everyone knows your name is bullshit. Not only do they know your name, they know your every move. At first, sneaking around seemed romantic, but after a while, it began to take a toll. It especially was wearing Echo down. She has more at stake to lose. Of course I argue that idea because I'd lose Echo, and to me, she's everything. But I worry just how far her dad would take it. I don't want to chance her losing out on getting signed to play college ball as a way out of here. Even though I'd pack her in a suitcase and haul her away from here myself, need be. I don't want to be the reason that dream of hers isn't fulfilled.

I sink back into our couch and groan loudly. Dropping my head back, I close my eyes. My mother called me downstairs for my birthday celebration, but it's the last thing I want to celebrate. For a moment, I debate packing my shit and hitting the road since I'm of age now, but what kind of future could I secure for myself doing that? Echo deserves better than the unknown. And that route, without a shadow of a doubt, would be unknown.

"Bro, why do you look like someone killed your puppy?" Dax jokes, landing next to me on the couch. The force bounces me out of my zone. I debate slapping his chest with my hand but think better of it. I peek over at him, and I swear he sits taller than me. His eyes are fixed on the TV, so I know he's not expecting a reply to his question. It's not like I was going to give him one, anyhow.

My mom walks in, carrying a cake covered in white frosting, with two lit candles on top. As she gets closer, I take notice of the image on the cake. It's one of my senior pictures with the one and eight candles to the side. My dad follows behind her, camera in hand. I'm so thankful no one else is here to witness this monstrosity of a cake.

"I get his face," Dax shouts, turning toward me to join in the singing. This time, I don't hold back as my hand slaps his chest. "Ow." He winces, not missing a beat with the song. My mom narrows her eyes, and my dad says cheese.

Picture-perfect family.

"Your brother's right, you know?" my mom admits as she hands me a slice of cake. I'm thankful it's not my face.

"Of course I am," Dax says with a full mouth. "What am I right about?" He licks his fork, getting up for a second piece.

She sits down in her recliner, careful not to drop her cake. Taking a bite, she slowly pulls the fork out of her mouth, looking off to the side as if she's in thought. I'd say she's choosing her words cautiously, but that's something my mother never does.

"I just think..." she begins, treading with ease. "That it's time for you to stop walking around here sulking, with that sour puss look on your face." She finishes, throwing caution to the wind in true Donna fashion.

"Uhhh," Dax stammers, sitting back down next to me. "I never said that." He looks at me, offering a weak smile, all traces of humor gone. Just like most of his boyish features. When he's serious, I can notice how grown he's starting to look; all defined features as he thins out with height.

"Not in so many words." My mom gives a wave of her hand, looking our way. "But I agree with Pastor Price." The mention of that prick's name has my body tensing and my jaw clenching. She better choose her next words carefully. I'm about to ask what exactly she agrees with, but she begins without my ebbing her on. "I'm glad whatever you and that girl of his had going on ended. It was only going to end in disaster and mess up your future," she says matter-of-factly like she's expecting a 'Mother of the Year' award.

"Oh, shit," Dax whispers at my side. "Abort, abort." I'm unsure if that's intended for me or our mom. Probably both. I sit my cake down on the ground before pushing to my feet. Out of the corner of my eye, I see Dax bend down and grab it. If I wasn't so incredibly pissed off, it'd make me laugh.

"You're glad?" I all but snarl, giving her a chance to abort like Dax insisted.

She straightens in her recliner and my dad stands for good measure, always being the middleman. Obviously, not where I got my balls from.

"Yes, I'm glad." Her shoulders rise and she tilts her chin up toward me, holding my stare. She's not backing down, and neither am I. "You have a prominent future in baseball ahead of you. There's no way I'm going to let some girl screw that up."

"Some girl?" I seethe, clinching my fists. If she wasn't my mom or a woman, I'd lunge at her. And I've been putting all the blame on Echo's dad, accusing him of being the culprit. Now I'm starting to wonder if my own damn mother conspired against us as well. My chest heaves and my neck feels hot. These people are turning me into someone I don't even recognize or like.

"Dustin," I hear from beside me, breaking through the noise in my head. I avert my gaze to Dax, who's standing at my side. His brows furrow and he swallows hard. "Let's go outside." His hazel eyes plead with me and my shoulders sag in agreement, not defeat.

Echo's dad and my mother might have won the battle, but they won't have the final victory.

I fling open the front door with such force Dax has to catch it before it slams into the wall. He curses under his breath, and my lip curves up at the corner. I walk off our porch and pace the sidewalk in front of our house, trying to calm myself down. *Happy eighteenth birthday to me.* The idea of taking off floods my thoughts even more.

"Do you want to talk about it?"

I stop mid-stride and look at Dax. He's sitting on the bottom step of the porch, with his elbows resting on each thigh, watching me intently. My heart drops, hating that I've put him in this position. He's too young to have to step in and play Devil's Advocate over something that doesn't even concern him. Hell, it doesn't concern anyone in our house, yet they seem to think it does.

I throw my hand through my hair in frustration. I want to scream, but the prickle behind my eyes says otherwise. The urge to drop to my knees and let it all out tries to push through my iron exterior but fails. To do so shows weakness, and weakness is a sign of defeat.

And I will never accept defeat.

I start focusing on my breathing, slowing it down so I can think rationally. I thread my fingers together, cradling the back of my head against them. Walking back toward the porch, I stop directly in front of Dax.

"What do you do when you feel like the entire world is against you?" I ask, letting out an exasperated breath. Dax scoots over and pats the spot next to him. Without hesitation, I sit and let my head hang down.

"You do what you're best at," Dax commands, placing his arm around my shoulders.

"And what's that?" I glance up, angling my head toward his. His eyes widen and his mouth curves up into a devious smile.

"You give the world the middle finger."

I laugh, being extremely thankful for this brother of mine.

He pulls me in closer, giving me a brotherly side hug, and continues, "For real, Dustin. When have you ever cared what people think? Don't start doing it now."

I'm never one to admit my younger brother is right about anything. But he's right about this. I just needed someone in my corner —someone who shows faith in me. Never would've expected that person to be Dax, but beggars can't be choosers.

"Thanks, bro." I stand up, clamping my hand on his shoulder. "I really appreciate you."

"I'm writing that down." He chuckles, teasing as he stands by my side. "Now go get your girl back."

I look at my watch and begin jogging backward to my Blazer. Super thankful practice for spring ball is in full swing.

"Can I have another piece of cake?"

I raise a brow, hoping he's kidding, but he begins rubbing his stomach.

"Eat all you want." I laugh before turning around, wondering where it all goes.

I head to practice early because the idea of walking back into our house isn't an option. I really need to regain my focus before dealing with my mother again. Now I get a glimpse of what Echo has been dealing with, and I feel like an ass for not being more careful.

I pull into the parking lot like hell on wheels. Echo and I have been avoiding each other. A lump settles in my throat, fearing she might really be done with me. The way she's always worried I'll get tired of the situation and not feel it's worth it...maybe she finally has instead.

Desperation to see her takes over—even just a glimpse. I scan the parking lot, not seeing either parent's car. To be on the safe side, I park behind the weight room so they don't see my vehicle if they show up to pick her up. The girls have been practicing at different times than us, and now I wonder if her dad is responsible for it as well. I open my glove box and pull everything out onto the floorboard. Ahh, that'll work. I grab an old receipt and write a quick note. I fold it in half and jump out of my Blazer, hoping my plan works.

I stand at the back side of the locker room that faces the school, knowing it's the side she always uses. My palms begin to sweat, and I rub them on the cool cement as my back leans against the wall. Butterflies engulf my stomach and for a heartbeat, I second-guess this plan. Then she emerges and all doubt ceases to exist.

She startles, then stops in her tracks, staring. The color leaves her face, and a mixture of sadness and madness fills her eyes. It's like she's battling which she should feel. I want to cup her face and pull her into me, but I don't want to overstep. I push off the wall, closing the distance between us.

"Dustin," she says breathlessly, dropping her bag. That's all it takes for me to close the distance and wrap my arms around her. "I've missed you." Her words are barely audible as her mouth moves against the crook of my neck. A couple warm tears fall to my skin before she sniffles and pulls back, gaining her composure. "What are you doing here?" She looks past me, scanning our surroundings.

I trail my finger down her cheek. "I came to get my birthday gift from you." I cock a brow and grin.

Worry fills her eyes, and she begins shaking her head, stammering. "I don't have a gift for you. I barely even leave my—"

I press my lips against hers, stopping her. Since time is of the essence, I refrain from deepening the kiss. I pull back, both of us breathless, with smiles on our faces. I push the loose hair behind her ear, then cup her chin.

"That was my gift. And it was the best damn gift ever." I lean in and kiss her forehead.

I grab the note out of my pocket, slide it into her front pocket, and kiss her one last time. Then I book it before we are seen together and my recovery mission blows up in my face.

Chapter Seventeen

ECHO

March 2001

*I will fight for you until my dying breath, or you tell me to stop—
and that last part is questionable.*

It's a bit Shakespeare-y, but it does things to my heart—like make it grow and beat faster. I close the note Dustin gave me in between the safety of my Bible's pages. I know my dad won't search the holy word for anything damning. His words give me hope. Hope I thought was lost after the night he showed up at my house.

Dustin is now eighteen, and I envy the idea that he can take off, leaving this world behind if he wants to. I have to wait until May but still wonder if I have the actual gumption to do something so rebellious. Practice for spring ball has finally begun, and I praise Jesus every day for the distraction. I also pray for a scholarship so I can move far away from my overbearing parents—well, mainly my father, but they seem to be a packaged deal.

It's hard to stay positive about something when it seems like the whole world is against it and you hold no control. I know Dustin said he isn't going anywhere, but he's young and has so much going for him. I don't want to put a damper on his last year of high school. How cool will it be to look back ten years down the road, only to be reminded of the girlfriend he could never be with?

Yikes.

Juliana, our catcher, sidles up next to me as I finish stuffing my school attire in my gym bag. Something in her hand catches my eye and I glance down. "This is for you."

I take it from her hand and begin reading the invitation. "A slumber party?" With a raised brow, I tilt my head in her direction.

She laughs and raises her hands in defense. "I know. I know."

Being this close in proximity to her, I fully drink her in and see the dusting of freckles peeking out through her dark skin, framing her dainty nose. Her tight mocha curls bounce around with each movement. A tinge of guilt builds within me, regretting that I haven't taken more time to build relationships with my teammates. I guess I'm still stuck in a nomad mentality when it comes to softball. Subconsciously keeping it all at arm's length, leaving everything on the field.

"But," she starts cautiously. "I just have a feeling getting out is something you desperately need."

More than she knows. I tell her I'll see what I can do but don't mention how nothing is my choice anymore. I would like to go—anything to get me out of the damn house. But just the idea of bringing it up isn't something I want to deal with. I take the invitation with every intention of throwing it away as soon as I get home.

"What's this?" my mom asks as she flips through the mail I set on the counter.

I look over from behind the fridge door, wondering what the heck she's referencing. She's holding up the rectangle invitation and I scold myself for forgetting to toss it. I want to be a smart-ass and ask, *Well, what's it say?* She's holding it, for Pete's sake. She knows what it is.

"Juliana is having a sleepover for all of us girls from the team. I meant to throw it away." I shrug.

"Well, are you going?" she asks, and this time I can't control myself.

Uncontrollable laughter bubbles up from deep down. "You're kidding, right?"

She stares at me incredulously like I just grew a third eye or something. Has she been oblivious to what has been going on in this house for the last few months? Has my dad been drugging her? I want to walk over, place my hands on her shoulders, shake...hard, and ask, *"Where have you been?"* But I refrain.

I slide the drawer open, grab a spoon, and hip bump it closed. Peeling back the top of my yogurt, I lean back against the counter and stare back at my mother. I'm waiting for her to answer my question just like she seems to be waiting for me to do the same. But I answered hers. It doesn't matter if I did so with a question.

I sigh with defeat. "I'm not going. When's the last time I've done anything?" I ask, raising a brow. I'm not trying to be a smart-ass this time around. I want her to think about it.

"You're right. Let's change that," she says with determination, tapping the invitation against the counter.

"Good luck with that." I snort.

"Ye of little faith," she quotes, and boy is she right. All the faith I had growing up has been squandered.

I HAVE NO idea how she managed, and I don't dare ask no matter how badly I want to say, *"Show me your ways, oh talented one."* I hug my mother, whispering a *thank you* and a *love you* in her ear. She worked some magic, and after more thought, I'm convinced I don't want to know the specifics. I have a feeling a sacrifice was involved.

"Bye, Dad," I say in passing without a glance back. I stopped telling him I loved him when he started being a dick. It's not like he's saying it to me, either. I feel his heated stare as I jog to the street where Juliana is parked. She waves and smiles at my parents, who are standing at the door like I'm off to my first sleepover. Well, on second thought, it might just be. They must be so proud that I'm finally growing up. I'd grow up a lot more if my helicopter father lost his pilot license.

"No hanging out with boys," my dad finally says. Out of all things, it's sad that's always his main concern. A *'bye, have a good time'* would've sufficed.

"Okay. I'll just become a lesbian," I mumble as I open the door and jump in her car.

"Wow. If your dad's glare could kill," Juliana says, wide-eyed with disbelief.

"We'd be six feet under," I finish.

"Or swimming with the fishes." She laughs and shivers in her seat before throwing her car in drive. "Oooh. I love this song!" she exclaims, cranking the volume up.

Nelly's "Shake Yo Tailfeather" pounds through the speakers, filling her little Honda Civic. The bass in her speakers could probably move her car just as much as the four wheels do. She opens her windows and sunroof while we cruise through town, blaring. This is something I've heard other kids talk about doing but haven't been privy to partake in. From my understanding, it's something that most teens do in small towns since there isn't much else to do. We're singing, dancing, and attempting to rap all at once. And it's great. It's freeing. All the bull crap seems to disappear. I'm able to let go and have fun.

And this is how my entire senior year should've been. But it's not my reality, and I'm not oblivious to the idea that this is most likely my only chance to experience this. So I dive in, acting silly and taking advantage of it. We passed by the sign leading out of town, and instead of questioning our destination, I waved bye to the sign that said, *"Jasper, Georgia will miss you. Come back soon, ya hear?"*

The tunes keep coming, and with each one, I become more pumped. I'm never allowed to belt out and dance to secular music at home. If my father knew I listened to it, I'd be grounded. I'm not sure why booty shaking or music that makes you want to shake your booty is considered so ungodly. To him, it all centers around sex...and to him, sex is of the Devil. I've come to terms that my father and I will never see eye to eye. He'll always be stuck in his ways, and I'll always be wrong for not wanting to be stuck with him and his ways.

Thirty minutes and some back roads later, we pull back into town, passing by that cemetery I had come across. The sun has almost set, and I begin to wonder what's on our agenda for the night. "Umm, are we picking someone up?" I scrunch my nose as we get closer to the back entrance of the school.

"Yeah, about that," she says, glancing my way with a smile. "I took the scenic route to make sure we weren't followed." What? To make sure we aren't being followed. I've never been out here when all the lights are off. It almost gives off an eerie feeling. Juliana drives to the very back of the parking lot, to the older field the middle schoolers use for games. I glance around, trying to figure out what the heck we're doing. I'm starting to question my ability to see the best in people. It's not like I even know this girl. Sure, we play ball together, but what if this is payback for someone else who wanted to be the starting pitcher. Or maybe they planned some last-minute hazing for me.

"Uh." I slowly swallow, looking over at her. "What are we doing here? You selling me off into human trafficking?" I hesitantly laugh.

A grin spreads across her face as she shakes her head. "You're not being sold." She giggles. "But other than that, I wasn't told any of the specifics." Juliana points out in front of us, and I turn my attention to the dugout. Butterflies slam into my stomach as I watch Dustin make his way in our direction with that cocky grin of his.

What did that boy of mine do this time?

Chapter Eighteen

DUSTIN

Echo has the cutest look plastered on her face. Shock, surprise, awe, love...it's all there, and I'm over the moon knowing I inspire it. It took lots of careful planning to make this night come to fruition. Juliana is pretty much one of the only girls at school I can trust since we've practically been friends since birth.

I walk over to the car and open the passenger door.

"What's going on?" Echo asks, looking back and forth between me and Juliana.

"Well, my dear," Juliana begins. "Mr. Prince Charming over there freed you from the dungeon." She reaches over and unfastens Echo's seat belt. "But we're on a time limit, Cinderella. So it's time for you to get this show on the road."

Echo grabs her bag, steps one foot out the door, and then looks back at Juliana. "Thank you."

"Any time, princess." Juliana looks past her, winking at me.

"You have some explaining to do, mister," Echo chastises with a grin as Juliana drives off. She sucks at playing tough. Even when she has all the right reasons to be mad, it never lasts. She can't be hard on someone even if she tries.

Because her heart is too soft.

She has the kindest soul. I just hope I'm not ruining her. Her dad seems to believe so; that I'm some kind of bad influence. I'm sure he even blames me for the strain in their relationship now. But I refuse to have that charge pinned on me. One day, he'll look at himself in the mirror and realize he's the true person at fault.

Hopefully.

"Good to see you, too." I smirk, pulling her into my arms and holding her tightly. God, it feels like forever since I've touched her. I slowly inhale deeply, pulling her scent in. Her bag hits the gravel and her body molds even more into mine.

"I've missed you." She breathes against my neck, holding on for dear life. Almost as if she's afraid to let go. The feeling is mutual. Apprehension creeps in as I start to second-guess this surprise of mine. My lack of patience could have irreversible consequences.

"I'm sorry," I say, stepping back. Echo gasps at the distance, and I shake my head. "I didn't really think this through clearly. I just wanted to see you."

She steps to me, reaching out to grab my hand. I pull away before she can, throwing it in my hair before resting both on the back of my head. And then I start pacing, anxiety seeping in.

"I'm so selfish," I admit loudly. "What if your dad finds out? What if I just f'd everything up?" I stop and face Echo. She's so ridiculously beautiful, standing completely calm, with a comforting gaze.

She holds her hand out, and I take it. "You are worth the risk, Dustin," she boldly enunciates each word. The tension in my body dissipates, but a sense of dread remains. I nod, and she pulls me in for a hug.

"I just don't ever want to lose you," I whisper, the enormity of it all hitting me out of nowhere.

"You won't. I'm yours forever." She kisses my neck, causing a wake of shivers. "Now, are you going to tell me what we're doing here?"

"Oh yeah." I smile with relief, thankful for her pulling me off the ledge of dread. "I thought you and I could do some stargazing," I say, pulling away from her, watching as her eyes go bright with excitement. I toss her bag over my shoulder and grab her hand, threading our fingers together. "Come with me if you want to live," I tease, using her favorite line from *Casper*, earning me a chuckle.

We walk in silence to the outfield where I have our blankets laid out and the early birthday gift I got for her. She looks back and forth between me and the telescope I have set up, mouth slightly agape. "You have a telescope?"

"No." I run my hand along the side of her face, wanting to pull her in for a deep kiss, but lean in for a peck instead. "You have a telescope." I clarify mere inches from her lips. "Happy early birthday, Echo."

"Thank you, Dustin," she says with disbelief. "But how am I going to explain walking in with a telescope?" She laughs, causing me to as well.

"Well, you see, I'm attached to the gift. So that just means I have to be with you anytime you want to use it." I shrug my shoulders.

"Well, good." She leans in, resting her arms over my shoulders. "Because I'm kind of attached to you."

"Just kind of?" I lift my brow, teasing her.

Echo rolls her eyes and smacks my chest. "Shut it. You know better," she teases back as she walks over to her telescope.

I sit down on the blanket and lean back on my side, propping myself up on my left arm. And I just stare, convinced I could easily do this for the rest of my life. While she's in awe of the sky up above, I'm in awe of the girl I love.

"See any little green men up there?" I laugh.

"No." She snorts, glancing back at me. "You look comfy."

"I am. You should join me." I pat the empty space beside me. I debate on patting my lap. Echo makes quick strides over to me, kicks her shoes off, and lies down facing me.

"I don't know what tomorrow holds." Her voice is low as she keeps her eyes fixed on the string of my hoodie she's rolling between her fingers. The admission causes my heart to drop to my stomach. Then her mocha eyes meet mine and my heart is back in its rightful position but threatens to beat itself out of my chest. "But thank you for tonight. For this. Whatever happens, you are worth it. This is worth it." She twists her hand in the front of my hoodie and yanks me to her, our mouths crashing together as if we've waited our whole lives for this moment. I'm positive we have.

The kissing is deep and hot...and needy. I drape my arm around her, pulling her into my chest as tightly as possible. She tosses her leg over mine, intertwining our legs together. My hand trails its way up and down her curves before I push it up underneath the back of her sweatshirt, feeling her bare skin beneath my hand. The simple gesture causes her breath to catch as she does the same to me.

She pulls away slightly, breaking our mouths apart. "I want you, Dustin," she says, intertwining her fingers in my hair at the nape of my neck.

I open then shut my mouth, no words forming. I watch her face for any inclination of resignation. I don't want her to feel like she owes me her virginity. I didn't bring her out here for that. Echo closes her eyes for a heartbeat as she shakes her head as if thinking better of the situation.

"No, I need you." Her eyes flare open with a level of desire I've never seen.

I nod, feeling the same need, and place my hand on her cheek, searching her eyes one last time before I completely make her mine. "Are you sure this is what you want? Here?" I glance around, feeling like I owe her more than a blanket pallet in the middle of a field for such a special moment.

"Here and now," she replies, pulling me on top of her.

My hips fall between her thighs, and I rest my body against hers, causing her to feel just how badly I need her. She moans against my mouth, and I resist the urge to growl. This woman has no idea the hold she has on me. Echo begins tugging at her sweats as she shimmies them down along with her panties. I prop myself up, giving her the space to do so, while holding her stare.

"Now," she says, biting her lip. I gulp.

I lean back onto my knees, slowly pulling her pants the rest of the way down. Nerves and excitement flood my body as I take in the beautiful sight in front of me. I want to touch her, taste her, take my time with her, but the way she tugs at the waist of my pants lets me know she's ready to fully feel me. Grabbing the other blanket, I push my pants and boxers down and cover us as I rest back between her legs. The closeness already has me wanting to come undone. She rubs her hands up and down my sides, then dances back and forth along my waistline. One hand begins to move lower, and I shudder.

"No." My breathing is ragged against her mouth. I rest my forehead against hers to calm myself. "I'm not going to last long," I admit.

"We have all night," she whispers, cradling my face.

Chapter Nineteen

ECHO

We don't move for what feels like forever and all too quickly, at the same time. I hold Dustin tightly against me, feeling as his heart rate begins to slow to normal. I kiss his cheek, telling him over and over how much I love him. The closeness no longer feels close enough as my arms continue caressing his back.

"I'm sorry," he says in a hushed tone against my mouth.

"What? Why?" I stare up, waiting for him to open his tightly shut eyes. They finally flicker open and showcase so many emotions, making it impossible for me to decipher where his mind is at.

"I just..." he stammers, looking off. I move my hand up to his cheek, guiding his gaze back to me. "I wanted our first time to be perfect." His lip quirks up with the admission. "You were gypped." He averts his eyes down and drops his head.

"Dustin, you're mine. Nothing could be more perfect than that." I rub his back for reassurance, then move my hands down to his hips, which are right where they belong—between my thighs. "And how could I possibly be gypped when I'm not done with you?"

His head darts up, searching my eyes as I bite my lip.

His hand grazes my cheek before stopping at my chin, holding it. "I don't think love is a strong enough word for what I feel for you," he admits before claiming me again. A delicious ache takes over all my senses as I lose myself to him.

STARING SKYWARD, WE lie in a blissful slumber, stargazing as I point out all the visible constellations. Our intertwined hands rest between us, and every so often, he pulls them to his mouth, lacing my hand with kisses. While the sweet gesture is simple, it causes me to lose my train of thought every dang time.

"And over there is..."

He slowly kisses each knuckle.

"Umm." I shake my head, regaining my senses. He snickers, knowing exactly what he's doing to me. "Oh yeah, and over there is Pisces." I use my free hand, pointing in the direction that is northeast of Aquarius the Water Bearer.

"Mmm-hmm." More kisses. "That's cool," he says, not even looking up.

"Yes, it is. Since it is your constellation." I roll toward him and tickle his side. He squirms against me, trying to push my hand away. "Ha, I found your weak spot." I laugh, moving my hand around to find more.

Dustin stills as he stops laughing and turns his body to the side to fully face me. "You're my weak spot, Echo." My heart completely melts within. He's mine, too. "What're your plans once we graduate?" he asks.

"I figured I'd start my career as a housewife," I tease, raising a brow as I carefully watch his expression. Instead of fear and trepidation taking over, his face is full of approval as he nods with a big smile like I just named the best life goal ever. "I wish," I admit, rolling my eyes. I quickly cover my mouth, shocked by my own admission. "College and softball are what I'm working for." The answer falls flat as I begin wondering if it's really my goal, or what's been pushed on me like I've been programmed from the beginning of my life. "How about you?" I return the question.

"Wherever you go." He leans in, kissing me as his hand wraps around the back of my head, holding my face close to his. "I kinda like the idea of you being a housewife." He smiles against my lips.

The loud crunching of gravel fills the stillness around us. Our heads jerk up, seeing headlights cascade over the field. And my heart drops to my stomach as dread floods in.

"Echo," a voice yells. I can hear the padding of feet, making its way to us.

I jump up with Dustin right behind me and watch as Julianna runs through the gate, heading our way. *Oh shit.*

"We have to go," she says with urgency, holding her arms out, waving for me.

"What the hell is going on, Julianna?" Dustin asks, stepping in front of me in a protective stance.

"There's no time to exp—"

The abrupt stopping on gravel as another car skids to a stop cuts her off. Nausea burns my throat as I realize what she was so desperate to convey.

She mouths, "I'm so sorry," as she begins retreating backward, keeping her eyes trained on us. Dustin's body tenses as he keeps his stance in front of me, shielding me from what's to come.

"Echo Dian Price." My dad's voice booms, startling me. My breath hitches and I turn statuesque, unable to move, think, or barely even breathe. His eyes are big, features tight as he makes his way closer, clenched fists at his sides. Dustin's arm shoots out in front of me to hold me back. My dad scoffs at the gesture, then his gaze falls past us, landing where we had spent the night lying. A mix of emotions fills his eyes, but anger is the only one that remains. "Get your stuff now." He seethes.

Tears begin to fall as reality sets in, and I turn to get my stuff.

"No." Dustin protests, grabbing my hand. He looks at me with such desperation as if he has a way for us to make it out of this unscathed.

But he doesn't. Nothing can save us from what's sure to come.

I cradle my hand against his cheek and rub my thumb against his bottom lip. It trembles. "The love I have for you consumes me," I whisper. He tightly closes his eyes, trying to blink back the tears to no avail.

My father steps in, breaking us apart. "I warned you, but you didn't listen." He sticks his finger in Dustin's chest, and I pray he doesn't get decked in response. "This is your fault." The words come out slow and deliberate as he stares at Dustin with rage. It's almost as if he's begging him to retaliate, but he doesn't. Although his fists are clenched and his chest heaves, my guy stands firm; unshakeable. "Come on." My dad grabs my arm and pulls me with him, leaving my belongings behind.

Halfway to his car, Dustin hollers, "Hey, Pastor."

My dad stops but doesn't turn around to acknowledge him.

"I'll pray for you."

The grip he has on my arm tightens and I snicker, knowing that guy of mine just hit my dad where it hurts; below the Bible belt. I glance over my shoulder and hold Dustin's stare, wondering if this will be the last time I ever see the boy I love.

13 YEARS LATER

Chapter Twenty

DUSTIN

May 2014

My head falls back and I breathe in the dry air surrounding me. It's been a month since I last saw her. I wish I could say the same about Brian. But we made it to our first post overseas a couple weeks ago and he's been up my ass ever since. I suppose it's not his fault. Besides getting ourselves reacquainted with the heat, we've also been taking daily classes, ensuring we're refreshed on rules of engagement and sensitive sight exploitation as we search buildings—among other things.

I'm trying to embrace the busyness of it all. It's usually my superpower.

But in the quiet moments, such as this, when the world around me slows down just enough...my mind roams. I can't seem to shake the feeling seeing her evoked. I'm just as wound up now as I was then: my heart in shambles. I can't erase the image of Brian walking up behind Echo and placing a kiss on her cheek like she's his. She is, but in another lifetime, she was mine. Who knows, maybe in an alternate universe she still is.

Being in the war zone has become my way of life for the last thirteen years, and I'm ready to immerse myself back into what I consider my normal. While it hasn't ridden my mind of all the noise, it helps quiet it, and for that reason alone, I'm ready to embrace the heat, the destruction, and the unknown with welcome arms. Except this time, it's different. Instead of running to escape, I've run into a trap. See, that's the problem with running. You eventually get caught.

I open my eyes skyward and take in the canvas before me. Darkness splattered with the most beautiful array of bright speckles hovers above. The proximity feels within reach. Maybe if I stretch far enough, I can steal a speck of brightness to illuminate my own darkness. And maybe if I grab enough, I can extinguish my dark altogether. I tightly shut my eyes and shake my head before lifting it back upright. What a ridiculous concept. But which thought is more farfetched? That I'm salvageable or wishing Echo could see the view above me. She would be in awe. And I would be in awe of her.

Fully dressed, with my rucksack in tow, I stand in the formation I'm all too familiar with as we wait to load up on the C-17 that will be flying our unit into enemy territory. Dread—a feeling I'm unfamiliar with—washes over me. I'm heading back to a combat zone and the only thing I'm dreading is being stuck with my new platoon sergeant. My second-in-command. Echo's husband. My newfound responsibility. The constant reminder of what will never be mine again sleeping in the same room as me.

I stare at the matte gray monstrosity of a plane before me. Its nickname is the Moose, but it should be the Meg. Alone, this plane could easily hold five Blackhawks, with their propellers folded down. But today, it will hold us along the outer walls with pallets of supplies between us, and our Stryker trucks beneath for the next three hours. As

I watch the trucks load up, I'm reminded of the nickname I gave Echo so long ago...Striker.

Conversations cease and the sound of shuffling feet fills the void as the two lines of soldiers work their way toward the ramp. I hang back, making sure everything is loaded—especially my men. Once the last man clears the ramp, I follow. Twenty-seven seats line each side wall. All metal and nylon, resembling a bunch of mini trampolines. Stopping at the second to last seat from the ramp, I sit; thankful that, unlike a trampoline, the material beneath me is taut against the metal frame. The spot to my right is vacant, and I pray Sergeant Trae Greyson, to my left, is quiet. I let my head fall back against the inner wall and glance above me. The plane looks like an unfinished contraption of wires and cables fully exposed. It reminds me of the atlas my dad used on family road trips; different colored lines going every which direction. Very confusing and hard to decipher to the untrained eye. I used to wonder if they ran out of money while assembling these beasts, but soon found out it serves a purpose. Not only was this thing built for maximum efficiency for capacity, but it was also built for maximum efficiency for functionality. It wasn't built to be pretty but effective, and time has a way of getting in the way of effectiveness. With everything exposed as it is, things get fixed in record time. Because when in a war zone, you don't have time to spare.

The clicking of seat belts steals my attention, and I grab the buckle, securing it across my waist as someone walks down the line in front of us, verifying all the cargo pallets are fully secure. I lean my head back again and let my eyes fall shut. I'm used to the heaviness they carry but hoping for some relief.

"Is this seat taken?" the lively voice asks, causing my heart rate to speed up with recognition. Of course. As if the universe hasn't screwed my life enough. I open my eyes and see Brian standing in front of me. I glance over at the empty seat and then up at him.

"Seems to be," I reply.

Then his chipper ass sits down, and I contemplate two things:

Suicide.

And murder.

Chapter Twenty-One

DUSTIN

"Here we go!" a soldier farther down yells with a little too much enthusiasm. The seat belt signal clicks on, warning us of the incoming nosedive. That's the thing about flying into enemy territory. You get in and out without getting shot down. Meaning you have a ridiculously short window to do both.

"I'm not sure I'll ever get used to this part." Brian rubs his palms up and down his thighs. "The whole not being able to see our surroundings as we drop out of the sky doesn't help." He looks over, giving me a nervous grin.

"At least we wouldn't know we were going to die. We'd just be dead. And it'd be quick."

"Tell that to the newbie."

I follow his gaze over to see a statuesque, paler than normal Greyson to my left, staring off with eyes wide as saucers.

"Breathe, Sergeant Greyson. Or you'll pass out," I say, nudging him with my elbow. "And clench your butthole. So you don't shit your pants."

The plane dips downward and we all follow suit, falling to the side before righting ourselves. Except Greyson. His body hangs over like a limp noodle. I grab his arm, pulling him upright against the side wall as much as I'm able to during the descent.

"I swear to God if you hurl," I mumble, securing my arm across his chest. He comes to, frantically looking around like a lost kid in a flea market. "Welcome back." I smack his chest a couple times as the plane straightens itself before coming to an abrupt halt, tossing us into one another like a pendulum. Once the jostling of cargo and bodies stills, the unbuckling of seat belts clanking echoes around us.

Echo.

And without warning, Greyson's body lurches forward, remnants of his last meal splattering on the floor.

THE SUN SHINES brightly, too brightly, and I wonder why the fireball is likened to happiness. Something that literally burns you shouldn't boost one's mood. Yet it does. Well, not here. Here it's a reminder of where we are—hell on earth. Besides the whole gnashing of teeth, I'm pretty sure the temperature here is set on *hell* degrees.

Thankfully, I'm familiar with this operating base and know where to find our company commander. We're only here until the alternating platoon returns and we move out, but I need to know precisely how long we have to get our Stryker uparmored. I begin making my way through the makeshift village we've created out of abandoned buildings and homes made of rock and cement.

"Hey, Adams. Wait up." The sound of feet padding the ground inches closer, but I don't wait. "Do you know our orders?" Brian asks, now walking in step with me.

"Heading that way now."

"Is it cool if I go with you?"

"Listen," I say. "I hate dumb questions. So instead of asking just do unless I say otherwise."

"Yes, sir." He gives a curt nod. Heavy, uncomfortable silence looms between us, almost diminishing the noises that fill the lively base as we continue walking. "It's just," he starts as we stop in front of the wooden door, "I want to make sure I'm familiar with all the whos and whats in case…"

"In case I'm incapacitated, and you have to fill in for me?"

He gulps.

The wooden door swings open, saving him from a response.

THE NEXT FEW days we spend up-armoring our Strykers we'll be driving to our post as well as putting a bird cage around them and adding sniper nets. Most would think these nineteen-ton monstrosities could withstand anything, but since explosively formed projectiles became a thing, we've had to adapt. So to keep the molten metal from melting through the Stryker, we now encase them with metal slats and bars all the way around, which is called the bird cage. It makes the new weight of the beast a good twenty-two tons.

Ever since coming back to life after landing, Greyson hasn't seemed to shut up. I'm unsure if it's nerves or age, but I'm just thankful he's playing twenty-one questions with the other guys and not attempting to do so with me. Greyson and Williams work on the Stryker to my left, working to get the camo net over the top to keep the snipers from being able to easily spot our men.

"Where you from?" Greyson asks.

"Oklahoma."

"How long have you been married?"

I glance up and watch as Brian looks off momentarily.

"Umm, almost thirteen years."

Holy shit. She literally shacked up with him right after she disappeared.

He continues, "She's my childhood best friend. Familiar and comfortable."

How can he reduce what she means to him to such simplistic values?

"All I've ever known. And same for her."

But that's a lie. She knew me. And truth be told, she still owns me.

"Pool, where you from?" Brian asks, hopping to the ground.

"Oklahoma," he says. Then as if it was planned, in unison they yell, "Boomer Sooner."

Naturally, both Brian's would be Okie's.

"Yo, Adams. How about you?"

I can sense all three looking my way, waiting for a reply that I don't care to give. I don't even want these guys to know my first name, let alone where I'm from. It's a tactic I started when I first joined to keep from getting close to anyone. The less information, the lesser the attachment.

"Smalltown Georgia." Roberts comes up from behind, bracing both hands on my shoulders. "Ain't that right, Georgia Peach," he teases, walking off.

And I hate him for it. Apparently, I haven't kept my wall high enough through the years and have let some mosey their way in a tiny bit. But when you're in a war zone, you do desperate things to keep your men alive. That's what I did with Justin Roberts when he was lying injured in my arms five years ago. He wanted to hear about my life to keep his mind off his wounds. And without hesitation, I opened up to him. I just hoped he wouldn't remember anything I had said.

"Remind me to let you bleed out alone next time." I finally speak up, but only to change the subject.

"Dang, shots fired," Roberts says, causing me to laugh. Every platoon needs a Justin. For someone who had such a rough upbringing, his humor and positivity know no bounds.

"You know I love you, man." I walk up to Roberts and give him a fist bump.

"Yeah, brother, I know. You ain't as hard as you try to act."

"I soften up just for you, baby."

And just like that, the conversation has been diverted.

Chapter Twenty-Two

ECHO

July 2014

Dylan and I are driving to a town I haven't been back to in over thirteen years. Ever since I saw Dustin, I've been out of sorts. I'd like to say we're driving there on the sole basis that I already miss Lynsie—which I do—but it's not the driving force within me.

"How much longer?" Dylan asks.

I glance over and smile at my son, who is intently playing some game on his handheld PlayStation Vita. "Are you hungry? We can stop at the next food exit."

"Yeah, I could eat."

My nerves are a bit shot. Okay, more than a bit. More like completely frazzled at the ends. Far worse than any split ends I've ever seen. At least with those I can snip them away. Can't do that with my nerves. Though it would be nice. Just a quick and easy trim, and I'd be all good.

That's a lie.

The closer and closer we get to my past, the more frayed they seem to become. And if I was able to just snip away the deadness, I'd end up having none to nurture back together.

"Whatcha want to eat?" I ask my son as we stand in line.

"Number five with a mountain dew. I'm gonna go take a leak."

I want to growl at his choice of word, but I don't. In all reality, it could be worse. "Wash your hands."

He looks back at me, curling his lip up. "Ma." He shakes his head, then turns back around.

We sit in silence as he chows down on his hamburger, and I pick at, dismantle, and eat tiny bites of the fries I ordered. I don't really have the stomach to order anything, but I can't make it obvious that my anxiety is at its peak. I'm trying to play it cool. But it's impossible. I've never been good at hiding my emotions—especially when I'm upset.

"So this town we're going to"—Dylan breaks the silence, dipping a fry into his ketchup—"is this the same town my dad is from?"

For being such a simple question, it carries one hell of a punch. It's fifty questions packed into one.

I've always been honest with Dylan. It's something Brian and I agreed on from the get-go—the reason Dylan has his dad's last name. But running into Dustin two months ago kind of wrecked that loyalty and trust thing I had going with our kid. As much as I wanted to run home that night and tell Dylan I saw his dad, there was no way I could. Far too many unknowns. I couldn't even tell Brian. There's no way I can tell him now. Not while they're overseas together.

"Yes. Yes, it is," I finally reply.

"Cool," he acknowledges. His face seems more accepting now that he's come to that conclusion, and I love the fact that he got his go-with-the-flow demeanor from his father. "Think you can show me around?"

"I'd love to." I smile at the idea but dread it as well. I just hope I'm able to keep it together in front of my son.

"Good. I'd also like to meet my grandparents while we're there."

I choke on a fry. "What?" I cough, then slurp a drink of my soda.

"Aren't my dad's parents still there?"

I stall. I know for a fact they are because that's one of the reasons Dax and Lynsie moved there. But I can't tell him that. And there's no way I'll be introducing him to his father's parents before I introduce him to his father.

"Honestly, I don't know," I lie. "Let's just worry about seeing one set of grandparents for now." I raise a brow, knowing he loves spending time with my parents.

His eyes light up with excitement at the realization. "You didn't tell me I was going to get to see them."

"I didn't really get to plan any of this out in advance. With everything that's been going on and all. I just have a lot I need to figure out."

"Ma," he says, bringing my attention back to him. "Add you and Grandpa making up to your list." He tosses his last fry in his mouth and crumples his trash together in a ball. "He misses you."

I want to counter and say, *"He's the adult...he's had plenty of chances to reach out and hasn't."* But my father isn't the only one at fault for this continued rift. I'm also an adult, and if we both wait for the other person to make amends, it'll never happen. We're too much alike. And truth be told, I miss my dad, too.

I nod in agreement. "You're right. It's time for me to stop running from my past." I let out a heavy breath and relax my shoulders. It's as if coming to terms with what needs to be done has lessened what I've been carrying for so long.

EVERYTHING LOOKS THE same as we pull into Jasper, Georgia. It's as if time stopped when I left. Memories play out in front of me as I drive down Hickory Street; the main street that goes straight through town. It used to be the main drag all school-aged drivers did on the nights after games. Or when the football and basketball teams played out of town. Fellow classmates who didn't go to the game parked backward in this gravel parking area, waiting for the buses to come strolling back in town. They'd always hoot and holler from their tailgates or the trunks they were perched on. It was something I never got to experience.

On my left, I see the diner Dustin took me to for our first date—good ole Tootie Fruitie's. Of course it wasn't considered a date to anyone but the two of us and possibly our waitress. I smile as I picture us sitting in the booth in the back corner.

"Please tell me this isn't the town," Dylan groans from his seat. "There's nothing here."

He's right. There's not much physically to this town, but it holds all my favorite memories. This town is where Dylan was conceived. To me, this town holds everything of value.

"Sorry to disappoint you, kiddo."

"Shoot me now. This is going to be so boring. Way to end summer with a bang."

"Way to be optimistic, buddy. We just got here. I'm sure there will be fun things for you to do." I haven't told him about the plans my mom and I discussed.

"Highly doubtful," he mutters as I start navigating through town, not even realizing where I'm going until I park in front of my old house. The house that now has a *'for sale'* sign staked into the front lawn.

My parents bought it when we moved here. I truly think they believed we'd live here much longer than we did. I'm sure they never expected things to go array in a town with less than five thousand occupants. As far as I've ever known, they never sold it after we moved but left it open to rent out to missionaries and such, people coming through needing a place to stay.

"This used to be the house I lived in when I was in high school." I look over at Dylan and smile, hoping showing him my memories of this town and how we're linked to it will bring some sort of understanding to him. After all, the little turd did ask me to show him around.

"Cool," he says, unmoved. "I hope the place we're staying at has a pool or something."

I try not to roll my eyes. "You better hope it has a pool or I might have to enroll you in summer school to show you how bad your summer can truly be," I half threaten.

"I'd almost willingly go." He laughs, finally returning to his normal joking self.

"I want to see something," I say quickly, unbuckling my seat belt, and open my door.

I make my way through the pristinely manicured yard, heading for the back fence. It still catches, so I push on the handle, lift up on the gate, and hit it with my hip. Voilà. It opens.

"I didn't know you were a ninja," Dylan says from behind.

Blowing the hair out of my face, I turn to face my son. Short of giving myself a pat on the back, I'm mighty proud of myself for remembering this nifty trick of the trade.

"Well, you know"—I try to play my skill off—"a ninja would have just jumped the fence or swung from a tree."

"I think you underestimate yourself sometimes, Ma." He pats my back, walking past me through the gate.

When did my son become so smart?

"So this is where the magic happened?" Dylan asks, looking around the yard. His question causes me to choke.

"Ahh, the magic, what magic?" I ask, propping my hand on my hip. I know he's smart and all, but my son doesn't need to know about any kind of *magic* yet.

"You know. Where grandpa helped you perfect that pitch of yours you've yet to show me."

"Oh." I let my hand fall and my body sags a bit. "That magic." I wave my hand. "Yes, this is one of many yards where grandpa taught me a few tricks. But this is the yard where I had finally perfected it." *And the last yard I ever played ball in with him. Or played ball period.*

"What kind of magic did you think I was talking about?" He frowns with suspicion.

I shrug my shoulders and turn away. "You know. Houdini," I say with the wave of a hand. I walk toward my old window to see if the carving from so long ago is still there. The old white windowsill is now worn and peeling, but the carefully knifed out D+E 4ever is still visible, barely. After all these years, the proof of the love we once had still exists.

Arms come around my waist from behind and I cover my mouth, trying to hold back a sob.

"That's why this place means so much to you. This is where all your memories of you and my dad are." Dylan isn't asking. He knows. He sees what I'm touching and can tell what it means to me.

As I let my finger trace the letters that represent the love we once had, I'm held tightly with the arms the love we shared created. Both of these realizations slam against me, forcing me to release the sadness I've been holding inside for so long.

"Excuse me, miss, but can I help you?" I know that voice. I quickly wipe my face with the back of my hand.

"Hey, Mom." I put my arm around Dylan, pulling him close to me. I'm suddenly nervous and hold on to him with everything I have. Because he is everything I have.

"Echo!" She hurries over and places her hand on my arm.

"It's good to see you." I'm shocked at my own admission and how easily those words slide from my mouth. But I can feel the heavy weight I've carried for the last thirteen years melting away. While my mother and I have had somewhat of a relationship since I took off, it still hasn't been what it should be. I've kept her at a distance, keeping her closed off. I only allowed her into my life for Dylan's sake. She wraps her arms around me and Dylan, and I don't fight it like normal. Instead, I hug her back.

"I've missed you too, Mom." My lip quivers with emotion as my body melts into her, finding comfort in her arms. Arms that I've truly missed and have at times wished could hold me and comfort me.

Over the years, I made it my mission to meet up with my mom at least twice or more a year for her to take Dylan for a week so he could have a relationship with his grandparents. I never wanted him to suffer and miss out because of me. Besides those times, emails, cards, missed phone calls, and scattered FaceTiming has only made up for so much. My dad is the only one I've stayed shut off from in its entirety. I've never had the inkling to change that until now. I'm just not sure how we can mend what destroyed us. It's usually easier to get over the past when you don't have it staring you back in the face. But when your past follows you to the present and will be in your future, it tends to make looking beyond it all the more difficult.

Dylan represents my past. He represents what my dad cursed and ruined. But to me, he represents love. He's the proof that earth-shattering love does exist.

"Excuse me. But you guys are kind of smooshing me."

My mom and I loosen our grip on each other and laugh as we both look down at Dylan, who lets out a sigh of relief.

"I wasn't expecting you guys to show until this evening," my mom says as we make our way through the gate, walking toward our cars.

"So what now?" Dylan asks, needing to be entertained.

I look out to the street where kids are playing. A teenage girl on rollerblades flies by, bopping her head to the music pounding through her headphones. She reminds me a lot of myself and how I used to jog everywhere I went since my parents never bought me a car. Heck, I probably would've anyways even if they had. A warm breeze twirls my hair around, and a faint smell of a grill in the distance catches my nose, causing my stomach to growl.

"So what brings you back? You didn't really mention why when you called last week." She's not prying. She's concerned. I get it, I really do. But it's not just a quick answer. If I tell her the immediate reasoning, I have to tell her everything that has led up to it for it to make sense why I'm so torn. Trust has been lost on both sides, and now it has to be gained. It's not that I don't trust her. It's more that right now I don't trust myself. I'm still trying to figure it all out.

"We just needed to get away for a while, and my best friend moved here at the beginning of the month, so you wanting to meet here worked out perfectly." Everything I said is the truth. Partial truth but truth nonetheless.

"Well, for whatever reason it is, I'm glad you got a hold of me." She knows I could have snuck back here and not bothered to inform her. Maybe if everything back home was where it was six months ago, that might have been the case. Hell, I wouldn't even be here if that were the case.

My mom stops at the back of her car and looks over at the house. "The only thing I had planned while waiting for you guys was to work on the house some. The people who moved out did minimal cleaning. The realtor told us we needed to get someone in to clean it if we weren't planning on making the trip ourselves. She also recommended doing some simple updating to make it more appealing. But we just haven't had the time to do that."

"You mean you." I point out. I don't see my dad making the four-hour trip here to help.

She looked downward and to my dismay, her voice broke slightly. "He's changed." But without clarifying, she veers off and asks, "So are you guys hungry?" There's hopefulness in her voice as she glances back and forth between me and Dylan. Dylan tugs on my arm, and I look down into his pleading eyes, begging for us to do something besides continue standing here.

I give him a smile before looking back up at my mother.

"Starving," I say, my appetite making its return in full force.

"It's such a pretty day out. What do you think about walking to the diner down the street?"

"Sounds perfect," I answer, wrapping my arm around Dylan as we head for Tootie Fruitie's.

The waitress seats us up front in a window booth. I smile as the cushions slightly squeak as the three of us sit down.

"Gross. Who farted?" Dylan asks with his face twisted in disgust.

"Oh, shush. It's the seats."

"Mmmhmm. That's what I'd say too." He grabs a menu, and I just shake my head, not even bothering to reply. I look over at my mom, who's watching the two of us with happiness in her eyes and a smile.

"Kids," she says, letting out a sigh of contentment.

"Yeah, they're so great," I reply sarcastically, then reach over, ruffling Dylan's hair.

"Ma," he whines, pulling away from me. "I'm not very hungry. So." He closes the menu and places it in front of him and looks at me. "What would you recommend?"

"Hmm." I scan over the options. "For a growing boy who isn't very hungry, I'd recommend a chocolate shake and fries."

"Eww." He scrunches his cheeks to his eyes. "Disgusting."

I laugh at his reaction. "That's exactly what I said to your dad the day he ordered it for us." I chance a glance at my mom, who I never got to talk to about my first love and our experiences. She watches Dylan and me intently, with sadness evident in her somber features.

"And what did he say?" Dylan always liked hearing stories about his dad when he was younger. But as he's gotten older, it no longer seems to be very important to him. I believe it's because the older you get, reality begins to fully sink in. You realize life isn't a fairy tale anymore.

A big smile spreads across my face as I hear Dustin's voice in my head. Then I say aloud, "Don't knock it till you try it."

"And did you?"

"I did." I nod.

"And did you like it?"

I scrunch my nose and shake my head. "I did not." I laugh.

"Guess I'll try it. It can't be that bad." He shrugs.

"Whatever you say," I mumble under my breath.

My mom remains quiet, watching intently.

Fifteen minutes later, I'm feasting on my burger and fries. I cut my eyes to the side, watching as Dylan lightly dips his fry in the chocolate shake.

"Gotta get more than that." I grab his hand and dip it in more, using his fry as a spoon. "Don't be *skeered*," I taunt.

He stares at it, and I have a feeling he's going to do so until the chocolate melts off. Then out of nowhere, like it's a now-or-never decision, he closes his eyes and throws it in his mouth. My mom and I watch as we wait for a sign. His face remains neutral and eyes closed until he finally swallows. He keeps us anxiously waiting, taking his sweet time. Slowly, his eyes begin to open, and he looks over at me, then at my mom. "What?" He knows what.

"Well, whaddya think?"

"I think it's not that bad." He grabs another fry, dips it, and then tosses it into his mouth.

I smile over at my mom and Dylan, who are now talking about the Atlanta Braves, his favorite baseball team. That's where my parents live now and apparently, they have season tickets.

My phone rings, and I instantly smile. "Hey, Lynsie."

Chapter Twenty-Three

ECHO

Walking into the house that holds so many memories hits harder than expected. It could be the emotional turmoil swirling within me, making me a mess of unending nerves. I feel as if I've walked into a perfectly contained time capsule. Or twilight zone. The same blue and green plaid sofa and love seat sit in the shape of an L in the living room, both still facing the older, non-flat screen TV with the heavy hunter green curtains hanging behind, blocking out the sun. I walk past my dad's old study, not bothering to inspect it, heading straight for the kitchen. The fruit wallpaper lining the backsplash between the wood cabinets peels in spots as though someone wanted to replace it but thought better of it. The same wallpaper lines the walls of the dining room in a six-inch strip atop the half-paneled portion of the wall. White stove, white dishwasher, and white refrigerator with a loud hum fill in the spaces between the wooden cabinets. As I make my rounds through the house, I cringe when I see the toucan and palm tree wallpaper still in the bathroom. It was bad when we lived here, and even worse now.

It's as if time stopped the day we moved. I know for my heart, it practically did. I look behind me to Dylan who has been on my heels, staying abnormally quiet. I giggle at the expression on his face as he looks at the bathroom walls in horror.

"You can hang out in my old room." I gesture down the hall and he walks past me without hesitating. I make my way back to the living room and sit next to my mom on the sofa. She sits with her legs crossed and her hands resting atop.

"There's a lot I need to fill you in on," I admit, breaking the ice. "I'm going to wait until Lynsie gets here so I can get it all off my chest at once."

My mom nods and asks, "I know you've mentioned her before, but can you explain to me who exactly Lynsie is and how she fits into all of this?"

"Yes, of course." I hit my forehead with my palm. "Duh." I bite at my thumbnail, trying to figure out where to start. "Lynsie and I met at the salon I work at a couple years ago. We didn't really become close until last year. Her husband, Lincoln, was a pilot along with his best friend, Dax." I straighten myself and rub my sweaty palms against my jeans. "Lincoln and Dax are both originally from here." I pause and watch her eyes widen. "But wait, there's more." I snort, sounding like an infomercial. "Lynsie's husband, Lincoln, died in a plane crash last year."

Her hand covers her mouth, muffling her gasp. "The one that you and Dylan witnessed at that air show."

I nod and swallow down the lump of grief and terror that seeps in anytime I envision that night.

"That's horrible," she whispers.

"Yes, it was devastating." I shake the memory away. "So after that, Dax was pretty much Lynsie's crutch. On top of losing her husband, she found out she was pregnant." I smile at the thought of seeing Blu. It's been so long. "Dax and Lynsie are now together, and they moved back here this past summer."

"Oh, okay. Well, that makes sense why you'd want to come back to this town. I figured it had something to do with—"

I hold my hand out, stopping her.

"Here comes the more part. Dax is Dustin's brother."

"Oh my. What are the chances of that?" she asks redundantly.

"And that's not even where it ends." A nervous laugh escapes my mouth. Speaking it all aloud sounds absolutely insane. "After thirteen years, I finally saw Dustin."

My mom uncrosses her legs, straightening her posture, but keeps her hands placed at her knees.

"It was at an award ceremony for Dax. That's how I found out, but we didn't get to really talk. A lot happened that night, keeping us from being able to." I stand up, pacing in front of the sofa, and rub the back of my neck.

"Well, what happened? Where's he been this whole time? Where'd he go after?" Her voice sounds invested, as if she's intrigued by my story.

"He's been in the Army." I stop dead in front of her and look down. "And he went to the war with Brian," I whisper. My knees begin to wobble, wanting to buckle beneath me. I pivot and drop to the couch.

"Oh, Echo." My mom's arms swiftly wrap around me, and she pulls me into her, rocking me in that loving way only a mother can. I finally break. I cry as one might mourning the loss of a loved one. And maybe that's exactly what I'm doing; mourning the girl I once was or the one I've become. "I love you." Her words flutter across my ear, warming my heart. I sniffle as I pull away and place my hands right below my eyes and wipe outward. Thankfully, I didn't wear makeup, or I'd look like a clown.

"I love you too, Mom," I finally reply, regaining my composure. I look around, grimacing. "No wonder you're having issues selling this house," I say, changing the subject. "I mean, it's not like people are dying to move to this town, as it is. This house solidifies why they shouldn't." I chuckle, hoping to lighten the mood for a short stint. "It needs a lot of work. Not hard work, just work." I shrug, angling my body in her direction.

"You want the job?" She cocks a brow, then adds, "I'll pay you."

"You don't have to pay me, Mom. I'll gladly help. I need the distraction." I place my hand over hers and give it a squeeze.

"Knock, knock," Lynsie says through the screen door. Excitement and dread hit me as I stand to let my friend in.

I give her a big hug as if I haven't seen her in years. It's only been a few weeks, but it feels like an eternity.

"Where's Blu?" I ask, taking notice of her empty arms.

Her smile is warm and comforting. "I just dropped her off with Lincoln's parents." We make our way to the couch, and I introduce Lynsie to my mom before we sit on the couch across from her.

I prepare myself for what I'm about to say. "Okay. I need to start from the beginning for any of this to make sense." I take a deep breath. For a second, I debate whether to continue to pull the breath in until I run out. Maybe I'll pass out and buy myself some time.

You can do this, Echo, I keep thinking over and over.

"Echo, you don't have to start from the very beginning. I know why you left." I peek over at my mom and can see the pain written all over her face.

Hell, this is just as hard for her as it is for me.

I swallow hard. "Yes. Yes, I do. I owe it to you, Dylan, and myself. I'm tired of living with this feeling. I've finally come to a point in my life where I'm realizing what matters most. I'm done being that stubborn girl."

My mom snorts, causing me to giggle.

"Fine, you got me there. I'll always be stubborn, but it doesn't have to be at the expense of others any longer."

The hope shining in my mother's blue eyes encourages me to push forward. The weight begins to lessen. Then I think about Dustin. This conversation doesn't end here. It ends with Dustin. He deserves to know what happened. Truth be told, I'm more worried about that conversation.

So I start from the beginning. Mom cries through the parts about me being eighteen, pregnant, and feeling alone. Sympathetic Lynsie sniffles beside me.

"We would have never made you give up your baby." My mom cries, pleading for me to believe her. I do.

"I know that now. But I was young, in love, and hurt. I was scared, and through the pain I was feeling, I wanted you guys to hurt, too. Brian had always been there for me. So the night Dad told me we were moving back to Oklahoma, I remembered what Brian said before he took off for basic training." He called me and told me he had joined the Army. His dad had recently been diagnosed with cancer and Brian couldn't deal with the reality and blamed God, not understanding why he wouldn't heal him. As I sit here and remember, I witness the chip on his shoulder form and realize it's the same timeframe mine manifested with Dustin's following shortly after.

Oh, the weight we have all carried for far too long.

I shake off the memory and continue, "I told him about Dustin and how hard Dad was being with it all. *He said, 'you could just leave and come with me.'* I thought he was joking." I laugh. "Until I called him, and he showed up." I wipe away the tears I didn't realize were falling as I look up at my mom. She's wiping her own tears away. "Eventually, he brought up the idea of marriage. I'd get his health benefits, and as his wife, I'd be able to move wherever he was stationed. I knew I loved him in a way." I tell her that it made perfect sense and for the last thirteen years, it's worked for us.

"Well, as much as I hate how it all happened"—my mother sniffles —"I'm glad it did all work out on your end." She starts shaking her head as more tears stream down her face. "I just hate all the time we've missed. I didn't get to see my baby grow up or have her own baby."

"I know, Mom." I get up and sit next to her, wrapping my arms around her. "I'm sorry about how it all went down. I'm sorry it took the past coming back into my life for me to realize all of this. I should've done it sooner."

"I'm just glad it's finally happened. It's an answered prayer." She pulls back, placing her hand on my cheek. "No matter what has happened in our pasts, I'm proud of the woman you've become."

I nod, choking back a sob. Those are words I've never expected to hear from her.

Proud. She's proud of me.

I let them anchor my soul because no matter what comes our way in the future, I don't want to lose what I'm feeling now.

"Now, finish the story. What brought you back here?" My mom prods.

"Honestly, after seeing Dustin, I've been a ball of confusion. I needed a break from the everyday and just wanted to feel close to him even though he's half a world away."

My mom pats my hand. "All I can say is sometimes there's something bigger in the works. Maybe this isn't a coincidence. You need to figure out what you want and what will make you happy. In the end, that's what will be best for Dylan."

"Can I add something?" Lynsie pipes in. She angles her body toward me. Our knees touch as she holds my hands in hers. She stares deeply into my eyes. "I know you have these feelings you're unsure of. But just be careful. Guard your heart. People change. Don't expect the boy you once knew. He's been gone for so long. No one really knows him anymore."

I see sadness in her eyes and know it's empathy for Dax and the lack of relationship he has with his brother.

But she's right. Not only was Dustin hurt by what happened

between us, he's been in constant battle since. I can almost guarantee the boy I once knew and loved no longer exists.

"ARE YOU SURE you're up for keeping Dylan?"

"I'm always up for keeping my grandson," my mom reassures me.

"I know, but it's last minute, and not during the normal time we usually do it."

"Echo, stop." She hushes me. "It's baseball season, remember?"

My eyes light up with a glint of envy.

"You need to take this time to put your needs first and sort out your thoughts." She looks around, swiveling her head and motioning with her hands. "What better way to do that than getting your hands dirty?"

"Any requests?"

"Nope. I trust you'll make it look a million times better than its current state." She grimaces, and I laugh.

I lean in and hug her, holding her tightly and telling her thank you. Pulling back, I place my hands on her shoulders and just gaze into her eyes, not being able to form any words. She does the same back until we both nod in understanding. "Okay, I'm going to go get the boy now. I haven't even told him he's going with you. He's going to be so excited."

I push open my old bedroom door, and it creaks just like it use to. I glance around, taking in the brightly lit room. The yellow paint only amplifies the brightness. My Switchfoot poster still hangs near the closet and I smile. My eyes drift to my broken bed and I gulp in remembrance of how it got that way. No matter how many times it's been fixed and propped back together, it still ends up falling back down to a slant.

"Whatcha playing over there?" I lean against the bedroom doorway as I watch Dylan. He's lying on his back on the floor, holding the iPad up. I always tell him to be careful. That he's going to drop it smack dab on his face. But he never listens, and because of that, we've had one black eye and a busted lip. Two separate occasions. Because apparently, dropping it on your face once isn't good enough.

"Minecraft."

"Nice. I still don't get the point of that game, but whatever." I walk into the room and kneel beside him. I grab the iPad and pull it from his hands.

"I wasn't done," he huffs.

"Sit up. We need to talk."

"As long as it's not *the talk*," he mumbles as he sits up, stretching his legs out.

"And what talk is that?" I raise a brow. "Never mind. We'll discuss that another time. You're going to go hang out with your grandparents for a bit while I stay here and work on this house."

"Are you sure, Ma?" he questions, taking in my old room. "This house needs an awful lot of work done."

"Yes, I'm sure." I ruffle his hair. "Ye of little faith."

"Oh, I have faith...in you. Not this house," he teases.

Heading out of the house, I get his suitcase out of the car and load it into my mom's trunk. I make sure he has all his electronics in the front seat with him, along with the snacks we bought on the way here. He just got done being trapped in a car for hours. I'm shocked he's so excited to be trapped in another one again.

I hug them both tightly, Dylan a little tighter, before waving them off. I watch as my mother's car becomes smaller and smaller until I can no longer see it. The urge to run after it and jump in with them crosses my mind.

A slender arm wraps around my waist, pulling me in. I look over at Lynsie and smile. "I really hate to leave you. Are you gonna be okay?" she asks warily. "I can go pick up Blu and come back here instead."

"Nah, as much as I want to see that baby of yours, I probably should get to work on this place." "Oh my gosh," Lynsie exclaims, dragging each word out. I look over and her eyes are as big as saucers and a smile covers her face. She starts jumping up and down. "You and I are practically family." In a roundabout way, she's right, and the realization makes a full smile take over my face. "I've always wanted a sister," she says, throwing her arms around me.

"I love you too, Lynsie." I tightly hug her.

I stand on the cracked sidewalk, the same one I used to watch the neighbor girls do hopscotch on. Giggling from behind pulls my mind back to the present. I turn to see a little boy a couple yards down, running as his dad chases him. It makes me smile. I can picture Dustin doing that with Dylan. He's missed so much. He may never forgive me.

Chapter Twenty-Four

ECHO

I wake up early, anxious and half out of my mind. I pull my jean shorts up, toss a tie-dyed tank on, then grab my sandals. Cash flies out of my purse when I pull my keys out and I laugh at my sneaky mother for stuffing it in there. I grab my phone and open my notes so I can type down a general list of supplies I need. I drive down memory lane and park right in front of the store. I walk in and the bell on the door takes me back to the only other time I walked in this store. I picture Dustin at the back wall on the step stool. The memory makes me smile, as all of them do except our last.

I smile at the chick behind the register, who greets me as I grab a shopping cart. I fill it with puddy, scrapers, sandpaper, brushes, a few rollers, tape, plastic, and four gallons of white paint and the plastic pan to pour it into. Surely that'll do it. I push my cart to the counter and sit my items on it. The young cashier isn't very chatty, and I appreciate it.

"Do you need help out?" she asks.

I smile and wrap my fingers around the handles of the paint, grabbing one per hand. "Nope, I got it."

· · ·

I'VE NEVER BEEN the Bob Villa type, but since recently becoming obsessed with *Fixer Upper*, I feel qualified to whip this house into shape. Or at least better shape than its current state. I start by filling the holes and imperfections in the living and dining room walls. My thought process is that once I'm done doing this, I can place the tape around the baseboards and trim and once I'm done with that, the putty areas should be dry enough for me to begin sanding. I'm trying to maximize my time and minimize my effort.

You know, work smarter not harder.

After sanding away all the imperfections, I walk through both areas and double-check my work. I cross the entryway into the room I've been avoiding—my dad's old office. An old walnut desk faces me with a matching desk and hutch filling the wall behind it. I envision him sitting behind the desk, peering up at me as I walk past. I pull open the blinds to the window he used to stare out, releasing a wave of light into the dim room.

I sit in the rolling chair and pull the center drawer out. I push around the notepad and the few pens before shutting it and looking through the other drawers. With the disarray the rest of the house is in, I'm shocked the desk seems to be wiped clean. I spin around in the chair a few times, stopping right in front as if I just spun the bottle and it's directing me back to the drawer. I slowly open it again and pull out the notepad and a pen. I click the pen and take a deep breath.

Dustin,

Hey! How are you? It's been so long.

"That's the dumbest thing ever." I rip the page and crumple it, then drop it on the ground. And proceed to do this five more times before giving up in frustration. "You need to eat. That'll help clear your mind since writing Dustin probably isn't a good idea." I push away from the desk and quickly exit the room and then the house after grabbing my purse. Slowly, I begin walking down the sidewalk with no clear destination in sight. Food. I need food, but other than grabbing something for lunch, I don't need anything else since I'm supposed to have dinner at Dax and Lynsie's tonight.

I don't take the main road, which would be the shortest way to the bakery downtown. Instead, I make my way through the neighborhood. I walk this route unconsciously, without hesitation. Once in front of Dustin's house, my senses return, and I come to realize how out of it I truly am being back here. The last time I was at this house was when I returned in hopes of finding him. But he was already gone. I glance at the side of the house, noticing the black tarp, and wonder if his Blazer is beneath. Before I'm able to give off any Michael Myer vibes, I take off and continue my journey for lunch.

I PULL INTO Dax and Lynsie's driveway and take in the surroundings. While it's not very far from my parents' home, it feels like it doesn't belong here. The gravel drive leading up to the spacious amount of land encompassing their two-story colonial-style brick home. I can only imagine how much Lynsie loves the symmetry of it all.

The part I love most is the huge pond they seem to have all to themselves. I can't help but walk out to it. Shadows embrace it from the surrounding trees while the sun kisses it good night as it settles in for the night. I'd kiss it good night too if I could do so without drowning.

I take the two steps up the porch and smile at the two rocking chairs to the side of the door. I can picture them both out here, watching the sunset as they rock Blu. The image warms my heart.

I knock, using the metal door knocker. I half expect it to start talking to me like the ones from *The Labyrinth*.

"Hey!" Lynsie almost squeals, opening the door.

I follow her inside and gawk at how tall the ceilings are. While the house isn't a complete time capsule like the one I'm trying to update, this one is a bit outdated as well. But that's what makes it fun—making it your own.

"It is so gorgeous out here. And this house... Y'all hit the jackpot." I check out the huge, open living room with the skinny brick fireplace that shoots up the wall.

"Thanks. We really love it out here." Lynsie looks around with a mile wide smile. I can tell how proud she is.

"I can see why." We make our way into the huge kitchen.

Dax is sitting at the table, nose deep in a book. He looks up just enough to say hi and then returns his focus back to his book.

"He has to study for that instructor job he's about to start."

"Ahh." I nod with understanding.

Lynsie walks over and grabs Blu out of her swing.

"C'mere, pretty girl." I hold my hands out with excitement. It hasn't even been a month, but she's grown so much. Her brown hair is filling in and twists at the ends to what looks like the forming of ringlets. I snuggle this precious baby, disliking that the closest thing I have to family moved three hours away.

AFTER DINNER, I head back to the house. I walk in, kick off my sandals, and stop in front of the office. The streetlight shines on the piece of paper I wrote Dustin's name on, beckoning me to finish what I started. I throw caution to the wind and decide to go for it. I can't just leave things the way we have when I now have a way to communicate with him. Even if I don't get a response, I can't keep quiet.

Ten rough drafts and lots of second-guessing later, I'm done. I neatly fold the letter and pull out the few envelopes from the back of the drawer that I missed earlier. I don't put my name on the envelope, just the address.

Then I write Brian. He never writes me back, but it feels bad not attempting communication. Plus, I need to tell him I've been here. With his, I don't write this address on the envelope because I plan on being back home before I expect to receive a response. And I can't chance someone noticing both men receiving mail from the same place.

Chapter Twenty-Five

DUSTIN

We've been here for a good two months, moving back and forth every ten days between the combat outpost and the forward operating base. When it comes to keeping my mind busy, I prefer our time at the outpost and our daily missions, no matter how minuscule some of them are. Those moments seem to keep the personal sharing to a minimum. Unlike now, as the guys sit around bullshitting one another. We arrived back at the operating base a few days ago and while I'm thankful for a shower and clean clothes, I could do without the *Kumbaya* sessions.

I sit in the back, cleaning my weapon as they watch *Field of Dreams.* Or more like have it on as background noise. Hell, I'm paying more attention to it than they are, but truth be told, I could recite the whole movie in my sleep. A fact none of them need to know.

My mind begins to drift back to my childhood and my obsession with ball. It's all I ever knew. It's all I ever loved. Until she moved to town. And while she wasn't in competition with my love for the game, she fell in line with it and easily became more important. The dynamics of my future shifted. Until she was gone, and my future as a third baseman disappeared along with her.

"Roberts. Greyson. Pool. Williams. Daniels. Adams. Adams. Dustin Adams."

I jump to my feet at the use of my first name. I haven't gotten close enough to anyone for that information to be known. First Sergeant Mills stands holding a handful of envelopes. I take in his deep brown complexion with eyes to match. The only thing darker is his hair that has a shading of gray setting in.

"You've got mail, soldier," he says, holding out the envelope. If it were anyone else, we'd have words. But Mills, he's put me in my place more times than I'd like to admit, and I respect the hell out of him for doing so.

"Lieutenant," I say and nod. I inspect the envelope, trying to get an idea of where it's from. The return address is for Jasper, Georgia, but I know it's not from my mom. I haven't given her the address. I rarely ever do.

Dustin,

Wow! I don't even know what to say. The multitude of crumpled papers at my feet is evidence of that. Maybe I should put them all together so you can witness the evolution of this letter. Actually, that's a horrible idea as my words have been all over the place trying to string together something that makes sense. How is that even possible when nothing seems to make sense?

I don't know if this is a bad idea, but the idea of not reaching out seemed worse. I don't have many regrets in my life, but the ones I do have seem to all involve you. More so the way I've handled situations. Most recently, the one at Dax's award ceremony. Truth be told, I keep playing the night in my head over and over, wishing I had handled it differently. Given the circumstances, there'd only be so much I could change, but maybe it'd be enough.

For the last thirteen years, all I've ever wanted was to see you again—to make sure you're okay. Then I finally had that chance, and I blew it. Things never seem to go as we picture them to, do they?

Well, are you okay?

So many words I want to say. Words that just seem pointless, yet I keep finding myself wanting to say them all to you.

Stay safe, D

Love, E

I stare at the letter in my hand as if I've never seen words on paper before. As if I'm trying to brand every single one of them in my brain so I can play it on repeat. I want to scar her words onto my heart so I never forget them—in case I never receive them again. I stare and stare, trying to decipher this feeling. It's foreign and somewhat obtrusive. My instinct is to fight it off. To be impenetrable. But something within is going to battle against that logic.

"Holy shit." Someone snickers. All eyes are on me as I've seemed to become the entertainment. "Adams is smiling."

"No, I'm not," I say, straightening my mouth.

"You can't bullshit a bullshitter," Daniels says, strutting toward me. "Who's got you smiling?" His eyes drop to the letter in my hand, and I quickly fold and tuck it in the envelope.

"Your mom." I sit back down to reassemble my gun. "You didn't know we had a thing?"

A look of disgust washes over his face and I snicker. He mumbles something about me being nasty as he retreats. I catch Brian sitting quietly, looking my way. He received mail, too, and I wonder what his wife had to say to him. He seems to be lost in thought, but his doesn't put a smile on his face like mine did.

Reality slowly returns, sobering my thoughts. She's married. Her husband is here. She was just being kind. Checking on me like one would an old friend. *An old friend.* That is what we had reduced one another to at Dax's award ceremony. Whatever her reasoning may be, that's what I have to tell myself. False hope or happiness are things I can't afford to creep in and cloud my judgment.

The guys start to clear out, heading to bed. All but Brian. Figures. He sits in a chair, leaning back with his legs outstretched, crossed at the ankles. His hands rest in his lap, clasped together as his head rests on the back of the chair. His eyes are closed, and I take the rare moment to assess him. With his naturally tanned skin, black hair, and knowing he's an Oklahoma boy, I'd venture to say he's part Native American.

"Where'd you say you were from, Adams?" Brian doesn't open his eyes or break form, confirming something does indeed have him in deep thought. I'm not sure I like where his thoughts might be going as he seems to be attempting to piece together a puzzle.

"I didn't say." Before he can prod any further, I gather my stuff and walk away, leaving him alone with his thoughts.

Walking into our shared room, I head up to the bunk bed we also share. For the sake of self-preservation, I've made it a point to avoid being around when he talks about his family. I don't want to hear about something that was supposed to have been mine. Something I feel he doesn't value the way he should. If I had what he has back at home, I'd be there, not here.

The picture I've avoided analyzing catches my eye, and I lean into the bottom bunk for a better look. I stare at Echo longer than I should, imagining she was smiling at me the way she was at the camera. I follow the arm draped around her to Brian. I can't be mad. I see the appeal. Stark contrast to me...and the very white, blond boy in the family picture. I lean further to get a better look. The door handle jolts, and I jump, hitting my head on the metal bars above me.

"Adams."

I grab the top of my head and turn to face Lieutenant Mills. "Sir," I say, dropping my hands and straightening my stance.

"I just received word your team will be sent back out sooner than planned. I'll give you further orders as I receive them but wanted you to give your team a heads-up."

"Thank you, sir. I'll inform them."

THE NEXT MORNING, we gather our belongings and wait for orders. I pull Echo's letter out and read over it again even though I can repeat it verbatim. I picture her sitting legs crisscrossed, writing it, scrunching her nose at each word as she second-guessed herself.

I do the unthinkable and grab a piece of paper and quickly write her back.

Echo,

Give me all the words.

Love, D

Chapter Twenty-Six

ECHO

August 2014

A man of so few words wants me to give him all the words. I walk around the house, trying to think of what to write. Going down memory lane sounds like an awful idea, but as I lie here on my old bedroom floor staring up at the ceiling, all I can think about is the constellation that used to be up there. A faint outline still remains.

Dustin,

I'm not sure I can give them all, but here are some words. I hope they hold you over until I can string together some more.

My parents are selling their old home, so for the last two weeks I've been staying here. I offered to fix it up some in an attempt to get it sold quicker. But I'm starting to lose faith that it will help. I've taped off every room in this house except for my old one. I just can't bring myself to do it. I just can't bring myself to paint over the memories, pretending they never existed. That you never existed.

I sit in here nightly, much like I am right now writing you, leaning against my old broken bed. Then I get pissed that the reason for my bed being broken is gone. Someone stole Orion's Belt, Dustin, so I need you to buy me another one.

I'm just kidding. I am upset about it, but it's not your responsibility.

I won't be here much longer, with school starting back soon. Plus, I've taken enough vacation from work. I might come down on some weekends to continue working on the house. It just depends on how busy life gets once I get back to it. I've loved being close to Lynsie and Dax again. I don't really have anyone else I'm close with back in Alabama. But they're not the real reason being here feels... right.

Yet, it doesn't fully feel right without you here.

I would like to say that all of this is making things messy, mudding up feelings. But the only reason it's getting muddy is because the feelings have never went away. They've just been hidden and are now being unearthed.

Maybe I shouldn't be telling you these things with

the situation, but feel that with the distance it's safe to just be honest with you and hopefully work all this inner turmoil out. I can't help but still feel drawn to you. You've always been my safe place. And I've missed you terribly.

Love, E

I fold the paper, second guessing whether I should be so vocal with my vulnerabilities with Dustin when he's the reason behind them all. I walk to the study and pull out the last envelope. The idea of just sliding the letter into the drawer and forgetting about it crosses my mind. Just because my feelings and thoughts are all over the place doesn't mean I should muddy up Dustin's, too.

Then lack of better judgement takes over and I address the envelope, put a stamp on it, and walk it to the post office. I have a lot I need to get done today at the house. Mostly just organizing all my supplies neatly in the garage for the off chance someone will want to view it while I'm back home.

Back home. What a foreign thought.

My mom is supposed to be bringing Dylan back to me tomorrow and I know he's not going to want to stick around here long. The idea of leaving has me feeling very apprehensive. I feel close to everyone I love here. Something about this place just feels right.

And I don't know what I'm supposed to do with that feeling.

Chapter Twenty-Seven

DUSTIN

Sleep? What's that? It's definitely something I don't get much of anymore. Over the years, I've come to terms with my restless nights. Screw the gunfire in the distance and ongoing mortar bombs being shot our way. I welcome those sounds. My self-inflicted sleep deprivation has more than prepared me for being overseas, in enemy territory, embedded in a war zone.

The mortars are always good at pointing out who the new guy is. While the seasoned guy is whistling Yankee Doodle Dandy, the *new guy* is taking cover. It's a pretty comical sight, though those bombs are no laughing matter. They're kind of like a launched grenade that flies up high in the air, comes down, and blows up. They are constant, even though they aren't accurate—which is a plus. They're one of the reasons we can't have mass formations. If we do take on mortar fire, it won't kill a big crowd. Some bases are fortunate enough not to experience them. But since most bases are bigger than the towns us guys grew up in, and the fact that mortars only have a kill radius of about ten feet, I'd like to believe we have the upper hand.

But that's impossible when there's absolutely no defense to them.

That's why I don't bother taking cover. If it's going to hit, it's going to hit.

You'd think being over here in a war zone would help me forget the past. It was finally starting to pull my mind away from the what-ifs and *what happeneds*...until she appeared out of nowhere like a mirage. Now my mind is a wreck, and my heart is in shambles. I thought I was finally over her. I was wrong, so wrong. Seeing her stopped my heart and kick-started it back to life all at once.

I make my way to the makeshift gym that consists of nothing more than a weight bench and punching bag. The small tent-like building is empty; just how I like it. The only time I'm able to find rest are the nights I stay up until I can no longer keep my eyes pried open, exhausting my body to its limits. Some nights usually end with me in the gym lifting, pressing, and punching until my arms and legs are completely numb. If only the effort could numb my thoughts and emotions. Then, and only then, I might have a chance of recovering.

Who am I kidding? For me, there's no such thing as recovery. I'm a lost cause and I'm even more tormented now.

I should be exhausted. If my body wasn't beat, my mind should be. So much goes into these—so much that could go wrong. We're venturing into the unknown. We have one full day of prep, one day of recovery, and however long it takes to complete the mission between the two.

For our next mission, we will be on foot. I like the idea of that far more than being confined to a Stryker. I just don't like the idea of being part of route clearance and being part of the team that clears the road of bombs. A bomb does far more damage than a bullet. Every job has a number associated with it called a military occupation specialty. Infantry is 11b. So a lot of the other guys like to call it 11 bang bang because we're always getting shot at. But I'd rather take on a bang bang than a kaboom kaboom.

I climb into bed, sweaty and fully clothed. I read the last letter I got from Echo one more time before tucking it under my pillow. I stare above, begging for sleep as the constellation taped above lulls my eyes shut.

I wake what seems like only minutes later as I lie on my bed. Dreams always seem to flood my mind no matter the amount of effort I put into wearing the damn thing out.

I quickly sit up and toss my legs over the side, placing my elbows on my legs. I rest my head in my hands as I start thinking about life and how messed up it is. Being in the Army, I've seen how cruel life can be. People die and you simply have no control over it, but that's just life in general. But the joke's on me now.

Oh, how the circle of life isn't some Disney theme song when it comes to me. I lost the girl and took off in hopes that maybe one day the moving around that comes with being enlisted would either bring the girl back to me or kill me, putting me out of my misery.

"Do you ever sleep, Adams?"

I look up and see Roberts making his way toward me with one hand scratching his nuts, the other resting behind his neck while he stretches.

"I'll sleep when I'm dead." I stand up, stretching before reaching back with both hands and pulling my shirt over my head. I ball it up and throw it next to my bed.

Roberts gives me an 'mmhmm' as he continues back to his bed. I hear him land on the mattress as soon as I hit the floor on all fours. One hundred push-ups are how I like to get my mornings started. I close my eyes and get lost in the weight of my body lowering almost completely to the ground. Letting myself quickly free fall and then slowly rise up is just one of the ways I like to torment my body.

Ninety-seven.

Ninety-eight.

Ninety-nine.

One hundred.

I open my eyes as I'm pushing the last one out and I see her face. Tightly closing my eyes back, I let myself collapse back to the floor, rolling onto my back. Maybe I should just take my thin-ass pillow and smother Brian. That'd surely put an end to my never-ending torture. I doubt that'd win me the girl, but that's a lost cause anyways.

I sigh as I sit up and grab another shirt to toss on. Killing Brian doesn't fit into the plan I made. In fact, offing him would be quite the opposite.

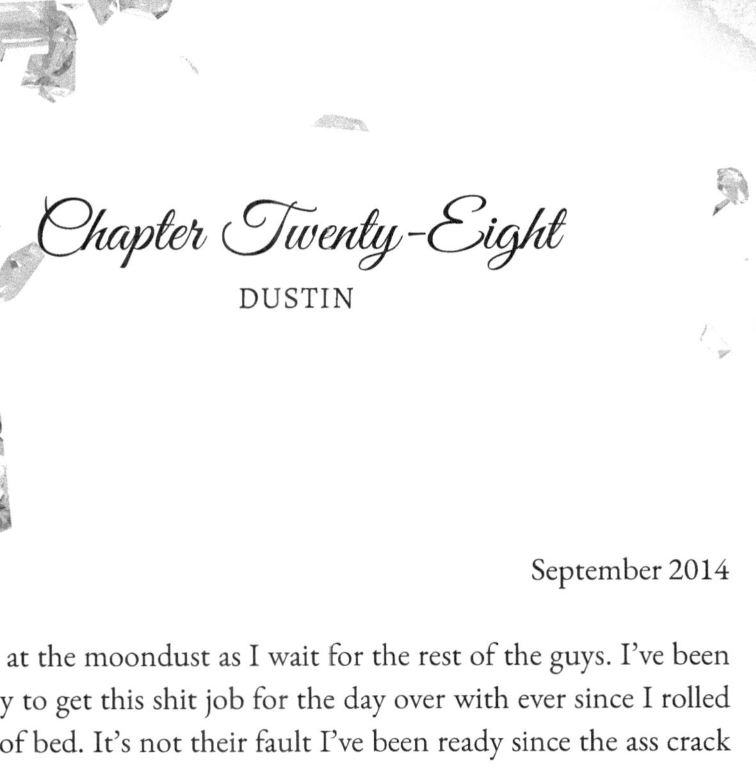

Chapter Twenty-Eight
DUSTIN

September 2014

I kick at the moondust as I wait for the rest of the guys. I've been ready to get this shit job for the day over with ever since I rolled out of bed. It's not their fault I've been ready since the ass crack of dawn. Surely it'd be easier for me to watch my own back than mine along with Williams' too. But since we're heading to what's been called a kinetic area, guess I'll wait for my fellow soldiers.

"Williams!" I yell once we make it outside the wire.

He looks over and lifts his head in response. "Adams," he says as he closes the distance.

"You'll be going with me today. I want the three of you." I turn, pointing to Pool, Greyson, and Roberts. "You three go east and secure the buildings. There's been talk of movement and we need to clear it out if there is any."

"Yes, sir!" they all say as they turn and start jogging away.

I turn without saying another word and start jogging toward the west end. I hear Brian close behind as our feet lightly push against the dusty earth. As the sun beats down upon us, sweat trickles down my face. The sky is constantly orange. I used to feel like I was on another planet, but being over here for as long as I have, US soil now seems more foreign to me. Sand land is miserable. Surely hell isn't much hotter.

As we approach the buildings, I slow down.

"Why have I been coming with you lately?" Williams asks from behind as his breathing returns to normal.

"What do you mean?" I pause but don't face him.

"Anytime we're sent out, you always make sure I go with you. And it's only always just us when we have to split up. Is there a reason for it?" He evens with me, standing at my side. I can feel his eyes on me while I debate a response.

The truth should work. "No reason. Besides keeping your ass alive." I look over at him and see a dumfounded expression taking over his face.

"That doesn't even make sense."

"Quit overthinking shit, Williams." I roll my eyes, taking a few steps forward.

"I know you know my wife. The tension was thick as shit when I walked up the night of the award ceremony." His words almost cause me to lose my footing.

I stand still, playing it cool. "It's a small world after all." I shrug like it's no big deal even though it's everything but.

"Yeah," he huffs. "There's just something else."

"Williams, I don't have time for your games right now." My anger's taking over as his bullshit starts to compromise our position.

"Where'd you say you were from?" he continues prodding for an answer he's not going to like.

"I didn't," I grit out.

"Your middle name wouldn't happen to be Ryan?"

I stop in my tracks. There's no way he'd know my middle name.

"Adams is a pretty common name. But I doubt there are multiple Dustin Ryan Adams from Jasper, Georgia." WTF is this guy, with the FBI? He continues, "I know how you know her. You're her—"

"Williams, just shut the hell up. Quit being an oxygen thief." I quickly pivot toward him, wanting him to just shut up about it all, and that's when I see him hiding. "Get out of the way." I jump into Williams, pushing him with all my might. No matter how many missions I've been on and all the training in the world, you never fully get used to the onslaught of bullets flying at you. So much enemy gunfire surrounds us. I fall to my knees as I take one to the side.

"Dammit!" I shout, looking down to see red mist oozing out. It's not that bad. I've seen plenty worse. I crouch up on my feet, peering around the building, trying to get a visual on the situation. I need to see where these bastards are hiding and need to see where my men are. I plan on getting us all back alive, but damn, it's hard to see through the dust and smoke.

"Don't do it, Adams."

I look back and see Williams on the ground, doubled over. *No, no, no.* I was supposed to keep him safe...in one piece. Rushing to his side, I push him back to assess the damage. One wound to his upper thigh. I need to get him to the medics.

I hear a chopper in the distance and know I need to get Williams there, now. I need to get us to where the other guys are. I hear *"dustoff inbound"* in my earpiece and wrap my arm around Williams and make our way to the location the MEDEVAC is heading. I grit through the pain as I practically pull him with me, his wounded leg being nothing but dead weight.

Finally, our other guys come into view, and I yell for Pool.

"Get him on that bird!" I order and take back off in the opposite direction.

Then out of the dust and smoke, I see the contraption flying toward my vicinity, and this time I'm not singing Yankee Doodle

Dandy. I hear screaming all around me as I fly backward. Pain soars through my body as I drop to the ground. I can't pinpoint the source. My ears are ringing, and my vision is blurry as I try to look around to get a sense of the madness that encompasses me.

I'm not dead and I need to get back to my men. No one will be dying on my watch. That much I know. I roll to my side and scream out in pain. I can faintly hear Pool yelling for help while shooting back at the enemy. I need to help. I have to help. I attempt to shove myself to my feet, but my arm gives out beneath me. The pain is sharp. A burning sensation seeps up my arm as I fall to the ground. My stomach rolls, and I force myself to move to my other side so I can at least hold on to my injured arm, possibly salvaging whatever is left. I grip my elbow, pressing it against me. I don't want to let my hand drift down. I don't want to feel what I already know.

The pain is unbearable. I can't keep my eyes open as I struggle to breathe through the searing agony. I lie on my back, welcoming the pain.

God, let it take over me.

Chapter Twenty-Nine

ECHO

He's injured. That's all I know. The severity is unknown. I pace back and forth, waiting for the plane to arrive. I need to see him, touch him...know he's okay. The uncertainty of it all holds my heart and mind in a vice grip. People start filing out through the secured exit. It has an automatic command that says, *'Don't Stop'* to keep people from pausing or turning around mid-exit, and I fight the urge to belt out *'Get it, get it'* every time someone walks through.

Fewer and fewer people funnel through and worry seeps in that I had the arrival information incorrect. I take a few steps closer to the glass wall that separates us from the rest of the airport, wanting to see farther down the gate area. A man in camouflage walking with a cane and a slight limp and his left arm in a sling slowly fills my vision. My heart races, leaping for joy as I see Brian in the flesh. A singe of pain squeezes it at seeing him injured. I want to run through the exit and help him as he struggles to keep his bag tossed over his shoulder and slightly trips in the process.

Why isn't anyone helping him?

Now I see why he's the last to make his way out. He doesn't want anyone to see him struggle. He walks through the exit with his head hanging low, and my heart hurts at the idea of him not even wanting me to see him in this condition. I run the few steps and cautiously throw my arms around his neck. He winces, but I don't retreat. Instead, I hold a bit tighter until I feel his body relax and his head falls into the crook of my neck.

"I'm so glad you're home," I whisper.

"Yeah, me too." He lets out a shaky breath against my skin, causing a ripple of goose bumps to form. Keeping one arm around his neck, I use the other to gently rub along his back. His body lightly trembles and I'm unsure if it's from the weight he's having to bear on his cane, or the weight of what he's been through causing it.

I pull back and cup his face in my hands, lifting it from its downcast retreat. "Hey," I lightly say, getting him to make eye contact with me. "Let's get you home."

He nods, mouthing *'home'* like he never expected to see it again. That realization slams into my chest so hard my knees almost buckle. But I manage to keep my wits intact for the sake of this man standing in front of me. This once strong, no fear man of mine who seems like a frail shell of who he once was. I might have been unsure of what direction my life should go a few months ago, but here in this moment, I know I'm right where I need to be; taking care of the man who made it his mission to take care of me thirteen years ago—what seems like a lifetime ago. Perhaps this is my sign to leave that life where I left it.

"Do you want me to carry that for you?" I touch the strap that's over his shoulder.

"I got it." He grips the strap tighter as if it's going to keep it in place. I want to take his cane and have him use me as his crutch instead, but I have a feeling he won't accept the offer.

"Okay. Is this it or do you have more?"

"Of course I have more," he bites out. "You packed it or have you forgotten?" His eyes are narrow slits as he waits for my response.

I slightly jump away from him, my eyes big as saucers with shock. His demeanor seems cold, and I gulp back the urge to cry at his sharp tone. *What in the actual hell?*

I shake my head and place my hand on his that's holding the cane. "You're right. I'm sorry." I apologize, attempting to sympathize with his current situation.

His face softens and the boy I've known my entire life returns. "I'm sorry," he quietly says. Turmoil swirls in his eyes, and I wish I could isolate all the different emotions. Not that it'd help him deal with them, but it'd help me decipher how to handle him.

I lean in and push my lips to his, saying what I've wanted to say since I first ran up to him. "I love you, Brian."

His shoulders sag like those words gave him permission to drop the weight of the world he's been carrying. Then his bag falls down his arm, stopping where his hand meets his cane and causing him to stumble forward. Instinctively, I place my arms out, grabbing the sides of his arms to steady him.

"Dammit, Echo," he bellows, and I release my grip, realizing my mistake. "My arm is in a sling for a reason." He grunts, steadying himself as he adjusts the bag back into place. His stubborn ass is going to be the death of me, but this new attitude he seems to have might be its competition as I've never been known for holding my tongue.

"I didn't want you to fall. It was instinct." I shrug. I don't apologize this time, but I also don't say what I really want to. *"Next time I'll just let you fall on your face."* Because I'm sure that would go over really well.

He starts walking toward the direction of the baggage claim, and I fall to his side, in silence. This isn't the coming home I envisioned, but I'm just so grateful he didn't come home in a casket. So many soldiers and their families pay the ultimate sacrifice, and I just can't even imagine being in that situation.

We stand and wait behind the other passengers as the conveyer sounds and begins to move with luggage. I watch as a few children peek around their parents' and eye Brian. I smile as he keeps his eyes trained ahead with a stoic look, not paying any attention to his surroundings. Once the crowd thins out, I break away and move closer to watch for his duffle bag. He belittled me earlier when I asked if he had more. I know he always has a duffle bag because I'm the one who usually packs it for him. I figured they might just ship it back versus him have to tackle one more thing with his injuries. I spot the olive-green bag and pull it off by the hand straps. I turn around to Brian, who's watching me with furrowed brows like he's trying to figure out how he can carry this huge bag. Grasping the handles with both hands, I carry the bag in front of me, stopping in front of him.

"It's okay to have help," I admit, hoping he realizes it's an act of reassurance and not belittlement. He nods, and a throat clearing to our side shifts our attention. An older man stands near us, looking at Brian in awe as if he's reminiscing.

He stands a bit straighter, in an attention stance, before raising his arm to his forehead, saluting Brian. It's in that moment I take notice of the veteran hat adorning his head.

"Thank you for your service, soldier." He gleams.

Brian straightens his posture and pushes his shoulders back, hiding the pain I know it's inflicting. He takes a deep breath and passes his cane to his hand sticking out of the sling. He's able to hold himself steady for a heartbeat as he lifts his hand in salute, mimicking the man as they face one another. Quickly, he returns his cane and shifts his weight before letting out a huge breath. The adoration and respect these two are showing one another cause tears to well up in the corner of my eyes.

. . .

THE CAR RIDE home is rather stagnant with silence. I want to ask what happened over there, but I don't want to upset him. I seem to be doing a good job of that already. Opening the garage door, I pull in. The one step into the house from here should be much more accommodating than the five leading up our porch. I jump out and open the door leading to the kitchen, flipping the light on. Then make my way back to the car, opening his door.

"You don't have to baby me," he grumbles, swinging his legs out as he steadies his cane.

"Trying to help and make things easier for you isn't babying." I roll my eyes out of his view.

We make our way in, and he stops at the fridge. Opening the door, he assesses the contents.

"No beer," he chastises, disappointment evident.

"Umm, sorry, alcohol was the last thing on my mind when I found out you were injured." I drop his bag on the tan tile and walk off to regain my shit before I lose it.

I hear him mumble at my retreat but don't bother asking for clarification. I hate that he's been wounded, but it doesn't give him the right to treat me like shit. Retreating to the master bedroom, I sit in the rocker near our bed. It offers me the same sense of peace the rocking gave Dylan as a baby. Once perspective returns to me, I sense a tinge of guilt, feeling I should be going above and beyond to cater to Brian. I can't take his attitude personal. God knows what he saw and endured overseas. Knowing he needs to fully relax after being so cooped up on a plane, I walk to our bathroom and draw up a hot bath. I make my way back to where I left him, hoping my gesture will help.

"Baby," I holler, heading down the hall. "I drew you a bath." I round the corner to the open living room to see a fully reclined Brian... asleep.

Looks like I'll be taking a bath.

I stay in the bath extra-long, making sure my skin is nice and wrinkly. I'm trying to relax and calm my thoughts, but they're all over the place and all too consuming. I crawl into an empty bed, a tradition I'm all too familiar with, and wonder if I'm abandoning my husband by doing so. That thought pushes me out of bed as I grab the blanket draped at the end and head for the living room. I lay on the couch with my head facing the opposite end so I can keep an eye on Brian throughout the night. He's still fully dressed in his fatigues, not even bothering to take his boots off. If I could do so without waking him, I would. But the idea of startling him in his sleep is something I take heed of. The last thing I want to do is jolt him awake.

The three pill bottles sitting on the end table next to him grab my attention, and I begin to wonder if the medication has a bearing on his mood, or if there's something more controlling it.

GROANING, CURSING, AND the shaking of pill bottles awakens me, and I peek my eyes open right as Brian tosses something in his mouth, then chases it with a big gulp of water. It makes me thankful there isn't any alcohol in the house. I can only imagine how that would worsen an already bleak situation.

"Do you need anything?" I ask, propping myself up, seeming to startle him as I do.

"What are you doing in here?" he questions as if it isn't obvious.

"I wanted to be nearby in case you needed anything." I offer with sincerity and a yawn.

"Go to bed, Echo. I'm fine." He groans, shifting in the recliner. "Or I will be once the pain pill kicks in."

I glance at my phone, see that it's already 6:00 a.m., and decide to go ahead and get my day started. I had planned on playing nurse to Brian, but I'm under the impression that me taking care of him in any capacity is the last thing he wants. So I'll just take care of me and wait for him to ask for help. I grab my blanket and fold it as I make my way back to our room. After sliding my feet into my sneakers, I braid my hair, push my headphones on, and start up my treadmill. No sense in me changing up the routine I've grown accustomed to. Thirty minutes into my intense walk, Brian shuffles in, eyeing me with suspicion. He mouths something and I'm unable to catch it before pushing my headphones down.

"Who you gettin' fit for?" he repeats, causing me to blink at him in disbelief. I study his face for a hint of humor, and it's void.

"Uh," I stammer, "myself."

"Yeah, sure." He slowly moves toward the closet. "Where's Dylan?"

I hit stop on the treadmill, letting it slow down beneath me.

"He's at a friend's house. I didn't know how you'd be feeling." I take my little towel and wipe the sweat off my forehead and the nape of my neck.

"And you didn't think to consult with me about that." He's leaned against the closet door, arms crossed, and it's as if I'm looking at a stranger. I'm unsure if he's asking or accusing, and I can't help but feel he's trying to push me away.

"Since when have I consulted with you in regard to Dylan?" I huff, a bubble of my own anger appearing. His back is now to me as he shimmies out of his jacket, wincing every so often. I want to help him. I want to walk up behind him and wrap my arms around his waist. I want to just touch him and push away whatever has him so angry. But then he speaks again, and it makes me want to throat punch him instead.

"Oh, that's right. Why would you since he's not my son." He all but sneers with a laugh.

"Screw you." I seethe, grabbing my phone and purse off the bedside table. I stop momentarily to give him the benefit of the doubt. I want to see if he still has a conscience or if that was left back in the war zone. My heart cracks a bit when he doesn't acknowledge me as he keeps slowly stripping off his uniform. Something within urges me to push my luck. I walk to the entrance of the closet, standing inches away from him, and whisper, "I love you, Brian." He slightly flinches before his body stiffens. "I don't know what happened over there." I let my fingertips trail down the exposed skin of his uninjured arm. His body sags, relaxing into mine, and I let out a breath of relief. "And maybe one day you'll want to talk about it. But please don't let whatever happened ruin us," I plead.

"Okay," he agrees with a nod, and I slowly wrap my arms around his waist, praying he doesn't resist. He pulls away, only to turn and face me. His deep brown eyes are rimmed red, with a pain I've never seen before. I caress the side of his face, noticing the random scars intricately placed around his cheekbone and down the side of his neck. He closes his eyes, causing the pain to spill down his face. Just because he left the war zone doesn't mean the war has left him, and I have a feeling the battle he's now waging is even bigger.

I cup his face in my hands and whisper against his lips, "I'm going to fight this with you." His body begins to tremble, and I push my lips to his, feeling such sadness and desperation. No way I'm going to let this man who has been there for me my entire life go through this alone. He has to know that. I let my arms fall and wrap them around his hips to keep him steady. I pull back and wait for his eyes to flicker open. The brown depths feel as if he's staring into my soul as he holds my gaze and it's the exact intensity I need from him. "It's my turn to take care of you," I admit. He attempts to pull away, but I tighten my grip. "You've been taking care of me ever since you sent that boy flying with his lunch tray." I smile, and the memory causes his lip to curl in a similar fashion. Boy, have I missed that boyish grin of his. "Please," I beg. "Let me take care of you."

He nods and drops his head in defeat. I wrap my arm around his waist and help him to the bed, thankful he allows me to assist. Brian sits and I stand in front of him. I run my hand across the softness of his fresh buzz cut, and he wraps his arm around my waist, pulling me closer. I yelp at the quickness, and he groans where his head rests against my chest. His hand moves all over my body, finding its way between my thighs as it navigates up. My breath catches at the feeling of his hand moving up my bare leg, caressing the hem of my shorts. This isn't what I meant by take care of him, but it feels too good to stop. He tilts his head up, and I lean down and kiss him. So much built-up need between us as our mouths open and our tongues intertwine.

I step back and kneel in front of him, watching as he watches me. One by one, I unlace his boots, slowly pulling each off. I stand and tug the bottom of his brown shirt, pulling it off from his uninjured side over his head and then slowly maneuver it around the cast. His breath catches as my fingers fumble to unbutton his pants. I lightly press against his chest, urging him to lie back as I unzip and carefully remove his fatigue bottoms and boxers. His lean, hard body lies before me like it's mine for the taking. But I don't want to take. I want to give.

Chapter Thirty

ECHO

We sit in the hot bath that he only agreed to take if I joined him. Like I would tell him no when I feel we might be on the upward trajectory. I revel in the closeness of my back against his chest as we sit with our fingers laced together. His casted arm rests propped on the side of the tub while he begins to move our interlocked fingers across my stomach. The movement slightly tickles, but I remain still as he continues.

"Have you ever thought about having more kids?" he asks, sending a shiver down my spine.

I begin to stutter, unsure if it's his breath against my skin or the question causing my reaction. "Sure, in a perfect world," I admit with a shrug, trailing my free hand down the top of his thigh.

"Huh," he says, pulling his hand from mine. "And what would be a perfect world?" I hear the agitation in his question and regret ever answering him in the first place.

I sigh. "One where I'm not the only parent ninety percent of the time." He wasn't wrong when he said Dylan isn't his, but he also hasn't been around to even be a father figure. His body tenses beneath mine and a coldness settles in as he pushes up from behind me, groaning in pain as he does. "Let me help you," I say as I stand and reach for his arm.

"No," he yells, voice sounding like thunder, rattling the walls. I jump back, retreating from him.

"Fine, figure it out yourself." I grab a towel and wrap it around me. "But don't blame me if you bust your stubborn ass on the floor." I wipe away the tears and head for the door.

"Echo, I'm sorry," he mumbles, the water splashing as he sits back down in the bathtub.

I turn around to see my husband hunched over with his knees pulled to his chest. His body heaves with cries of brokenness I've never heard from this man of mine. I practically slide on my knees the short distance to him and wrap my arms around his shoulders, pulling him into me. I don't know what he's been keeping inside. I just pray he can get it all out.

"I don't know what's wrong with me," he admits through ragged breaths.

"Shhh." I rub his back, trying to calm him down.

"I just find myself getting so angry, and I don't know why." He looks over at me, eyes filled with agony, pleading for understanding. I move my hand to his face and cup it, offering what he needs. "I don't know if it's the pills, the pain, the experience, or the situation that's pushing me over the edge." He shakes his head as if he's trying to rid the demons. I want to ask about it all and pick at his brain to see if it'd help but feel it might have the opposite effect. I want to ask about the rest of his unit, but I refrain. I keep the possibility of Dustin being injured in the back of my mind, knowing that if he were, Lynsie would let me know. But also knowing he has a family to take care of him, while I'm essentially all Brian has.

"You need to talk to someone." I let out a shaky breath. "And while

I'd love for that to be me, I don't think I'm going to be what you need to get through what you experienced."

He nods in agreement.

"Now let's get you out of this tub." I kiss his forehead and pull him against me again for a hug.

"I love you. I don't know what I would ever do without you." His admission ties my heart in a knot.

Chapter Thirty-One

DUSTIN

"We tried to preserve as much of your arm as possible, but there was just nothing we could do from the wrist down. The burns, shrapnel damage, and crushed bones were just too much. Honestly, you're very lucky to have the majority of your forearm left."

I snort when the word lucky comes out of his mouth. Yeah, I'm some ungrateful asshole who wants everyone to pity me. I do realize I'm lucky to be alive. But you should only consider yourself lucky when that's what you're wanting.

"My men?" I croak, my throat feeling dry and scratchy. I could give two shits about my own flesh wounds. I need to know the status of my platoon.

"No casualties." The doctor looks up, finally making eye contact. I can see the sympathy in his crystal blue eyes before he quickly adverts his gaze back downward to my arm where he continues business as usual. "You still have full mobility of your elbow, which will allow you the ability to wrap that part of your arm around in a gripping motion. I know it doesn't seem like much, but if we'd had to amputate"—I shudder at that word, but he continues without noticing—"from the elbow down, you'd only have from the bicep section up." He gestures with his own arm what he's trying to explain. I get what he's saying. The puppet show isn't necessary.

"How much longer will I be here?" I ask, needing to get to get an idea of when I'll be discharged from the hospital. My facial hair scratches my neck and I can imagine I look pretty unkempt and rough.

"Well, if everything goes smoothly with no infection, both of your wounds should be fully healed in four weeks at the earliest."

"I have to stay here for a month?" My voice comes out louder than I intended. I grip the bedsheet with the only hand I have left, and breath in and out, reigning in my temper.

"Ideally, no." The nurse attempts to be calming with her low tone and sympathetic stare. "If you have somewhere to go and no infection, you should be able to leave here in ten to fourteen days."

I don't want sympathy but have a feeling it's a look I'll receive from here on out.

I lean my head back as my eyes begin feeling heavy. I refuse to look down at my wounds. I'm so drugged up; I can barely feel them. I don't need to see them. Seeing them will make them more real. The doctor's lips continue moving, but I don't care what he's saying. All I can do is think of the fingers I'm trying to move that no longer exist. It's such a weird, empty feeling.

"HOW LONG HAVE you been having nightmares?"

I open my eyes, trying to focus on the nurse in my room. I push the button, elevating my bed into a sitting position.

"What makes you think I've been having nightmares?" I ask before taking a drink out of my now lukewarm water. My throat is dry and scratchy. Must be the meds.

She walks up to the side of the bed, and I lean forward a bit so she's able to readjust my pillow. "Your heart rate increases, your body begins to tremble, followed by beads of sweat near your hairline. You shake your head back and forth, and when you finally do wake up, it's as if you're startled." She takes a step back, eyeing me, waiting for an answer.

I contemplate telling her the truth, but then think what the hell and decide the truth won't affect a stranger. "I only have nightmares when I'm awake. Sleep is the only time I'm able to escape them, for the most part." I attempt a shrug.

She looks at me with a faint expression of sadness. Like she's all too familiar with the nightmares I just explained. But it leaves as quickly as it came.

"Then why do you seem scared if they aren't nightmares?" She pulls up a chair and starts to slowly pull off the dressings. I wince as I bite through the twinge of pain. For the most part, I'm so medicated it doesn't bother me, not until they have to change the dressings on it.

I take a deep breath before releasing a heavy sigh. "Because sometimes dreaming about something you once had and knowing you'll never have it again is frightening to come to terms with."

She nods, and I see understanding in her eyes.

Since being in the hospital, all I seem to do is dream about her... what we had...what I miss...what I will never have again. It's as if my subconscious mind is playing out the time we had together on a constant loop, reminding me why I'm here in the first place.

Just like the meaning of her name, a repetition of sound, everything about her ripples through my soul. But unlike her name, the vibrations never cease. To this very day, they're still very much moving throughout my mind, my heart, and every fiber within me.

The love I feel for this girl is an untamable force of nature just waiting to be unleashed again. It calls out to me, begging for one more chance. It's her or no one. I will never feel these feelings for anyone else.

But she's taken, and it's eating me up inside. The one thing I want more than anything in the world is unattainable.

"Well, maybe getting you out of this hospital and back to your home state will help." The nurse gives me a smile as if me going home will fix all my problems. Little does she know home is where they all began.

I'm leaving here worse off than I ever imagined, yet far better off than I deserve to be. I'm a jobless, handless, Echoless man with nothing left to offer. But I wouldn't do a damn thing differently. In some screwed-up way, I protected what I love, and there's no way I can regret that decision.

Chapter Thirty-Two

DUSTIN

The abrupt bouncing as we land jars me awake, bringing me out of my haunting memories. It's bright and sunny, and I'm more than ready to get off this cramped plane. But what I'm not ready for is what lies on the other side of the door—the one I follow all these passengers through. Passengers who'll most likely be greeted by loved ones whom they are happy to see. I shouldn't harbor these resentments that I do, but I haven't figured out how to shake them. So instead of unpacking and dealing with them, I've kept them stowed away like carry-on baggage.

It's not that I don't love my parents, because I do. They gave me a great childhood, but I can't get past the idea that my own mother played a role in the demise of Echo and me. The idea of being dependent all over again and temporarily having to reply on them is the part I'm less than thrilled about. The idea of starting over from scratch and no longer having the only career I've ever known is something I haven't even begun to process. I don't even know how. Where would I even start? Where do you go when you give your entire life to a career you were willing to die for, and when you survive a blow that was intended to kill you, you're no longer needed. The idea that I've been reduced to damaged goods is a bitter pill to swallow.

I wait for the plane to empty before stepping out of my window seat and reaching for my carry on. If I'm going to struggle, then I'm going to do it on my own—with no bystanders. I awkwardly pull my cell phone out of my pocket and turn it back on. The stewardess announced we arrived thirty minutes early, so I'm not sure my parents have made it here yet.

As I slowly and dreadfully trudge my way to baggage claim, the airport bustles with people rushing to make their flights. I'm more than thankful for this sling my arm is hiding in, here in this crowded place. No one can see that I'm missing the rest of my arm from mid forearm down. The last thing I'm up for are sympathetic glances and invisible pats on the back from civilians.

My phone chimes and I move to the closest wall, making sure to get out of the way from all the moving people.

Mom: We'll be there around 2:30. There was an accident that backed up traffic.

Me: I'll be in baggage claim.

I finally make my way over to where even more madness resides, waiting for the luggage conveyer belt to start up. The tug of war over suitcases will be commencing soon as the alarm goes off, alerting the passengers. I stay back, not wanting to get in the middle of it all. I'm not in a rush by any means. My bag can circle until the place clears out for all I care.

Being in uniform with a sling, holding my arm in place, doesn't hide the fact that I'm a wounded soldier. I'm proud that I've served my country. It's not that I'm ashamed of my injury. I just curse the meaning behind it and what it now stands for. It doesn't represent the war of US soldiers against foreign men. No, to me, it represents the war between my heart and mind. The hardest battle I've found myself in to date.

After the crowd has thinned, I decide to get closer. A few moments later, I spot my dust-colored bag. The same bag I've lived out of for the last thirteen years. It's been a faithful duffle bag, never allowing me to carry more than I need or could handle. But now, as I attempt to seize it, I'm wondering how well I'll be able to handle both bags.

I drop my gym-sized bag down, getting my arm ready to reach out for my large duffle. I quickly grab the strap and give it a strong tug, making sure to get it the first time. I fling it across my shoulder, resting it on my back as I bend down to grab my other one. Trying to balance it all is a bitch, and my phone falls out of my pocket with me bent over, clanking on the ground.

"Dammit," I breathe out, barely audible to the people around me. I'm not trying to make even more of a scene. My phone is scattered around me. It's an older flip phone and the back has come off, allowing the battery to fall out as well. *Just my luck.*

An older gentleman next to me picks up the two pieces that rest at his feet while I gather the actual phone part and my bag and quickly stand back up before I topple over.

"Here you go, son," he says politely, handing me the battery and back piece to my phone.

I try to reach for them, to take them from his offering hand, but my one good hand can't hold them all, and out of instinct I turn my arm that's in the sling, forgetting there isn't a hand there. He notices, and a pained expression quickly crosses his face, but it's gone before I can let it bother me.

"I know you're more than capable," he says, but I hear a bit of uncertainty in his voice. "But would you like me to put it back together for you real quick?"

I debate the idea momentarily, but my pride kicks in. "I got it. But thanks." I nod, and he nods back in understanding. I maneuver my hand, lift up the flap of my coat pocket, and drop the part I have in before holding out my hand for the parts he's still holding. He hands them over and I drop them in with the rest, giving him a curt smile before turning to walk away. I need to find somewhere to sit before this frustration I'm feeling becomes evident. I'm no longer in a war zone. I'm in an airport, and I have to keep my emotions in check. Once I sit, I can readjust my bag situation and fix my phone as I wait.

I make my way to the most secluded spot I can find and throw my bag down before falling into a chair. I push myself as far back as possible, letting my head drop back. I pinch the bridge of my nose and squeeze my eyes tightly shut, pushing away the liquid I'm unfamiliar with.

I will not cry.

This is nothing to cry about. I need to get myself in check. I'm just having a bad start. That's all. I rub my hand over my face and sit up with determination. Leaning to the side, I pull my phone out of my pocket, piece by piece. I can do this. No big deal. It's only a hand. Sure, it's an adjustment, but it could be far worse.

I carefully sit each piece on my leg. I grip my phone and, using my thumb, I pry it open. I place it open side down on my thigh and carefully reach over, grabbing the battery. Before placing it in, I inspect it, making sure I put it in correctly. I angle the battery into one side slowly, drop it down, and use the tip of my thumb to push it all the way in.

Like a glove!

Sweet! One piece down. One more to go. I got this. I lower the back evenly over the battery. Holding it in place with my thumb, I grab my phone, careful not to drop it. All I have to do now is slide the back into place. I feel the excitement of being able to accomplish something so simple. Something I took for granted before.

Almost got it back together. So close.

"Oh, Dustin!" The screech from my mother causes my focus to break and I drop my phone...again. *FML!*

Chapter Thirty-Three

DUSTIN

Having Dax show up with our parents is the only saving grace this experience has to offer. I love my mother, but I have no doubt if I were in this back seat alone, I would've already opened the door and let myself fall out of this moving car. I know she's excited to see me and trying to hide the sadness and pity she's feeling, but I'd almost welcome the sadness and pity over her naming off all the things I should partake in back home.

I want to ask her if she missed the memo...that I'm missing a hand. And then remember I never told her or anyone the extent of my injuries. With the sling on, it's not obvious I'm missing my hand.

"Ma." I try to interrupt the convo she seems to be having with herself. "Ma," I say again, a little bit louder. "MA!" I yell as my dad slams on the brakes in traffic, causing us all to plummet forward in our seats. Thank God for seat belts or Dax and I would've face-planted the headrests.

My dad apologizes and my mom finally looks back. "Yes, honey?"

I sigh and throw my hand through my hair, dreading the inevitable pity I'm about to receive—from all parties in the car. "I know you're trying to help."

She nods, saying, "Yes."

"But you're not."

Her face falls at my bluntness.

"I'm not going to be able to do all the things you've been mentioning. No big projects with Dad. No doing the lawn care for all the little old ladies. No helping coach the baseball team."

"I'm sorry," she stammers. "I wasn't trying to volunteer your services out. I just thought..." she starts, but I interject.

"I was sent home for a reason, Ma." My voice drops.

"Right, you're so right. You were sent home to recuperate, not work." She goes on her tangent, apologizing and saying it was a dumb idea, but she knew I wouldn't want to be couped up in the house. I let out a heavy sigh, drop my head back, and tightly close my eyes. Scrunching my face together, I pinch the bridge of my nose, feeling the oncoming headache.

"Mom." Dax steps in, coming to the rescue. "I'm going to say this in the nicest way I possibly can. Be quiet and let people talk." I glance over at my brother in awe, wanting to high-five him. "You don't know what's going on. None of us do. So for the love of God, let Dustin talk before you make him clam up again." I hear a slight huff from the passenger seat, but nothing more. Dax looks over at me and smiles, gesturing with his hands. "The floor is yours."

"Yes, I'm back home to recuperate, but my career with the Army is over."

"Oh, thank God!" my mom says with glee.

"Mom," Dax warns. My dad remains quiet, per usual.

"For shit's sake," I mutter under my breath, pulling the sling off my arm. The black amputee compression sock covers what's left of my forearm to my elbow.

My mother lets out an audible gasp, throwing her hand to her mouth in horror.

"What happened?" she shrieks.

"Looks like he lost his hand," Dax replies matter-of-factly and I suppress a laugh. He's not going to pity me, and for that I'm grateful.

"Dax." She gasps and turns in her seat, looking behind her toward my brother. I can hear the butt chewing now for him being insensitive about the situation. But she seems to have forgotten we're adults now, and he stops her dead in her tracks.

"No, Mom. I hate that Dustin is injured. I would never wish that on anyone. But I'd much rather have my brother return with a missing hand and bruised ego than not return at all. Some people aren't that lucky." His words drive the point home and I'm left wondering if it stems from him losing his best friend, or if he knows something I don't. Like what happened to Brian. All I can do is hope he survived the attack or this missing hand and losing my career would've all been for nothing.

We all sit in silence for the rest of the ride, and for once, I welcome it.

"HEAD ON IN. I'll grab your bags," Dax says.

I look up and glare at him as he holds the door open, waiting for me to get out.

I grit out, "Thanks," causing my younger brother to chuckle. I hold back the smile threatening to spread across my face. I'd be lying if I said I hadn't missed him. I've avoided this house and my family like the plague. I shouldn't have taken everything out on them by staying away. It's just this town only reminds me of what I've lost.

I pause and look up at the sky. It's not bright and lit up with stars. Tonight, it seems a bit gloomy. Like it's welcoming me home but knows I'm not happy about it. The constellations are more vivid in the vast openness overseas. Now I can barely make out the Big Dipper.

As soon as my feet hit the threshold, I'm hit with the same floral scent my mom has used since I was a kid.

"Are you hungry?" She wraps her arms around my good arm, pulling me toward the kitchen, and I fight the instinct to pull away. "When everyone heard you were coming home, they started flooding the house with all these meals and desserts. It's just so nice to be in such a supportive community. Everyone has missed you." She rambles and rambles, and I start to block her out.

"I'm not hungry," I grumble as my feet come to a halt.

Her face is a mixture of shock and sadness once I turn my stone-cold expression her way. I can see tears forming, and for a second, my façade falters. I don't want to be the cause of her sadness. She's done nothing wrong. But just like she's always been, she doesn't know when to quit. So I'd like to say she brings it all on herself.

"Are you sure? Mrs. Trudy brought over lasagna. I know that's your favorite." She walks off, expecting me to follow. Her voice returns to its chipper tone.

"I said I'm not hungry," I bite out, trying to control my annoyance. It's as if being in this house has altered my ego.

"Dax," my mother calls, keeping her back to me. "Will you go ahead and take Dustin's bags up to his old room?"

I want to tell her thank you...maybe even apologize for my harshness, but anytime I show the slightest bit of anything besides rudeness, she seems to take it as some mother-son bonding time. And that's something I'm just not interested in.

"I swear. That woman hasn't changed," I huff as soon as I reach the top step.

"And neither has your room." Dax snickers as he opens the door and pushes it in. "Welcome back to two thousand one." He drops my bags near the closet.

"If only I could go back to two thousand one," I murmur as I scan the room I left behind so long ago.

"Why in the world would you want to go back to high school?" Dax crosses his arms as he leans back against my dresser.

"No reason." I drop down on my bed and start messing with the sling. It's been rubbing on the back of my neck all day and I'm ready to get the pain in my ass off. I know I look like a monkey, dipping my head and reaching behind with my hand to pull the strap up. I don't bother to look at Dax. I know he's watching me—probably with a mixture of amusement and pity. I know he feels bad for me being injured. What family member wouldn't? But unlike the rest, he'll never make me feel it. I don't want to feel or see the sadness that my missing hand causes people.

I groan, carefully sliding my arm out, then toss the contraption across the room. "That's a bitch to get off when you only got one hand." I attempt to make light of the situation.

"Are you sure you aren't hungry? Mom bought some bananas, strawberries, Poptarts, Fruity Pebbles..." He taps his chin thoughtfully. "And pretty much anything you liked as a kid. Which means the whole store." He laughs, shaking his head.

"Glad to see you're still a comedian." I begin to unbutton my fatigue jacket. I'm ready to be out of this uniform once and for all. No use in dragging out the inevitable.

"Well." Dax cocks a brow. "You did take all the asshole genes." While his tone is light-hearted, his words ring true.

"Boys!" We both look toward the door. "I made you both a plate of food!" our mother yells from downstairs. I half smile because it brings back so many memories. But then remember I told her twice I wasn't hungry and my smile dissipates.

Dax shakes his head and snickers. "She never listened when we were kids. Why do you think she would now?"

"Because we're adults," I say, stating the obvious. "Well, at least I am."

"Hey now." Dax holds his hands out in defense. "I'm just a kid at heart." He closes his eyes, lifting his nose as he sniffs. "A hungry one."

Dax leaves the room, and I welcome the solitude. I stand up and walk to the door.

"Where's Dustin?" Ma asks.

"He's upstairs. Remember he told you he wasn't hungry? I know you're only trying to help, but this is a huge adjustment for him." I can hear the plea in Dax's voice practically begging her to back off. He tells her all these things and I love him for it, but I know it's pointless. It's like everything you tell the woman goes in one ear and out the other. She hears you loud and clear. I think she has selective memory. Not memory loss. I believe she just remembers what she wants and when she wants.

I remind myself that being here is only temporary until I get my own place. *My own place.* I haven't ever had one of those. I don't even have a clue where to go from here. The only thing I've ever known besides baseball and this town has been the Army. I'm just uncertain where I fit into the world anymore, since the one constant I had was stolen from me.

I close my door and pull one arm at a time out of my jacket, cautious not to hit my injury. I stand, staring into the mirror that's still mounted to the back of my door. I inspect how I look. I look like shit. Both arms hang at my sides. I hold my arm out in front of me. The instinct to move my fingers is there, but they aren't. I bend my arm at my elbow, noticing that for the most part I have a fully functioning arm. This will be an adjustment for sure, but that's all.

"It could've been worse," I say to myself in the mirror as a reminder. "You're too prideful for any pity parties—even personal ones you want to host for yourself." I hold my injured arm up to the mirror. "As much as you'd like to think you'd rather not be, you're lucky to be alive. Time to start living like it." I let out a deep breath and twist the knob to the door.

Time to go act like I'm hungry.

"See, I knew he'd want to eat!" my mother exclaims, accepting the victory, and I almost retreat back to my room. I sit down across from Dax where the plate she made me sits.

I look straight at my brother and want to reach across the table and slap the smirk off his face—just like old times. I bet this time I could get away with it. My, how the tables have turned. I can hear Dax being all whiny like, *"Mom, aren't you going to get onto him?"*

The image makes me snort. Everyone looks at me, and I deflect. "Where's that woman of yours and my niece?"

"Technically," my mother starts, and I instantly stop her in her tracks, knowing how she's about to clarify Blu not being biologically Dax's daughter.

"Screw technicalities," I blurt.

My mother gasps.

Dax chuckles from across the table.

And my lips curve up into an involuntary smile.

I don't want to smile. But I can't control it and it kind of feels nice.

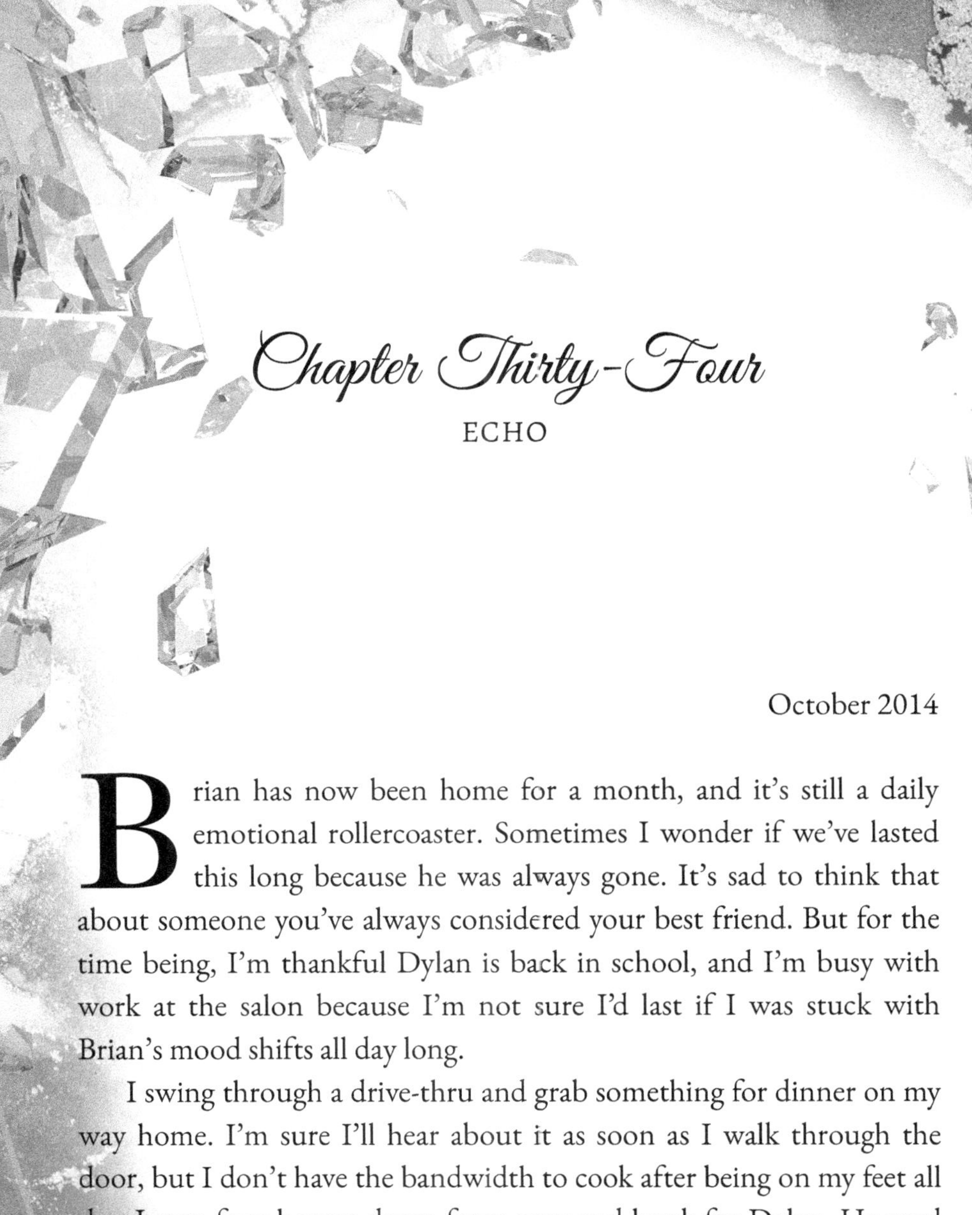

Chapter Thirty-Four

ECHO

October 2014

Brian has now been home for a month, and it's still a daily emotional rollercoaster. Sometimes I wonder if we've lasted this long because he was always gone. It's sad to think that about someone you've always considered your best friend. But for the time being, I'm thankful Dylan is back in school, and I'm busy with work at the salon because I'm not sure I'd last if I was stuck with Brian's mood shifts all day long.

I swing through a drive-thru and grab something for dinner on my way home. I'm sure I'll hear about it as soon as I walk through the door, but I don't have the bandwidth to cook after being on my feet all day. I stop four houses down from ours and honk for Dylan. He used to walk home after school, but now he walks the extra distance with his teammate, Brock. He avoids being home alone with Brian at all costs. I wanted to fight him on it and tell him to push past the awkwardness; that Brian needs us...but then my maternal instincts reminded me that

193

it's not my son's job to put out that amount of effort for anyone—especially an adult.

And just like that, I'm seventeen again, feeling like a stranger in my own home. I told myself when I ran away, I'd never walk on eggshells again, yet here I am, dancing my way across them as if my life depends on the performance.

Dylan makes his way to my car and a steady ache fills my chest. I was hoping this situation would rectify itself, leaving my son unscathed. But the more it drags out, the less faith I have it will all pan out. While I owe Brian everything for all he's done, my son and his well-being will come above even myself.

Dylan gets in and shuts the door, sitting his backpack between his legs. I ruffle his golden locks and smile at him.

"Ma, stop." He swats at my hand, causing me to giggle. "Mmm, what's that smell?" He takes in a long sniff and turns to the back seat.

"It's shake and bake, and I helped." I sing like he knows the commercial. He raises his brow, and I roll my eyes. "It's KFC. You know, finger lickin' good."

"All you had to say was chicken," he remarks, obviously too cool for my antics.

"That's boring," I mumble, pulling into our driveway. My phone rings, and dread sinks in as I see Lynsie's name on the screen. "Can you take the food in?" I see the reluctance in his eyes as he hesitates to reply. "I have to take this call. It won't take long." I put my hand on his, reassuring him.

"Fine," he grumbles, reaching in the back seat for the bags.

"Hey, Lynsie." I answer as soon as his door slams, evidence of his annoyance.

"Hey, girl. How's it going?" Her easygoing tone calms my shot nerves. "I haven't heard from you in a while. How's Brian?" She's asking about me and Brian. She's not calling to deliver another blow that I'm unsure I'd be able to withstand.

"It's fine," I lie. After getting out of my car, I walk to the porch and take a seat on the bottom step.

"Uh, girl, who do you think you're talking to?" Lynsie calls me out, almost bringing me to tears. I wish she were here sitting in front of me so I could just let everything out instead of feeling like I have to hold it all together for everyone.

"It's been rough," I admit, keeping my voice low.

"Rough, how?" Lynsie asks, her voice now full of concern.

I sigh, unsure how to fully explain it. "Like I never know what to say…what's going to set him off."

"Is he being violent?"

"God, no. I don't see him ever getting abusive." I look back, making sure the door is still shut.

"Abuse isn't just physical," Lynsie replies. "It starts with words."

"I know." I pause. "It's just like Dr. Jekyll and Mr. Hyde. There's so much going on with him and I just want to help." I swallow, pushing down all the emotion threatening to expose itself. "But I don't know if I can." Admitting it aloud hurts worse than keeping the knowledge hidden.

"Just promise me you'll get out before it gets bad. You can show up here in the middle of the night for all I care."

I nod as if she can see me. "I promise," I whisper, meaning it. I hear the door open and don't have to look back to see who's there. I stand and regain my normal spunky voice to end the call. "Well, hey, girl, I need to get off here. Thanks for calling. It was good to hear your voice."

"You are welcome here all hours of the day or night." She emphasizes and finishes with, "I love you."

"You too, Lynsie." I hang up and turn around to see Brian in the doorway, eyeing me with intense curiosity.

"Hey, babe," I say, pausing to kiss his cheek. He turns to the side, allowing me entrance, and I make my way toward the kitchen. The door shuts, and I hear him follow behind me as his cane taps the ground with each step. While his arm is finally healed and out of the cast, the nerve damage to his leg hasn't let up yet and it's possible it never will.

"What was that about?" he questions.

"What was what about?" I ask nonchalantly as I begin getting dinner out of the bags.

"Don't play dumb with me." He smacks the counter with a tight fist. "What did your friend want?" he bites each word out. I finish placing everything out, taking my time to reply. Me doing so seems to noticeably irritate him, but when I reply off the cuff, matching his temperament, it never helps the situation. So I'm damned if I do and damned if I don't.

"Well, honey." I pivot away from him to open the cabinet door. I go to pull the plates out and his hand tightly wraps around my wrist in a vise grip. The hairs on the back of my neck stand. It's as if I no longer have control of my own hand. The glass falls from my hold, hitting the edge of the counter before falling to the floor, breaking at my feet. My head swings to Brian, who seems to be unbothered by the destruction. Why would he be? It's all he's known.

"Mom?" Dylan hollers from down the hall.

I hold Brian's stare as I reply. The last thing I need is my son being brought into this.

"It's okay. I just dropped something," I calmly reply even though every fiber within me is on high alert. The holding of my wrist continues like he's holding it hostage for information. "Let go of me now." I seethe. "Or nerve damage won't be your only disability." I glance over at the block of knives. He winces and releases my wrist. I know it's not the threat that struck a chord. It's me calling him disabled. A word no soldier ever wants to hear. He drops his head and retreats toward the living room, which has basically become his room since he's been back. I press my hands against the edge of the counter and close my eyes, taking deep breaths to steady my erratic heart. I wipe the few tears away that manage to seep through my exterior and bend down to pick up the broken pieces. It's not like Brian is going to help. He hasn't done anything besides be a hermit since he's gotten back. Oh, and a dick.

Once the mess is cleaned up, I fix a plate for Dylan and carry it back to his room. He lifts a brow, eyeing me suspiciously as I hand it to him. "I know. I'm breaking my own rule." I smile and lean against his doorway, crossing my arms. "I think there can be an exception to the rules sometimes."

"I like this exception," he admits, sitting down on his bed as he takes a big bite of his fried chicken leg. I watch my son, all carefree and full of life as he plays his Xbox. Oh, to be a kid again. "Ma," he says, shaking me out of my trance.

"Yeah, hon?"

"Is everything okay?" His eyes fill with worry, worry he should never have to feel. I've never been one to sugarcoat the truth with him, and I'm not going to start now.

I walk over and sit on the edge of his bed, resting my hand on his knee as he sits criss-cross applesauce. "Honestly." I sigh. "I don't know." I look at Dylan and give him a weak smile. His head drops and I place my finger under his chin, lifting his gaze back to me. "There're a lot of unknowns." I shrug. "But I promise you, everything will be okay. I'm just trying to figure out how to get to that point," I stammer as tears well up in the corners of my eyes.

Dylan pushes up on his knees and tosses his arm around my neck. "I love you, Ma. And have your back no matter what."

I wrap my arms around his torso, pulling him tightly against me. Hugs like this with a teenager are few and far between, and I'm not going to squander this moment.

"I love you more than you will ever know. Everything I do is for you," I whisper.

I make my way back to the kitchen and make a plate for Brian, put the leftovers in the refrigerator, and then I carry his food to the living room. He's asleep, naturally. I sit the plate on the end table so he will see my attempt.

And then I head to my room to do something I haven't done in more than a decade.

Pray.

Chapter Thirty-Five

DUSTIN

I roll out of bed before the sun rises and immediately make it before throwing my running attire on. You can take the man out of the Army, but you can't take the Army out of the man. While my life these last years has been chaotic, it's been organized chaos. This flying by the seat of my britches is going to be an adjustment, as is. I need some sort of routine to keep from losing my ever-loving mind. My feet lightly pad down the stairs, and I slowly open the front door, making sure it doesn't slam behind me. It used to have a habit of doing so when I'd try sneaking out in high school.

The morning air is cool unlike the dry heat I've been accustomed to overseas. At least I don't have to worry about sand being blown in my face every turn I make on my morning run. The quietness is also something I'm unfamiliar with. While I enjoy it feeling like a ghost town this early in the morning, all it does is amplify the noise in my head. Everywhere I look holds memories of Echo, and before I know it, I'm stopping at the fence to the softball field.

I grip the chain-link fence and stare out into the outfield. It's as clear as day. As if it's playing out in front of my very eyes. We lie on the blanket, staring up at the starry sky. A picture-perfect night with the most perfect girl. The night she gave herself to me, and I her. The night we solidified our future plans.

The last night I ever saw her.

My grip tightens against the metal, and I quickly release it as I back away, refusing to let all those feelings make a return. But isn't that what happens to undealt with feelings? They always find a way to resurface. I circle around the front of the school just as the sun begins to peek in the horizon and hightail it back to the house.

"I thought I'd find you out here."

I jerk my head toward the house and see my dad standing at the top of the porch stairs.

"Old habits." I shrug.

"Die hard." He finishes. Not where I was going, but it's fitting. "You might want these." He flings his hand in my direction, throwing something, and before I have time to process it, my right hand flies up, catching the keys. I glance down at my old set of keys, and a sense of freedom fills the void.

"You would've felt like shit if I hadn't caught these." I laugh.

"I have more faith in you than that, son." He shakes his head and rubs the back of his neck. "You've always been too quick for your own good."

"Not quick enough." I remind him, lifting my left arm.

He winces and then stammers on his words, trying to change the subject as he walks down the stairs. "Not knowing when you'd be back for it, I've made it my personal mission to keep your Blazer maintained." He pulls the black tarp back, exposing my greatest earthly possession.

"Whoa, Black Betty." I sing to my blacked out beast of a vehicle.

"Start her up." My dad nudges with a smile and I quickly comply, flinging the driver's door open. I slowly slide the silver key in and turn.

The rumble surrounds me and a smile fully encases my face. "Take her for a spin."

I reach to shut my door, temporarily forgetting I don't have a hand to grab it with. I go to rest my hand on the steering wheel, being so used to driving with my left hand, but fall short with the missing length. My excitement is dwindling away.

"You only need one good hand to drive with, son," my dad says, hopping into the passenger seat. His words and calm demeanor ease my frustration. He's always been so even tempered, completely the opposite of Mom. Maybe that's why their marriage works.

I drop the gearshift into drive and peel out, slinging loose gravel around. Instead of apologizing, I laugh and my dad does, too. We drive the entirety of the town, hitting some back roads before I end up in front of the house I've been avoiding but drove to without a thought. I slam on my brakes and slide much like I did that night when I confronted her father. I throw the Blazer into park, get out, and jog straight to the backyard. I remember Echo said in her letter she had been here working on it. But I have to see if it's still there.

I pull the latch to the wooden gate up, lifting it slightly off the ground some before bumping it with my hip. I round the corner and take in the overgrown jungle that has taken over. It reminds me of an abandoned amusement park. A place that looks like the people just vanished—which is what they did. I walk up to her old window and let my hand drag across the windowsill. It's badly peeling as the paint chips off as I slide my fingers across, feeling for it as if it's Braille.

Unexpected emotions well up within me.

"This is why you left," my father states, walking up behind me.

"It destroyed me," I admit for the first time in my life.

"I wish you had come to us about the situation. We heard the rumors swirling through town but didn't realize how bad it truly was. You shouldn't have dealt with it alone."

I snort. "Maybe you. Maybe I should've come to you. But not Mom. Mom was part of the problem. She didn't want us together either. She didn't want anything to get in the way of my future in baseball."

"So she's the reason you enlisted?"

I'm not sure which *she* he's referring to, but I nod.

Chapter Thirty-Six

ECHO

I glance in the mirror and wonder when I became a shell of the woman I once was. How much do we give of ourselves to save the ones we love? Do we self-sacrifice our entire being in hopes it will make a difference? How much do we give without a guarantee of a return investment?

We're told sticking through the hard times makes us stronger, but what if it cripples us from within. Feeling obligated to hold someone else's head above water when they're drowning you is a messed-up situation to be in. Yet here I am.

I don't know what my future holds. I've been too busy trying to dodge insults and mood swings to bother thinking ahead. For the sake of my son, I've been in survival mode. For the sake of Brian and his mom, I've been in don't kill your husband mode.

I don't excuse his behavior, but he took on some demons while overseas and I'm not sure I'm powerful enough to exorcise them on my own.

But when he's not being a jerk I want to kick in the nuts, I see the boy I grew up with. The one who took me under his wing and has taken care of my son and me this entire time. Yes, our hard times look completely different, but how could I abandon him when he needs me the most?

I have a feeling he's about to find out. I remind myself why I'm in this situation in the first place. Every decision I've made in life has always been for Dylan. It will be the same reason I exit the situation if things don't change.

"I'm heading to the airport to pick up your mom. Do you need anything while I'm out?"

"I don't know why you invited her to come visit," he mumbles.

"Okay, so no. You don't need anything."

"You already mother goose me around. I don't need two of y'all doing it," he slurs.

"Well, one of us needs to make sure you still know how to wipe your ass." I stop in front of his trusty recliner and take notice of the beer cans sitting on the table beside him. "Are you drunk?" I walk over and start grabbing cans. This isn't the scene I want his mother to walk straight into.

"Beer. You can get more beer."

"Yeah, I think that's the last thing you need. You just drank an entire brewery," I say, walking to the trash can. "Good God. It's not even noon, Brian." I quickly return to grab the last two cans.

"It's five o'clock somewhere." He laughs, then grabs my wrist, startling me. "Not that one." He pulls the half-finished can from my hand. "Don't be a wasteful bitch." He smiles as I stare down at him.

I'm at a loss for words, which never happens.

"Now now. Go fetch my mother," he says, smacking my ass when I turn around.

I hope he realizes his days are numbered. One day, he's going to push me past the point of no return. I only invited his mom in hopes she can reach him because I'm at my wits' end. He won't go to therapy, he won't talk to anyone, and he stays medicated and drunk eighty percent of the time. And in asshole mode a good ninety-five.

PAULA AND I haven't had the closest relationship throughout the years. It's hard with so much distance involved. But lately, she's been on the receiving end of many late-night phone calls with me crying. She's always so calm and collected while I'm on the other end of the line feeling unhinged. At this point, she probably thinks I'm the one who should be taking medication. That's what I would think when our conversations go from me saying, *"'I'm going to strangle him in his sleep,' 'I can't deal with this anymore,' 'Can't I just trip him and blame it on his injury,' 'I'm not strong enough for this,' 'I love him, but I can't fix him,' 'I want to be there for him.' 'I want to see this through,' 'I won't leave him,' 'I bought a shovel today.'"*

I would obviously never cause harm to him, but some days he is so hard to deal with.

I hug her as soon as I see her and the tears fall instantaneously.

When did I turn into such a sap?

"Thank you for coming. I didn't know what else to do." I hold her tighter, praying she's the solution.

"You shouldn't be dealing with this alone," she says, calming my spirit as she rubs my back.

As we pull into the driveway, I give her a warning. "He was drunker than a skunk when I left. So I don't know what condition he will be in."

She nods and I wonder if she's ever dealt with a drunk person in her life.

I go to open the door, and it swings open.

"Mom," Brian exclaims, standing in the entryway freshly showered and shaved. Things I wasn't sure he still knew how to do. He throws his arms around her. "I've missed you." He looks up at me and smiles, but it doesn't reach his eyes.

Jekyll, is that you?

No, Hyde. It's always Hyde.

Chapter Thirty-Seven

DUSTIN

Taking my morning walk, I stop dead in my tracks. She's here.

"Echo," I whisper in disbelief.

She slowly lifts her head, and her eyes go wide with realization.

"Dustin." She all but runs to the end of the walkway, stopping herself from embracing me—like something's holding her back from doing so. I can think of one thing in particular. With mere inches between us, she looks up, entrancing me with her brown eyes. "You're here."

"I'm here," I repeat, unsure of how to react with her so close.

"You're alive." She steps back and begins assessing the damage.

"Yes, I'm alive." I might be alive on the outside, but I'm just a shell. Her hand brushes across my face. I shiver at her touch. She begins tracing the new scars, working her hand down my neck. The first tear falls as her hand begins to tremble down my arm, reaching where it now ends. Instinct sets in and I begin to pull away.

"No," she says, throwing her arms around me. I do the same, cradling her head to my chest. "You're alive. That's all that matters."

I want to argue, to disagree that it's not all that matters, but I also want to keep her in my arms for as long as possible. I don't know what's going on, but she's here for a reason and I plan to be whatever she needs. Because standing here, holding her, is the most alive I've felt in years. But all too soon, it ends as she begins pulling away. No matter the duration, it'd always be too soon.

"Did you just come to hang out on the porch?" I tease.

She laughs and it's the most glorious sound in the world.

"No, I'm waiting for my mom to remind me what the code to the lockbox is so I can get in."

"Oh, well, you don't need that. I can get you in." I jog off to the side and make quick work of the pesky gate door. I slide her bedroom window open and crawl in. It's always been my way into this house.

"Tada," I say, opening the door. "It's magic."

She laughs, walking past me. "Thanks, Houdini."

I want to reply that she's the one who disappeared, but I sense now isn't the time to joke about our past.

"I'm just going to go back here for a bit." She points toward the hall. "I'll be back out soon."

I count to ten and push off the wall as soon as I hear the door shut. More than anything, I want to rush to her side and hold her while she sorts through her emotions. But the bare minimum, I'm going to sit on the porch and be here when she comes back out. I lean my head back and daydream about when times were simpler. Times when I only had to navigate her controlling father, not a husband. Maybe I should have just saved myself instead of making it my mission to keep him alive. I'd still have my career, my hand, and probably could've won back the girl. Now the odds are more heavily stacked against me.

As long as she's happy. That's all that matters. But is she?

Lynsie pulls up, slams her car door, and jogs my way.

"Where is she?"

"Hi to you, too," I say, pointing at the house.

"Please tell me you didn't leave her in there alone." She runs up the steps.

"The house isn't haunted, Lyns."

"It might as well be with everything going on."

I jump to my feet and put my hand on the screen door, keeping it closed. "What's going on?"

"It's not my business to tell."

"Lynsie, please. I need to know she's okay," I beg.

"Fine. For the record, I hate being the middleman." She walks the length of the porch a couple times before stopping right in front of me. "It's Brian."

"What about him?"

She huffs. "He seems to be having some anger issues."

Heat rises within me, and I see red. I grab the door handle and pull. It doesn't open. I glance down and see Lynsie's foot propped up against it.

"What are you going to do, huh? Go in there and cause a scene being all mad. The last thing she needs is another angry man."

My body relaxes, submitting to her words. Going in and hulking out was never my intention, but that's exactly what it'd look like.

"Sit back down, Romeo. I got this." Lynsie pats my shoulder before walking inside, and I sit back down for what feels like an eternity.

THE SCREEN DOOR creaks open, and I jump to my feet, turning to face Lynsie. I glance inside, hoping Echo isn't following behind. I'm not ready for her to leave. I'm not sure I'll ever be.

"Is she okay?"

She stares out toward the street, contemplating her response.

"Yeah, yeah. Of course," Lynsie says, shaking her head before making complete eye contact with me. She smiles, trying to reassure me, but her eyes are filled with worry.

I cock a brow, calling her out on her bullshit.

"I just wish there were more I could do." Lynsie begins pacing back and forth. "I wish I were closer so I could be there for her and help like she was for me when Lincoln died." She sobs, and I pull her in for a hug.

"Is there anything I can do for her?" I ask, wishing I were the remedy.

"No." She sniffles, pulling away. "Just be whatever she needs without expectations. Like your brother was for me."

I watch as Lynsie leaves before making my way in to the end of the hall. I knock on the closed door before slowly pushing it open. She's lying back against her old broken bed, looking up at the ceiling, and my heart cracks a bit.

"Are you up for some company?"

"Only if you're the company," she replies, keeping her gaze above.

I walk over and sit down next to her. I stretch my legs out before me, crossing them at the ankles as I lean back with her.

"I took it," I say, twiddling my thumbs.

"I knew it." She smiles and relief washes over me. "You were the only logical explanation." Echo turns her head sideways, facing me, and so many feelings hit me all at once.

"But why? Why'd you take it?"

"It made me feel close to you. I put it up everywhere I went. Instead of feeling like I was worlds away, it made me feel like I was lying right here next to you." I wipe away at the runaway tear, not wanting to put my emotions on display. Echo reaches over and catches the rest that spill over, wiping them away with the pad of her thumb. She then grabs my hand and weaves our fingers together. We sit in silence, holding hands, and I couldn't think of a better way to spend my day.

"Did you know that Brian was injured?"

"Yes." I pause. "I was there when it happened."

"Oh."

"But I didn't know the extent of everyone's injuries. I was the last one to leave the hospital and was sent straight home."

Her hand tightens around mine.

"Do you suffer from PTSD?"

Normally, these questions would make me feel as if I'm being interrogated and I wouldn't answer them, but with Echo, I'd talk about the weight of animal poop if it meant I was privileged enough to have a conversation with her.

"No, I don't. Mine's all natural."

She snorts. I begin rubbing my thumb in circles against the delicate skin of her hand.

"Something happened to Brian over there. It's damn near like he's been possessed."

Dropping her hand, I turn and face her. "Did he hurt you?"

She looks down and shakes her head.

"You're going to have to do better than that." I lightly grab her face, directing her to look at me.

"He didn't hurt me. He's just mean." She sniffles. Her eyes meet my stare as tears begin to spill down her face.

I open my arms and, without hesitation, she's in them again. I hold her tight against my chest as she cries. I begin talking once her body starts to still against me.

"The mind can be a scary place. While I'm not excusing his behavior and really want to hurt his feelings or face for the way he's made you feel, I believe Brian left a physical war to now be trapped in a mental one."

"And how does one win that war?"

"They first have to realize they're in it," I say, brushing the hair off the side of her face.

She sits up and wipes her face of all evidence and then stands.

"Okay. I came here to get away and get my mind off things." She holds a hand out to me, pulling me up. "Help me get my mind off things."

THIS WASN'T WHAT I was expecting when I agreed to help get her mind off things. I believe I was tricked by a pretty girl. I roll the paint roller through the pool of white as Echo does the same from the other side of the kitchen.

"I thought you finished this back in August."

"No, I only managed to get the front part of the house done. So just the back part minus my old room, and the porch are all that's left." She stretches her body skyward, trying to reach as much of the wall as she can.

"You okay over there?" Lynsie walks in, eyeing me with one brow raised, completely amused by catching me watch Echo.

"Did someone call for beer and pizza?" Dax announces, carrying two boxes of pizza in one hand and a twelve pack in another. Lynsie's empty-handed as she should be.

Echo turns around, giving Lynsie a big smile. "So glad y'all could come over."

"What? You had to call for backup? I wasn't good enough company for you?" I tease her.

"Oh hush." Echo waves me and my bruised ego off. "I merely called in reinforcements."

"It's good to see you, Dax." She walks up to my brother and playfully smacks his cheek. "I see that peach fuzz is finally thickening up," she jokes as she rubs his facial hair.

I run my fingers along my wooly beard, jealous. I have facial hair. Why isn't she touching mine? Lynsie glances over, catching me in the act, and she snickers. I drop my hand before Echo catches me, too.

I really like the idea of my brother and his wife being here because it'll keep any other awkward moments from happening. But I don't like the idea of this project being cut in half. The four of us will knock this out in no time. Then what will I do to justify staying near her?

"So, Dax. Do you plan on starting your own woodcarving business?" Echo asks, striking up conversation as we all sit around the pizza, eating.

"Actually." Dax takes a gulp of beer, rinsing down his food. "I do plan on it. But it'll happen slowly. Once this instructor job starts at the end of the month, I'm not sure how much time I'll have for it. Plus, we're going to convert the garage into a studio for Lynsie before I figure out how to go about mine."

"What's this woodcarving business you guys speak of?" I ask with a frown. Then it hits me. My mind was such a haze that night, but I remember Dax mentioning a memorial he had made. "Wait, like the wing that was on display at your award ceremony?"

Dax nods. "Yep." He takes a big bite of pizza, talking as he chews. Some things never change. "It's something I kind of took an interest in after you left." He says it so nonchalantly like it's no big deal and I wonder if he's trained himself to feel that way.

Shit, maybe that's because he doesn't know what all happened. Echo has to have told Lynsie. That's what girls do, right? And Lynsie has to have told Dax. That's what wives do, right? Maybe I just need to quit assuming shit. Especially since Lynsie isn't Dax's wife yet.

Good ole oblivious Dax breaks the silence he doesn't even realize took place. "But I don't want my business just to be carvings. I'd really like to get into distressing furniture and even making signs and such."

I want to tease him and ask where his balls went. Maybe call him Martha Stewart. But the fact is, he has his shit together. He has his woman, his daughter, and he has plans. He knows what he wants in life and he's going after it. Why should I tease or belittle him when he has everything going for him and I have nothing? He's my brother, and even though I'm jealous as hell, I'm happy for him.

"Sounds like a great idea, man. I really hope it works out for you."

Dax looks up, and all the goofiness his face usually holds is gone. It's almost as if he's been waiting for my recognition all these years. That knowledge twists knots in my gut. It's something I should've given him long ago, but instead, I ran and stayed away—keeping the one person I should have held on to at arm's length.

"Thanks, bro. That really means a lot."

I just nod. No need to get any mushier than we already have.

"All right." I stand. "We got some work to do. Ladies, resume your posts on the inside. Us men got this out here." I smirk, and Echo doesn't even bat an eye. She instantly fires back, showing me that spitfire of mine still exists.

"Yeah, I'm sure since you *boys*," she drags out, "have a third to do compared to us."

"Don't y'all worry your sweet little asses," Dax chimes in, smacking Lynsie on hers, causing her to yelp. I wish I had the right to do the same to Echo. My hand practically itches wondering what her 'sweet little ass' would feel like in my palm. He finishes with, "It's not like we won't be in there to pick up the slack once we finish."

"Yeah, yeah. I give y'all two hours, and then we'll see who's slacking," Echo challenges and all I can do is eye her and her delicious curves.

I'm in trouble if I can't keep my thoughts on the straight and narrow. And I don't know how I'll do that being in her vicinity.

Chapter Thirty-Eight

ECHO

"I just don't know what to think. So I'm trying not to. After Dax's ceremony, I thought Dustin despised me."

"Yeah, I don't think that's the case at all," Lynsie says, and it brings my eyes back to hers that are filled with such understanding. "I think that night was mixed with a lot of shock and anger. He was caught off guard, just like you were. I think he's trained himself to use anger as his go-to emotion."

"Yeah, but thinking he wanted nothing to do with me didn't stop me from writing him while he was at war."

"What? You didn't tell me you wrote him," Lynsie shrieks.

"Well, it felt borderline wrong, so I thought it was safer to keep to myself. It was only two letters. Because then the accident happened."

"But all this anger everyone seems to reference to, even himself, I've yet to see."

"It's because you, and only you, can calm the storm that brews within him."

I think about her words for a second, letting them sink in. "But why do I feel like I can cause the storm as well?" I cross my arms.

"Because you can."

I swallow. "I don't want to be responsible for that."

Lynsie and I finish what Dustin and I had started in the kitchen before moving to the master bedroom.

"So you're going to open your own salon? That's exciting." I wipe the beads of sweat off my forehead before dipping my brush into the paint.

"Yes, I'm crazy excited. The only thing that would make it better is if you stayed here to work it with me," Lynsie offers, and it's highly tempting.

"I'll definitely keep that in mind."

"Please do." She giggles.

"Has there been any wedding talk yet?"

"No," she answers, disappointment evident.

"Well, we all know it's going to happen," I say reassuringly.

"I know. I'm just ready to fully be his. I don't need to get all gussied up. I'd be more than okay with just walking to the courthouse and having it done."

"Impatient much?" I tease.

"Very." She snorts. "And don't get me wrong, I'm very blessed with what I have. I know I sound like a spoiled brat."

"No, you don't. I get it. You have the man, and even though what you guys have is concrete, you want to make it official. There's nothing wrong with that."

"Thank you for that. I'm glad someone gets me. Not like I have anyone else to talk to about it, but still. I really wish you lived here." There's a longing in her voice.

"Who knows what the future holds." I shrug, accepting the uncertainty of it all.

"Man, my arms feel like jello," Lynsie says, flapping her arms up and down.

"Yeah," I say tiredly. "Painting is for the birds."

Lynsie and I walk out onto the porch to see the guys hammered and laughing.

"Glad to see you guys bonding," Lynsie deadpans, walking up to Dax, and wraps her arm around his side.

"It's the Bud that binds us," Dax says, doubling over with laughter.

"I got nothing," Dustin throws out, laughing.

Lynsie and I look at each other, shaking our heads and giggling at these two.

"I think it's time to get you home," she says, patting Dax on the back.

"Aw," he whines.

I cover my mouth to stifle a giggle.

"Yeah, what he said," Dustin chimes in. "Don't be a fun hater, Lyns."

"I'm just being a regret avoider," she corrects him, smirking. "He needs to get to sleep. He'll be thanking me tomorrow when he isn't spending all day feeling like shit."

"Hmm, good point," Dustin replies thoughtfully before tilting his head back and finishing off his beer. "I never sleep."

"Bye, guys," Lynsie says, pulling Dax behind her.

"Bye, guys," Dax says, mocking her.

"Bye, thanks for your help... Lynsie."

"Hey! I helped!" Dax yells back.

I just shake my head as I sit down near Dustin. "Did y'all accomplish anything?" I smack his thigh with the back of my hand.

"Well, that depends on who you're asking and what it's pertaining to."

I glance over at him to see him looking my way with one brow cocked. I hold his tired gaze for longer than I should. He wasn't lying when he said he doesn't sleep. It makes me sad, and I wonder what he sees when he does close his eyes.

I glance down, looking at his arm that's resting on his khaki shorts.

I've wanted to ask him about his injury since first seeing him, but it seems wrong to do so. But I no longer care, and he's drunk.

"Does it ever hurt?"

He doesn't ask me what. He knows exactly what I'm referring to as he takes his right hand and rubs over the white cloth that's covering part of his forearm. "Sometimes. Every now and then I'll get these phantom pains."

"Do you take meds for it?" I hate the idea of him being in pain, but I also don't want him turning into a loose cannon like Brian.

"I did in the beginning. Now I'll only take over-the-counter stuff."

"Does it help?"

"For the most part. If not, I find something to busy myself with and get the focus off it."

"Is that why you started this project?" I gesture to the fully finished porch swing that's waiting to be rehung.

He looks out onto the street, deep in thought. "No, it's pain related, but a different kind."

"Why endure the pain if you have something that can subside it?"

Again, he's silent, still for several long seconds. Like he's trying to work out how much he wants to tell me. "Because I'm still trying to figure out if it's my antidote or my kryptonite."

Chills sweep through me, bad and good ones simultaneously. He's referring to me, I know it. I can either heal him or destroy him. I hold the power. But I don't want to be the one responsible for his potential downfall. He sighs and gives me the answer I was after. "Because I don't want to become dependent on it."

I force a smile, trying not to let him see the storm inside me, the sadness I feel for our lost future, the sadness from all the pain I've caused him over the years, and the euphoria to think that he still might love me. I have to clear my throat to get the words out. "Oh yes, I forgot how independent you are." I stick my tongue out, trying to lighten the mood. But the way he's staring at me makes me think I did anything but. He quickly glances from my eyes to my tongue, then back to my eyes. He gulps hard, then turns his head away from me. I do the same as I rest it back on the house. Today has been one hell of a day —emotionally and physically.

Chapter Thirty-Nine

DUSTIN

I knew she was asleep before her head landed on my shoulder. First, she went quiet on me, but I thought she was just enjoying the calm between us like I was. I wasn't drunk like everyone thought. I was just really enjoying the time with my brother. It's something we've never been able to experience. I kept myself away and shut off from everyone and lost out on so much. I intend to restore what I can.

Even with this woman next to me. I want to fight for her, but it feels so wrong when she's married. I despise the idea of stealing another man's woman. And I hate the idea of putting her in that predicament even more. I know how big her heart is. I know how much she always wants to do what's right. Do I give her an ultimatum that's eventually going to hurt someone? One where she knows, no matter the outcome, she'll be inflicting some sort of pain?

She already has too much she's dealing with. *Brian.* Was everything I did to protect him for nothing? Am I now the reason she's suffering?

It just doesn't seem fair. But do I just lie low and not show her she's worth fighting for? Do I just pretend the last thirteen years have meant nothing...that the months we were together and what we shared meant nothing? All I know is I can't walk back into her life and just be like, *"BAM! Time to make a choice."*

I contemplate these thoughts as I sit, enjoying the closeness of her leaning against me—not to mention the light snores that escape every now and again. I can only imagine how truly exhausted she must be. I want to stay like this all night, soak it up for as long as I possibly can. What I really want is to be able to experience this nearness while she's awake. But when it's like this, it's innocent. It's subconscious.

For now, I'll take what I can get. And what I'm getting from something as simple as this is that after all this time, she's still drawn to me. That in itself is a victory.

As much as I'm loving this, I need to put her in bed. She needs all the rest she can get. Emotional exhaustion is worse than physical, and she's dealing with both. I don't want the closeness to end. I want to be selfish, but when it comes to her, it's impossible.

I slowly pull myself away from her, steadying her head with my hand. I get on my feet but stay crouched. I slide my left arm behind her back, pulling her into me so that her head rests against my chest. She makes a few noises but doesn't wake. I push my right arm under her legs, wrapping it around to pull her snuggly against me. Once I know I fully have her, I push up.

Using the tip of my shoe, I fling the screen door open. I don't fully walk in because I don't want it slamming behind us. I hold my foot out, letting the door catch on it, slowly allowing it to close behind me. The house is brightly lit. Pretty sure the girls have every damn light on. I make my way to the couch and carefully lay her down. I'd put her in bed, but it's broken and I don't want her rolling out of it. The other two rooms have beds, but with them just being painted, I feel the couch is the safer choice.

I unzip her sandals before pulling the quilt over that's hanging off the back of the couch. She looks so peaceful. I pray for the day I can slip in behind her and hold her all night. I know I'd actually be able to sleep with her in my arms. The effect she has on me is unexplainable. But something about her evens me out, grounds me, and excites me all at once.

I brush the hair off her face, pushing it behind her ear. I lean in and press my lips against her forehead. I'm treading on dangerous territory. But hey, it's something I'm good at.

"I wish you were mine," I whisper as I reluctantly pull away from her.

"Me too," she mumbles as she turns to her side.

I turn all the lights out except the hall and lock up behind me. I gather the trash from dinner and toss it into the bin on the side of the house. I need to get back to my parents' house so I can shower and get some shut-eye, but my mind is on high alert, and I know I won't be able to sleep. Instead, I begin to finish what Dax and I barely started tonight. That guy can be such a distraction. One I welcome these days.

THE PORCH LIGHT is on when I get to the house. I really hope no one is awake. I slowly turn the knob, thankful it's unlocked. I would have slept on the porch before I rang the doorbell. The lamp in the entryway is on, and I shut and lock the door behind me. It's quiet, almost too quiet. I turn to head up the stairs.

"Dustin," I hear, and I silently curse. So close.

"Yeah." I step back and turn toward the door that leads to my dad's office.

"You doin' all right?" my father asks hesitantly, worried, and guilt slaps me in the back of the head, calling me a fool.

"Yes. Just dealing with a lot of stuff."

"Understandable," he says, standing up and making his way to me. "We know this isn't easy for you." I go to speak, but he stops me. "All of it. Not just the wound. We know your world has been flipped upside down. I can't imagine how you're feeling about everything. But all I do know is that we love you. We will always be here for you, no matter what you face. Please, don't shut us out, son," he pleads, placing his hand on my shoulder.

"Okay." I nod. "I won't," I promise.

He grips my shoulder as he pulls me into him. I stand with my arms at my sides, trying to wrap my mind around what's happening. It's been so long since I've received a hug from my dad. My arms begin to move up, embracing him much like he is me. He tightens his grip, and I can't help but do the same as I feel his body tremble against mine.

What have I done to the ones who love me the most?

I pat his back and then peel myself away. I don't want to allow myself to get emotional. I want to shower and hit the sack, and I tell him that's what I'm going to do as I turn away to head up the stairs. After grabbing a towel out of the hall closet, I close myself in the bathroom. I pull back the curtain and turn the shower on, undressing as the steam begins to fill the room.

I pull off the dressing over my arm and inspect the area. I haven't really done so since the incident. I've known it was gone. What was the point of really looking at the damage? That had been my mindset. But for some reason, I feel the need to change that. I was expecting what I see to sicken me, but it doesn't. The scars from the stitching are barely visible and I question why I've been keeping it covered if it's fully healed. Has it been because I didn't want others to see it, or because I wanted to keep it hidden from myself?

I step into the shower and my body stiffens at the heat prickling it. Pushing myself fully under the stream of water, I welcome the warmth. It's relaxing as it cascades down my body. I reach over and grab the body soap my mother must've bought. I use my thumbnail to push the lid up and squirt some onto my chest since I don't have my other hand now. You never realize how much you needed both hands until you're left with one.

I can't help but think of Echo and how I spent basically the entire day with her. My mind begins to wander to the short shorts she was wearing and the fitted tank that showcased just how well she's filled out over the years. I shake my head of the thoughts, knowing I'd much rather wait for the real thing.

Chapter Forty

ECHO

The sun peering in through the cracks of the blinds wakes me up. I flop around like a fish out of water, not knowing where I'm at. I sit up, realizing I'm on the couch. I need to find my phone and check the time. I couldn't have slept in that late, could I? I mean, I was completely worn out last night. I don't even remember going to sleep. I sit up and scratch my head. The last thing I do remember is sitting next to Dustin on the porch.

And that was all she wrote.

I look down, seeing that I'm still in the shorts and tank I had on yesterday. The only thing I'm lacking is my sandals, which I notice are sitting perfectly next to each other at the front door. I know for a fact that I'm not responsible for that neatness. There's only one person who would do something so orderly, and he was that way before the military.

Light floods through the windows, reminding me why I loved this house so much. There's just something about natural light flooding in that literally brightens my mood. I'm convinced that people who purposely keep their houses dark are vampires. It's a fact. I know it. I glance down, spotting my phone on the coffee table. "I spy with my little eye," I say as I grab it.

Okay, it's only nine thirty. That's not too bad. It's probably the latest I've slept since having a child, but at least I didn't sleep the day away. I still have plenty I need to take care of. But first, I need coffee. That's essential. *I wonder if vampires drink coffee.*

I walk back to the room and grab my flip-flops. No sense in changing my clothes since I'm just going to be painting again today. I pull off the hair tie I have around my wrist and toss my hair up on the top of my head. Yanking open the front door, I freeze in my tracks.

The porch.

The porch is finished.

Dustin must have stayed up all night to accomplish this. And it looks amazing. The wood pillars look brand new, and the dark stained wood looks like it doesn't belong to this house. It all looks too pretty to be on the outside where it will be weathered and instead, belongs inside where it can be taken care of. It's so pretty that I don't even want to walk on it.

I kneel and press my finger against the wood, making sure it's dry. I lift my finger away from the wood to see no fingerprint impression. I place my hand down and lift it, checking other places around me before stepping on it. Dry. He must have finished sanding the pillars, cleaned off the porch, stained it, and then painted the pillars last. They still have a shiny, damp, sticky look to them.

I jog down the steps and head for my car, feeling giddy and hopeful as I head to the diner.

I MUST HAVE missed the morning rush. It's not as packed as I expected. There're only a few booths filled with customers. The waitress is busy helping bus the dirty tables, so I make my way over to the empty bar counter. I take a seat on a round red stool that spins.

"Sorry for the wait, hon. What can I get for ya?"

I glance up from the menu and smile. It's the same waitress from thirteen years ago. She's not the same, though. The gap in time is apparent with the silver trendles that spill from the sides of her ponytail. She doesn't return my smile as she waits for me to answer. I hate how she looks, worn out and over life. It makes me wonder what's taken place this past decade to cause such a drastic change.

"I'll just have a coffee for now."

She nods. "One coffee coming up."

I watch as she grabs the cup and pot of coffee, pouring it to the brim. She reaches over and grabs the saucer containing the different creamers on the way back, then sits both in front of me.

I look at her name tag. "Thanks, Bonnie," I say, holding her gaze and giving her a sincere smile.

"Anytime. Know what you're havin' yet, doll?"

"Think I'll have some pancakes." I close the menu and sit it back in the holder.

She walks away and gives my order over to the cook. I sit with my thoughts, trying to sift through them, but there're far too many. Talking behind me breaks through my internal noise.

I slowly turn my head around, making it appear as if I'm checking the door, waiting for someone. The booth is at an angle where I can't see the woman, but I can see the man, and he saw me. I smile because that's the polite thing to do when you and a stranger make eye contact —even when it's not accidental. He gives me a short, curt smile before returning his attention back to the nagging across from him.

"He was gone all night, David. All night," she says with frustration.

Surely that's not who I think it is and she isn't talking about who I think she's talking about...in public.

"He wasn't gone all night," he quietly counters.

"What could he have been doing? It's not like he was sleeping. That's what he's hopefully doing now."

Would it be highly inappropriate for me to place myself into their conversation and politely let her know that her son was at my house most of the night, fixing up the front porch? I have a feeling that wouldn't go over well. More importantly, Dustin would hate me for doing so. If he wants her to know his business, he'll tell her.

"Good, he needs his rest," he replies with tired patience.

"What?" she screeches. "He needs to be on a normal schedule."

"He's not a newborn, Jill." He leans into the table, lowering his voice. "Are you going to keep finding stuff to gripe about, or are you going to drop it and just be thankful that our son has returned...alive?"

I hear her gasp like he just sucker punched her. A sense of pride bubbles up within me, thankful that it seems like their dad does in fact have a backbone.

"Glad to see whose side you're on," she huffs.

"This isn't about sides. The sooner you figure that out, the better off you'll be," he threatens unapologetically.

Dustin's mom balks, throwing her hand over her chest. "And... what exactly is that supposed to mean?"

"You're pushing your son away."

"I am not." I hear the table rattle a bit and the bench squeaking. "I cannot believe you'd even say that." A few random noises follow, and I watch as she leaves, walking like a madwoman.

Yikes!

"WHAT THE HELL?" I start laughing as I look through the texts Lynsie sent me.

> Lynsie: This is as far as I could get him last night.

The text is followed with a picture of Dax half on, half off their porch. It looks as if he walked up to it and then crawled up it like it was his bed.

I call her as I walk out of the diner. I need to tell her about her in-laws.

"Hey, boo!" she answers cheerfully.

"Oh my God. I cannot believe he passed out like that. Did he fall off?" The image of petite Lynsie trying to get him inside the house is comical in itself.

"Yes." She laughs. "Then he came running inside like a bat outta hell, saying some animal was after him. It was probably one of the rabbits we have around our yard."

"It was a bear!" Dax yells in the background, making me and Lynsie giggle.

"Whatever you say, babe," she says, pacifying him.

"I say it was a bear, and he wanted to eat me!"

"Okay, okay. Inside voice, please." Lynsie goes into mommy mode on him.

"Man, that's funny." I needed a bit of a pick-me-up. I should've known I could count on Dax to deliver.

"So did you have to put a certain man to bed last night? Or should I say 'to porch?'"

I can practically hear her eyebrows wagging through the phone.

"I heard that," Dax says, in a hushed tone, taking heed of Lynsie's instruction.

I sigh. "Actually, no. He literally took me to the couch."

"Say what?"

"Yeah, I guess I passed out right after y'all left, and I woke up on the couch."

"And with no Dustin beside you," she says with disappointment.

"No. But he must have pulled an all-nighter finishing the porch. Since Dax was, you know, deadweight last night."

"Classy, Echo. Classy." Dax's voice booms through my phone like he's speaking right into the microphone.

"Love you, Dax," I say.

"Mmmhmm. I can feel it."

I proceed to tell Lynsie what I overheard at the diner, feeling like I now fit in perfectly with the rumor mill. Lynsie tells me how Mrs. Adams can be hard to deal with because, in her mind, she just wants what's best for her boys. She's stuck in her ways and believes what she thinks is the way it should be. But Lynsie reassures me that she can be just as amazing. It's just an adjustment getting to know her. Lynsie, of all people, would know with what took place at Dax's ceremony.

"Dustin just doesn't take her shit," Lynsie admits. "And she can't stand it. He thinks that it'll put her in her place if he doesn't allow her to run over him, but I have a feeling it might do the opposite."

"That doesn't sound good."

"Dax has already mentioned letting Dustin stay in the garage apartment if shit hits the fan at his parents. It'll probably happen sooner rather than later."

Chapter Forty-One

DUSTIN

More than anything, I wanted to lie next to her and watch her sleep all night. I wanted to at minimum lie on the floor next to the couch to protect her. But seeing the ring on her finger sobered my mind, bringing me back to reality before my head was too far in the clouds. So instead of staying close to her, I stayed up finishing the porch and left before I could get my hopes up even further. Yesterday was perfect, which is the problem when the situation at hand is anything but.

I know Lynsie told me to be whatever Echo needs, but there's too much on the line for me to keep tiptoeing around. There are far too many unknowns. I've kept my distance all day, which has proven to be extremely hard when you naturally gravitate toward someone. I drove two hours one way just to be intentional with the space, but as I'm pulling back into town, I drive straight to the person I've been avoiding.

I have to know.

It's time to pull the Band-Aid off.

I knock on the screen door.

Echo walks up, smiling like she's been waiting all day to see me... which I'm sure she has. "Hey you," she says, pushing open the door. "Hey you," she says.

"What happened that night?"

Her smile falls from her face as I catch her off guard.

"Which night?"

I raise a brow, encouraging her not to play dumb with me.

"A lot." She leans back against the entrance to the office and stares at me. Her gaze darts to the ground as apprehension consumes her before finally letting out a heavy sigh. "Apparently, my dad had been on the fence about moving us back to Oklahoma because Brian's father had been diagnosed with cancer and they were in need of a new pastor. Finding us together that night solidified that decision for him."

As if I only take one thing from what she just said, I reply back with the most chick question ever. "So Brian? You knew him before me?" The idea of him having stronger ties to her than me stings a bit.

"Yes, since third grade." She looks over at me and clarifies. "It was never like that...until it was. Our marriage began as a convenience. He was my escape route from my parents."

"I thought I was supposed to have been." I can't hide the hurt in my voice.

"I thought so too. I came back. I needed to tell you. But when I got here, you were already gone. Your mom was so distraught that I couldn't tell her. When she said you joined the Army, I knew the chances of ever finding you again would be damn near impossible."

As things start clicking together, I feel my anger rising. "Tell me what? That you were marrying your childhood best friend like I never existed?" My voice booms more than I anticipate. Echo's eyes widen, but she doesn't jump. Which is good because I don't plan on coddling her.

"No." She shakes her head. "I came back here before ever reaching out to Brian. He was my only option. I only married him because I was pregnant." Her eyes plead with mine. I see the tears forming and I don't care. I want them to spill over.

"Wow, you wasted no time."

Bang. Bang. Bang.

My eyes cut to the screen door, and I laugh. "Well, well, well. Lookie there. Mr. Convenient decided to show up." Brian swings open the screen door and walks in with a cane. I notice the limp he's trying to hide, but he's too focused on the situation at hand to do a good job at it.

"What the hell, Echo? You take off in the middle of the night without a word and run back to your first love?" Brian says, glaring at the two of us. I want to be pissed, but his admission renders me speechless.

"It's not what it looks like," she replies, looking absolutely defeated at this point. As if the last thirteen years have sucked the fight out of her and she's deciding to throw in the towel. She lets out a heavy sigh, pushing herself off the wall. Then her stance changes and it's as if the fight returns. "Wait, you knew this entire time?" she questions Brian.

"Knew what?" He attempts to play dumb.

She steps closer to him, almost pinning him to the screen door. "Knew who Dustin was to me. Knew he was injured and didn't tell me." She jabs a finger into his chest.

"Yes." He looks down, not willing to fully own up to his mistake. "It all came together right before we were injured."

Echo paces the space between us almost as if she's doing eenie meenie minnie moe to pick between us. "It all makes sense now," she whispers.

I want to ask what, but this new turn of events revolves strictly around her and Brian. I'm just an innocent bystander.

"The injury, the unknown with your career, the pills, the drinking..." She stops in front of him. "You being a complete asshole, talking down to me, making me walk on eggshells in my own house." Her voice rises with each statement. "It was all because you knew Dustin would be back in my life?"

Okay, at this point, I feel like I'm intruding on a married couple. But I can't help but wonder what she means by I'd be back in her life. Just because our worlds had collided again, didn't mean we'd become a permanent fixture in one another's life.

"It's everything. It all became too much. My career, all I've ever known is up in the air because of the nerve damage in my leg. Besides you, it's all I've ever had. And I only had you because of it."

Damn, I want to hate Brian, but right now all I can feel is empathy for him. Because same, bro. Same. No matter who she ends up with, she's not receiving a whole man. She deserves someone who is complete, and knowing that's not me torments me.

"You don't treat something you want to keep like shit and expect it to stay," Echo says flatly before walking out the door, letting the screen slam behind her. I want to chase her, but it isn't my time. This isn't my fight. More than anything, I want her to be mine, but on her terms and not because she's confused.

Brian finally makes eye contact with me, and I watch as his gaze travels down my arm to where my hand should be, and he winces.

"Listen, man," he starts. "You saved my life, and I never got to thank you."

I head toward the front door, stopping in front of him. "You sure aren't acting very thankful to be alive." His body begins to sag, and I get the feeling that standing for this length of time is probably painful for him. I lean in, mere inches from his ear. "You lay a finger on her and you will wish I had let you die. I didn't save your ass for you to come back and be an ass."

"Why did you save me?"

I push open the door and step onto the porch. "Lack of judgment."

I hurry down the steps, hoping to catch Echo before she takes off, not wanting us to end on bad terms. And not wanting to add to the shit plater she's already getting served by her husband.

Brian walks out with his head hanging low. I watch as he limps with his cane and feel partially responsible for his injury.

"You're riding back with your mom," Echo yells over her shoulder. As if he knows he's lost the war, he just says okay and walks to the car he arrived here in. An older lady with short gray hair holds the door open for him while he slowly climbs in. I can only imagine the blow to his pride all of this has been. Brian is in a shit position. We all are.

She walks around her car and leans her back against the driver's side door, facing me. With her arms crossed, she stares off into the distance. Dusk has settled in, and little specks of stars are starting to appear.

"Asshole for an asshole." She laughs. "Those seem to be my options."

I want to disagree, but she's right and nothing I have done proves otherwise.

"I'm only angry because I can't have you," I whisper, not knowing what else to say, but wanting her to also know where I stand. Her eyes dart to mine as if my admission is surprising. As if I could never want her. Even when I don't, I do. "But I don't want this to be a choice. I don't want you to feel like you are a rope getting pulled in two different directions."

Echo walks up to me, places her hand on my check, and I resist the urge to melt into it. "We've all been running, it seems. I think it's time we all work on ourselves and let everything unravel naturally." She gives me a weak smile. Tears trickle down her face and it's my undoing. I wrap my arms around her, pulling her tightly against me as if it's the last time I'll see her. Because it very well could be.

"I'm worried about you," I admit.

"I know."

I pull away and cup the side of her face in my hand, searching her eyes. "Promise me, Echo. Promise me you will get out before things go too far."

"Brian's harmless."

"We're all harmless in the beginning. Then life throws a bunch of shit our way."

"He just needs help." She diverts her gaze from mine.

"Yes, psychiatric. You can't fix him."

"I don't want to fix him." She wraps her hand around my wrist, slowly pulling my hand from her face. "I don't know what the future holds, Dustin. But right now, I have an obligation." She cups my face with her hands and stares intently into my eyes. "I promise you I'll stay safe, but you need to promise me something, too."

Can't she see I'm putty in her hands? I'd promise her all the stars in the universe.

"I need you to promise that you'll work on yourself. Not get trapped in the what-ifs. Restore the relationships you can. And most importantly heal this," she says, placing her hand over my heart. I nod. It's the only response I'm capable of giving. She then stands on her tiptoes and leans in to kiss my cheek. "I know the Dustin I love is still there," Echo whispers.

"He is," I confirm. I'm engulfed with a flood of emotions. That seems to always be the effect she has on me. I know she isn't mine, but I can't help but panic knowing she might be walking back out of my life for good. "But what if I don't see you again?" I barely get the words out. My throat feels tight as if I'm physically having the life choked out of me.

She wraps her arms around my waist, and this time I allow myself to melt into her. "You and I are bound for life. This isn't over."

I find comfort in her words and loosen my grip.

She pulls away and gives me a sweet smile. It's a reassuring one. Her hand glides down the side of my face, over my beard. She gives it a little tug once it reaches my chin. "I'm kinda digging this. And this," she says, ruffling my hair to lighten the mood. Something I've always loved about her.

"Just tell me when and I'll get rid of it."

She scoffs. "Or how about I just do it for you if that day comes?"

"Deal." I smile, loving her plan even better.

"Speaking of." She opens her door and bends over, reaching inside. I avert my eyes. The last thing I need is my mind wandering to the gutter. "Here," she says, handing me a business card.

"You want me to drive five hours for a haircut?" I ask, raising my brow.

"No." She laughs like it's the most incredulous idea.

"I would."

Her laugh falters and we stare at one another. I want to tell her to stay, to pick me. But I could never say those words knowing she has a family. I might be a selfish prick, but even I have my limits. Maybe just when it comes to her.

"I was just thinking if you wanted to continue our letter writing, you could send it to my work." She looks down and kicks at the scattered gravel.

"Is that what you want?" I ask.

"I don't know what I want." She shrugs, looking back up. I can see the defeat in her eyes even though she tries to hide it. She's carrying so much and all I want to do is lighten the load. "All I know is I can't go on living like you don't exist."

I slide my arm past her, leaning in close as I do. She sucks in a breath, eyeing me as I inch closer. She's vulnerable. I'm sure she'd let me push the limits. But that's exactly why I don't.

"It's getting late. You need to hit the road. I'll lock up the house." I lift the handle up, pulling the door open for her.

She slowly crawls in and buckles. It takes every ounce of restraint for me not to yank her out of this car and hold her. "Bye, Dustin." Her voice cracks and her eyes begin to water. And I shut the door before I lose all resolve. I watch the woman I love drive away and I want to burn this town down. I didn't even get to spend two full days with her, and I'm left feeling as if all the oxygen is being squeezed from my lungs. I shouldn't have let her go, yet I told her to.

Chapter Forty-Two

DUSTIN

I walk inside and work my way from the back of the house to the front, shutting off lights and making sure all messes are cleaned up for the slight chance someone schedules a viewing. I walk into the office area and tug the string to let the blinds down. A notepad with familiar penmanship filling the page sits in the middle and I envision Echo sitting at the desk as she wrote me my first letter with crumpled pages surrounding her on the floor.

While it doesn't look addressed to anyone, I don't want it to be left out for anyone to read. I round the desk and pull open the middle drawer. The big capital lettered words catch my eye, and I can't look away. I slowly sit in the chair, second-guessing my actions.

THIRTEEN YEARS AGO, I fell in love with a boy. All it took was one sideways grin, with his perfectly dimpled cheek, for me to know I was a goner. My days and nights were consumed by him—if not physically, he was there mentally—always on my mind. I loved him with everything within me. The love we shared was the kind romance novels were made of.

In the blink of an eye, the boy I loved was ripped from me. My overly religious parents didn't like their daughter falling in love. It was simply unacceptable to them when I was supposed to be focusing on God, school, my future in softball; nothing else. But he was my future, and I came back for him.

I was barely showing when I showed up on his porch, looking for him. It wasn't easy getting back to Georgia from Oklahoma, but I hoped I made it before he took off for college. I knew he was excited about all the scholarship offers he was receiving. His distraught mother informed me of his enlistment and all hope I had vanished. My heart shattered as I realized the dreams I had for our family would never see the light of day.

Eighteen, pregnant, and with no other option, I decided to take a friend up on his offer. A friend who took me under his wing back when I was in third grade. It was through our agreement I realized the different types of love. He was everything I needed when I had nothing. I love him for the life he brought me when every option I had was filled with uncertainty. I will forever be in his debt.

THIRTEEN YEARS LATER, I ran into the boy

I had lost, yet he's no longer a boy. He's a man. A deeply wounded man. Although his flesh on the outside is no longer fully intact, the wounds don't compare to the scars and pain he's carried around on the inside for so long.

THIRTEEN YEARS LATER, and I still have the same feelings for him...but they seem more intense. Was my first love my one true love? Now that he's reappeared in my life, my thoughts are consumed by him. But now they are paralleled with guilt. I love two men, but I love them differently. And, as of right now, I only know one for sure loves me back.

I'm caught between what's wrong and what's right...what's fair and what's unfair. I know what my heart wants, but is what it wants what's right? Feelings can cloud moral judgment. I don't want what I feel to take over what I know to be right. But I'm having a hard time sorting out the differences. I'm walking an emotion-packed tightrope, and I know I'm going to fall. I'm just unsure who's going to catch me.

I have a child. Her son is mine.

I'm a father.

Tears stream down my face as regret slams into me. I was such a dick to her. She tried telling me I have a son, and my mind took the whole thing south. Way south. I don't deserve her, and I pushed her back to the man who's been holding my place, playing daddy. I rip the paper from the notepad and fold it up. Holding the words to my heart,

I vow to fix this. No matter how long it takes. Time no longer holds any bearings.

I've already gone thirteen years.

I'd go an eternity.

Chapter Forty-Three

ECHO

Driving away from Dustin is the hardest and easiest thing to do. What I still feel for him after all these years scares me. There's so much at stake that I don't want to make the wrong choice. I don't want to be responsible for inflicting pain on anyone but feel that's inevitable. So for now, I need to focus on being a supportive wife and being a present mother.

Above all, Dylan is my number one priority. He needs to have a relationship with Dustin, but how do I breach that when the situation at hand is so messy? I don't want to prolong the reunion any further or steal more time away from the two of them, but it just doesn't feel like the right time when my world seems to be imploding.

"I'm glad you came home," Brian says, standing for me as I walk through the garage door. He begins to approach me but thinks better of it. His hand shakes holding the cane that's propping him up. "Where's Dylan?" he asks once I shut the door.

"Still on fall break with his teammate down the street." I bypass him, heading for our room. I'm just drained. Emotionally. Mentally. Physically. I'm tapped out. The door to the guest room is closed, but the lights are on. I'm glad to see he hasn't run his mom off yet. I was expecting him to send her packing once I agreed to come back. "How long's your mom staying for?" I ask, feeling him trail behind me.

"Until my first therapy session. I think she wants to make sure I actually go."

"I'm about to go to bed." I make my way to the bathroom first. I really should shower but don't care enough to.

"Can I sleep with you?" Brian whispers as I walk to my side of the bed.

"Are you sure you want to? You haven't slept in here since you've been back."

"I slept in here the two nights you were gone. I wanted to feel close to you." He looks down. "I thought I lost you."

"Pretty close," I admit, pulling the blanket back. I gesture toward his side. "Yes, you can sleep in your bed." I know that isn't the answer he wants, but it's all I've got.

We both crawl in, me faster than him. Lying in the dark, the silence gives me peace as I drift asleep. The bed begins to shift, and I feel Brian inching closer my way.

"Can I hold you?" His hand reaches out for mine. I hate that he has to be so hesitant with me when he used to be more dominant. But his actions have switched our dynamics. I don't reply. I just scooch closer to him, tucking myself against his side, and pretend.

THE BED IS empty, and the sun is shining brightly. I fling the blanket back, worrying that I'm late for work. I grab my phone off the side table and let out a sigh of relief that it's only Monday and the salon is closed. I walk into the bathroom and decide it's now time for a shower and to brush my teeth since I bypassed both last night. *Gross.*

A sound I'm unfamiliar with fills the house as I walk into the kitchen. Brian and his mom laugh while they dance. It's very endearing for me to see because I remember it being something they did when Brian was younger. His dark eyes shine brightly, and he looks so carefree. I just want to bottle this moment and feeling for us all to refer back to when facing bleak times.

"Good morning, Echo." Paula beams. "Want to join in?" she asks, holding an outstretched hand.

I lean back against the wall and shake my head, smiling. "No, I'd much rather enjoy this view. It's good for my soul."

Through all the bad times, moments such as these are what we have to hold onto to keep going and fighting for the ones we love.

Chapter Forty-Four

DUSTIN

December 2014

It's been two months since I last saw Echo. I thought about writing to her but needed to get some things figured out first. First, I've had to come to terms with the fact that I'm a dad and figuring out what to do with that. Then I realized that I needed to get my shit figured out, which led me to closing on my very first home today.

I never desired to be a homeowner until I knew I had a son. I stand on the porch of Echo's childhood home and unlock the door to what I hope to be our home one day. No matter what, I want it to be a safe place for her if she ever needs to get away. And worst-case scenario, it's a home I can have for when my son comes to visit.

Either way, I have a son.

I walk through the office opening and decide it's time. I need to finally acknowledge the situation. When I have so many thoughts going on in my mind, it's so hard for me to hone in on them. So I write the only logical things that come to me and call it good.

Echo,

I have a son...tell me everything, please.

Love, Dustin

Then I walk out of the house and make a list of items I need to complement all the painting that's been done. I make my way the short distance downtown, stopping at the post office first for envelopes and stamps. While I'm there, I pull her business card out and address her letter before tossing it in the outgoing mail. Then I drive to the hardware store. While I'm in there buying the tools necessary to pull all the carpet up, I stop in the back to have a duplicate key made for me and request a special inscription on it.

* * *

"WHY ARE YOU doing all of this?" my mom asks, standing on my porch. I kind of bought this house behind everyone's back. I didn't want to chance someone talking me out of it.

"Because I need my own space."

"We've barely had you back. Is living with us so bad?"

I laugh. She doesn't want me to answer that honestly.

"I'm barely down the street, Ma. Quit tripping."

"Yes, hon. Let's go home and let Dustin get back to work." My dad urges. Always the sensible one of the duo.

"No, I refuse to leave until he opens up to us. He always keeps things in and never talks to us. I want to know what's going on. You don't just buy your old girlfriend's home for no reason." She all but laughs and it makes me want to kick her in the ankle. My dad gives me a sympathetic look, apologizing for his unruly wife standing all defiant with her arms crossed.

"Fine." I let out an exasperated breath. They need to know. Might as well get it out now. "You're right. There is something."

"Everything okay?" my dad asks.

"Everything is better than okay." I grab the top of his arm, reassuring him. We walk inside, and I direct them both to sit on the couch. "I need you both to take a seat. There's some news that I recently found out about and need to share with you."

They both cautiously sit, unsure of where this is heading.

"Okay, well, for any of this to make sense, I have to backtrack to thirteen years ago." They both listen intently as I unravel my complicated history with Echo. Their mouths hang slightly agape as I recount how we fell in love, she was ripped away from me, and how my anger and hope of finding her led me to the Army. Toward the end, my mom's eyes begin misting up.

"It all makes sense now," she mumbles.

"I have a grandson?" My dad's face instantly lights up.

I smile. "Yeah, you do. He's thirteen and his name is Dylan Ryan Adams."

"Thirteen years old," my mother sobs. "So much lost time."

I gulp. So much lost time indeed. But I aim to rectify the hell out of it. "Don't go into this thinking that. Go into this thinking of all the time you'll have with him now."

She nods her head in agreement.

I walk into the office area and grab the envelope I received that morning in the mail. Echo wrote me back, telling me all about our boy. How much he weighed at birth. How he's a third baseman, just like I was. How smart and funny he is. Also, just like me. And sent many pictures to accompany the letter. From ultrasound to this year's baseball picture. He's such a stud and although I haven't officially met him yet, I'm so proud to be his dad. I just pray he accepts me.

"He's so handsome." My mom cries, looking through the pictures. "He looks just like you did at that age."

"I know." I feel so much joy, my heart is going to explode.

My mom's chest begins to heave as more tears stream down her face. "I'm so sorry, Dustin. I'm to blame for this, too. I just wanted you to have a great life. You had so much talent." She holds up the picture of Echo young and pregnant. "I remember her stopping by shortly after you enlisted. I was so wrapped up in my own feelings I didn't take notice of who she was. I've always been so selfish when it comes to you boys."

I want to scream "Hallelujah! Finally!" But I don't think throwing her admission in her face would help benefit the situation. I sit down next to her and pull her in for a hug. We're all to blame. I'm just glad we're all seeing that because now we can move forward.

Chapter Forty-Five

DUSTIN

January 2015

Echo and I continue to stay in contact through our letters. She keeps me informed about all things Dylan and I keep her informed about the progress I'm making on the house. We don't talk about us as I know she's focused on being a present mother and wife, and I don't want to take away from that. I'm just trying to follow Lynsie's advice of being whatever she needs. I do ask about Brian out of general concern for Echo's and Dylan's well-being. She always says he's doing better and staying consistent with his therapy, and I leave the prodding at that. I've come to the conclusion that no matter what happens between Echo and me, I want a relationship with my son. While I want her and for us to be a family, Dylan and his needs have become a vital part of my life.

Once the flooring is complete and I'm done with all the final touches of furnishing the home, I decide to write Echo and hope I'm not pushing my luck this time. But I have to make sure she knows without a shadow of a doubt that there's always a place for her here. That no matter how long she's been gone, she can come back.

How do you tell someone you've never stopped loving them and never will? That you will love them as long as it takes someone to count every single star in the sky. That your love expands the depths of the universe and transcends time. That you would literally die for them and almost did. That every decision you've ever made while apart was subconsciously for them. How do you say all of that and more without using words?

Echo,

If you need a safe space, come home.

Love, D

I fold the note around the spare key I made just for her and put it in the envelope.

Chapter Forty-Six

ECHO

February 2015

It's pitch black when we pull into town. My hand trembles as I pull the envelope out of my purse that contains the key Dustin sent me last month.

He even engraved D + E on the key itself. I've kept it tucked away in a hidden pocket in my purse since I received it. I couldn't chance Brian ever finding it. I just experienced what finding less does.

"Let me help, Ma," Dylan says, turning the flashlight of his phone on.

"Thanks, son."

I go to slide the key in but hear it unlock from the inside before it swings open. Dustin stands in the doorway, wide-eyed and shirtless. The tenseness in his body evaporates as soon as we lock eyes.

"I'm sorry to just show up," I stutter, looking at the ground.

He pulls me inside, turns the entryway light on, and inspects my face. Besides my running mascara, I'm sure the handprint is still evident. Along with the bruises where he grabbed my arm with such force I was pulled backward to the ground.

Dustin's face turns every shade of red before he storms off to the back of the house. I pull Dylan farther inside as we stand and wait for his return. He comes back fully clothed, and dread instantly washes over me.

"This is your safe place. Make yourself at home. I'll be back," Dustin says, grabbing his keys.

"Wait. Wait. You don't have to do anything. Dylan slugged him with a baseball bat," I plead. Possibly just making the situation go from bad to worse. He slows down enough to finally realize I'm not alone. I watch as he looks at our son. A sense of pride and emotion washes over him before he compartmentalizes it to the back and anger regains control at the realization that his son was also in harm's way. I try to stop him as he walks past us, but not even a freight train could slow him down from his new mission.

I tense up, anticipating the slam of the screen door. It never happens. He must've put new doors on. Then I do a three-sixty and realize we aren't standing on carpet but wood floors. He really has completely revamped this house. "Was that my dad?" Dylan asks.

I look down, offering a weak smile. "Yeah, that's him," I say, ruffling his hair.

"He's pretty badass," he says with awe.

I laugh, not having the energy to correct his language.

"Like a real-life G.I. Joe."

"Yeah, I'd have to agree. But this isn't at all how I wanted you to meet him."

"Life isn't a script, Ma. You're going to have to let things take their course," Dylan replies with a long yawn that follows.

"You need rest. Go pick out a bed, Goldilocks."

He takes off like a kid on an Easter egg hunt. "Whoa, cool. Ma, come look," he hollers from down the hall. I round the corner, and tears fill the brims of my lids as I take in the bedroom. It's baseball themed and I have no doubt that it was designed for the boy tucked in the bed.

"Looks like it was made just for you, huh?" I sit down next to where he's lying. He nods as his eyes fight to stay open. I grab his uncovered hand and run my free hand through his hair. "I love you more than anything, Dylan Ryan Adams. Thank you for protecting me today."

"I will always protect you, Ma," he mumbles.

Part of me wants to mold myself against my son and tightly hold him. I want to protect him from the ugliness of the world. But I've done a shit job of doing so. I failed him as a mother. I compromised the very essence of motherhood—to protect your child at all costs. I let love, loyalty, a lifelong friendship, the feeling of obligation like I owed Brian my life cloud my judgment. And who paid the cost? All of us.

Thirteen years ago, I fell in love with a boy and our love caused a war zone. And the casualties just keep piling up.

A light tap at the door brings me back to my current reality.

"Echo, it's me."

I slowly stand, careful not to wake Dylan, and stare down at him a beat longer than I should.

"I'll do better," I vow.

I turn around to see Lynsie in the doorway. All the emotion I've been holding in begins to fester as my chest heaves, beckoning me to release it all. I quickly make my way out of the room, pulling the door shut before I lose it.

"Oh, no. Echo." Her voice cracks as she takes me in. She pulls me against her. Wrapping an arm around my head, she cradles it against her. Uncontrollable sobs flow from within me as we slide to the ground, Lynsie never losing her hold on me.

"He was getting better." I pull back, pleading with her eyes. "He was getting help. I never would've stayed if I thought he would turn violent." I look down, shaking my head as more sobs erupt. "Never. I never would have."

"Shhh," Lynsie coos, pulling me back against her. One hand rubs my back, while the other massages my head. Both motions relax me, calming my erratic body movements as I try to regain normal breathing. This brings me back to when I did the same for her. And that reality sobers me right up. Why am I having a pity party? I'm alive and so are all the people I love—even Brian.

"I'm okay," I say through sniffles, peeling myself away from her. Lynsie cautiously lifts my face, tilting it to the side, and winces at the sight. I'm sure I'm a sight for sore eyes.

"Is that a handprint?" She seethes.

"Yeah, he slapped me."

"What the hell, Echo?" A mixture of emotions crosses her face as she releases her hold on me.

"I'm okay," I say again, hoping she believes me. Hoping I believe myself.

"Why do you always do that?" She holds my gaze. "You don't always have to be so tough. It's okay to not be okay."

"I just can't find it within myself to have a pity party when people have been through far more traumatic things."

Lynsie looks down and fidgets with her nails before releasing a sigh. "Trauma is trauma. No one event is greater than the other. You're allowed to feel whatever you feel. Don't try to confine it."

I nod, acknowledging her words. I hear what she's saying, but I'm not convinced it applies to me.

We make our way into the dimly lit living room, and I drop onto the new sectional as exhaustion settles in.

"I'm going to get a wet rag." Lynsie offers a weak smile. I must look like absolute shit. I hear a drawer in the kitchen slide open and shut. I'm about to yell that I don't know where the wash rags are when she comes walking back with a wet one in her hand. She sits beside me, asking, "Do you mind?" before carefully wiping off my face. The gesture is so gentle and loving I almost break down again. "There. All better," she says as she finishes up.

Lynsie asks if I want to talk about it. I don't *want* to talk about it, but I'm willing to. I let my head fall back against the soft cushion and close my eyes, taking my mind back to how it all started. Then go back even further.

"Well, like I said, he was getting better. After I went back home the last time I was here, I told him to get help, or I was walking. He agreed and has been attending therapy ever since. He even weaned himself from the pills and quit drinking. Things were good. Well." I pause. "Good enough."

"What do you mean by that?" The couch shifts and I open my eyes, seeing Lynsie angle her body in my direction before bending her legs criss-cross applesauce. I do the same, facing her, and she grabs my hands, holding them between us.

"Things were good in the sense that Brian was doing better. But I wasn't happy. I was content. Which I realize is what I've been most of my life."

"Do you think the two of you only worked so well because he was gone for a majority of the marriage?" She asks the question I've asked myself many times.

I finally answer it.

"Yes." I let out a shaky breath. "I do think that's why we've managed to stay married. I do love him as a friend and for what he did for me, but that's the extent of the emotional attachment."

"Then you were essentially just trying to get him back on his feet before figuring out what to do?"

I nod. "I couldn't leave him when he needed me the most. And I also didn't want to get into a situation where I was running back and forth between him and Dustin. Just because I've felt lost ever since Dustin reappeared, I didn't want to drag either of them into it. So I shut that part off to deal with the situation at hand. I told myself I'd get Brian better and then figure out where to go from there."

"But something happened?" Lynsie swirls circles on the tops of my hands, keeping me calm.

I close my eyes, visualizing how mad Brian was. A shiver runs down my spine as I begin telling Lynsie what led to this point.

"Brian," I hollered. "Are you ready? We need to leave." I was so excited to finally not be sitting at one of Dylan's games alone. Everyone else had their significant other, yet I was always solo. In the span we'd been married, I could count on one hand how many games he'd attended. Little did I know we wouldn't be making it to the game after all.

He didn't reply, so I headed down the hallway toward our room to see what the holdup was. Out of the corner of my eye, something caught my attention as I passed Dylan's room. I slowly backed up, peeking through the opening. Brian had found my box.

"What are you doing?" I pushed the door open and charged toward him. I grabbed the old jersey and softball he tossed on the bed and attempted to yank the letters out of his hands.

"What is this...some kind of a shrine?" He let out a maniacal laugh and I became transfixed with his deep brown eyes. There was darkness to them I had not seen before.

"Memories," I muttered. I could see him yelling but couldn't hear what was being said. It felt as if my subconscious was separating itself

from my body. Then, without warning, someone cranked up the volume and it all became too loud.

"That shit in your hands is memories. These letters from y'all playing pen pal are not memories."

"Then what are they?" I asked, feeling fight and flight, deciding which needed to suit up.

"After everything I've done for you." He took a step toward me. "I took you and that bastard son of yours in." Another step. "I, not this guy"—he waved the letters in his hands—"have been the one raising him and you wouldn't even give him my last name."

I laughed, catching him off guard. "You've raised him? All you have been in Dylan's life is a backdrop. I've been a married single mother for the last thirteen years. I never gave him your last name because you"—I point a finger at him—"haven't earned that privilege."

I should have expected it, but my guard was down. Before I could deflect, his hand slammed against my face with the loudest slap I'd ever heard. I dropped the items in my hands as I instinctively reached for my face. Heat, as if his hand was molten lava, engulfed the side of my face. I expected his demeanor to change, that it in that moment it would've clicked what he had done, but that didn't happen. I turned to run, but his hand wrapped around my bicep like a vice, pulling me back with such force I fell to the ground. In horror, I stared up at the man hovering over me, wondering what his next move would be. And what mine would be.

Before I had time to react, a loud crack sound filled the room. Brian fell to the ground with a thud, half groaning, half crying as he held his knee.

"Don't you ever touch my mom again," Dylan yelled, holding the metal bat up in the air like he was going to make it rain metal all over Brian.

I jumped to my feet and put my hand on the bat to keep him from swinging. "That's enough, son." I smiled, reassuring him. Dylan backed up but kept his grip tight on his bat as a precaution.

. . .

"Then I quickly grabbed all the items to Dustin's shrine, and we got the hell out of Dodge. And that's how we ended up here." I glance up at Lynsie, half expecting her to be asleep with how quiet she's been. She sniffles, wiping away a stray tear.

"I'm so sorry you had to go through that." She leans in, wrapping her arms around my neck.

"It's—"

"No." She pulls away just enough to rest her forehead against mine. "It's not okay."

THE BUZZING OF my phone awakens me. The buzzing ends before I can get up and I decide against moving. I almost drift back asleep before the buzzing starts again. This time it's louder and doesn't stop. Lynsie stirs and I realize her phone is going off too and I begin to wonder if we're under some type of weather warning. We look at each other, both still half asleep, then grab our phones off the table.

Seeing his name on my phone screen has me wanting to do anything but answer. I'd rather chuck my phone than talk to him. But something must be wrong for us both to be receiving calls at this hour. My mind goes to Dustin. And without hesitation, I hit the green button.

"Brian, what—"

"Echo, something happened." That's not Brian's voice on the other end of the line. It's Dustin.

Chapter Forty-Seven

DUSTIN

I sit in the waiting room, hunched over with my head hanging low. My body begs for sleep. Thankfully, it's trained to go without. But everyone has their limits, and I feel like my body is tired of me pushing mine. No one here will give me any updates since I'm not immediate family and the closest immediate family he has should be about halfway here by now. I stand up, deciding I need to stretch my legs and find myself a heavy dose of caffeine. After that long drive, I didn't plan on being stuck sitting in a hospital for God knows how long.

I could just leave and start my trek back home, but I'm not a piece of shit. I didn't leave Brian stranded on enemy ground, and I'm damn sure not going to do so now. While I'm still angry as hell at him for putting his hands on Echo, I want to see him get help...but from a distance. A very far away distance.

After walking around the hospital five times, familiarizing myself with every bathroom area, coffee station, exit route, and location of the cafeteria, I make my way back to the waiting area. Echo stands at the counter, looking how I left her—hair piled on top of her head in a messy bun, sweatpants tucked into Ugg boots with an oversized hoodie on. I turn around to see Dax walk in the automatic door and relief washes over me, realizing he drove her here.

I meet him halfway and give him a bear hug. The events of the last ten hours have really shaken me up. "Thanks, man, for coming."

"Of course, bro." He asks what happened as we make our way to the seating area. I open my mouth to begin telling him, but his eyes get huge as he looks past me.

"What did you do?" Echo screams, pushing on my shoulder from behind. I turn to face her and my heart damn near cracks. The side of her face is still puffy and slightly red. What looks to be the beginnings of a black eye forming. Her arms hang at her sides with her hands fisted. "Brian was alive and well when we left him. What did you do?" she demands.

"Mrs. Williams," the nurse hollers, breaking through the tension.

Echo stares at me momentarily before dropping her shoulders and unclenching her fists. I hope she can see in my eyes what I try to convey. Without another word, she turns her back to me and follows the nurse.

"How was the drive?" I ask, sitting down next to Dax.

"Uhm." He rubs his hands on the tops of his thighs. "It was pretty somber. Not gonna lie. It took me back to when I drove back home with Lynsie for Lincoln's funeral."

Guilt and regret begin to settle in, making me wish I had just driven home and picked Echo up myself instead of putting the burden on my brother.

The automatic doors open, and my body instantly stiffens as Echo's parents walk in. I knew this day would come, but I had hoped it'd be on my terms and not thrown at me without warning. They glance over as they walk past us. Mr. Price makes eye contact with me, holding my gaze. His eyes widen as recognition sets in, but the worry for his daughter and Brian overpowers it.

"You don't have to stay," I tell Dax.

"Nah, bro, I'm not leaving you to the wolves." He bumps his shoulder into mine. "But how about we get out of here for a bit and go grab some breakfast."

"Food sounds good."

"Yeah, DFF, baby." I look at him and cock a brow. "Down. For. Food." He clarifies.

As we walk to the door, I look down the hall. Echo's dad stands outside of the room, and I wonder how long it's been since they've seen each other. Just as I go to turn away, the door opens.

"Dad." Echo cries, throwing her arms around him.

Through the cries, I hear him say, "I'm so sorry, baby girl."

I'd never wish the reason we're gathered at the hospital on anyone, but I'm glad to see healing is able to come from it—in this circumstance.

* * *

MOST OF THE day has now passed and I contemplate leaving—especially since that's the only way I'm going to convince Dax to leave. Brian's mother arrived a little while ago, and I have yet to see Echo again since her glorious entrance.

I tell myself I'm staying because of my duty, but the truth is, I can't leave her.

"I'm going to go find a vending machine." I look over to see Dax asleep with his head leaning against the wall. I pass a couple different machines before I find one with peanut M&M's. I buy two packages and make my way back to my seat. I turn the corner, almost running right into Echo.

"Hey. I've been looking for you," she says, leaning back on the balls of her feet as her hand plays with the string of her hoodie. "I'm sorry." Her hand reaches out and rests on my forearm as her gaze finally finds mine and holds it. "When you took off last night, I feared the worse."

"You had every right to," I confirm.

"When you called, I thought you hurt him."

"Echo, I don't want to stand here and play Good Samaritan. After you showed up last night, I wanted to end Brian's life. I didn't want him to have the opportunity to ever hurt you again." I sigh, running a hand through my hair. "But he robbed me of it." I let out a laugh, feeling somewhat maniacal due to the lack of sleep. "I wanted to kill him, but he beat me to it." Tears begin to spill from my eyes.

Echo grabs my hand, holding it between us as I continue.

"I just keep playing the scene over and over. I walked up to the door and banged on it. The house was brightly lit and the TV was playing loud. That's when I looked in the window. My heart dropped, and I called nine-one-one as survival mode took over. I kicked the door in and ran to his side, checked for a pulse. It was faint. I jammed two fingers down his throat, praying his body would do its job and vomit up some of what he ingested."

Echo throws her arms around me, holding me as I relive the horrible moment. One arm rubs my back while the other wraps around the nape of my neck.

"All I could think was I had to save him for you. I couldn't let him die." I whisper

"But why?" She pulls back, placing both hands on the sides of my face. Her fingers play with my unkempt beard as she searches my eyes.

"Because I couldn't chance you having to live with that kind of burden."

She nods in understanding, spilling fresh tears. "You did that for me?"

"Everything I do is for you."

"YOU GET LOST, bro?" Dax asks as I take a seat.

"Yeah," I say, tossing the extra bag of M&M's on his lap.

"Best brother ever," he whispers. I laugh, thinking about how he truly is the best brother ever. His lightheartedness brings a light into this world that we all so desperately need.

Echo walks over to us, standing in front of me, and Dax begins smarting off.

"I never doubted my brother," he says matter-of-factly like I'm incapable of causing harm in his eyes.

"Not even a little bit?" She lifts her hand, holding her thumb and pointer finger close together, scrunching her face.

"Okay, maybe." Dax shrugs.

I slap his chest and Echo laughs.

Her parents come out from down the hall and tell her she's needed. She glances at me and then back at the hallway and I can tell she's torn. I grab her hand and squeeze. She looks down at my hand around hers and then her eyes drift up to mine and all I want to do is get lost in them.

"Hey, it's okay. Go." A twinge of pain stabs my chest, realizing those are the last words I told her the last time I had seen her.

She nods, then hugs both parents, saying something to them before continuing down the hall. They make their way over to me and Dax and sit. The closeness has me feeling a bit on guard.

"Echo told us you saved Brian's life. Thank you," her mom says.

My erratic heart slows a bit at her words, and I turn my gaze toward them and nod in response.

"Pride is an ugly thing," Echo's dad says, looking my way. "And this is all my fault." He shakes his head back and forth. "I set this all into motion so long ago with you and my daughter. I've caused all this brokenness."

Thoughts consume my mind at his admission—something I never thought I'd hear. I shift in my chair, knowing this conversation needs to happen now.

"Permission to speak freely, sir," I say. Now is the time to get it all out. None of us need to continue carrying this weight. With no objections, I continue, "Sir, to be honest, I carried a grudge, a hatred like no other for you most of my life. It molded me into a cold, calculated man, leading me to serve five tours overseas. Then I saw your daughter again and time stopped." I rest my elbows on my thighs as I lean forward. "My anger at you subsided and was redirected toward Brian." I nod, looking in the direction of the hall he's down. "Poor guy didn't even do anything to deserve it. I loathed him because I wasn't him. I was downright jealous. But because of Echo, I made a vow to protect him because I couldn't stand the thought of her world being shattered if something were to happen to him. It's always been because of Echo. What I did. What I do. And what I will do. I can't seem to stop fighting to keep her safe. Even if she's not mine."

"Please don't," Mr. Price says.

My head shoots up, making sure I heard him right. He holds my stare, and I can see a sea of regret swarming in his brown eyes and I wonder whose sea is deeper, his or mine.

"So yeah." I look away, letting out a deep breath. "I used to blame you for wrecking my world and destroying my future. But we're all responsible for our own actions and choices that have led us to this point. In regard to this situation"—I point down the hall—"the only thing you're responsible for is being a controlling douche thirteen years ago. You aren't responsible for that. Brian is."

"He said you saved his life twice." Mr. Price says with a sense of awe. I just nod. I'm not much of being an attention whore. Now my brother, on the other hand...

"Third time's a charm," Dax mutters, earning an elbow jab from me to his side.

Before I can tell him now is not the time to be joking, I look up to see Echo making her way back out. She eyes us suspiciously as we all now sit in silence.

"Everything okay?" she asks, raising a brow, looking from me to her parents, then back to me.

Her dad sighs, then says, "I think it's going to be." Then places a hand on my shoulder and grips it. His gaze falls to my missing hand, and I see him wince once finally taking notice of my injury. "Did you sustain that while saving Brian?"

"Yes, it was the main *physical* wound I suffered."

He nods and I feel he's able to read between the lines. The physical wounds will never overpower the emotional scars. He begins to shake his head as his chest shakes. "So much destruction. So much pain. So much division. We've all lost so much." He looks around at all of us, even nodding at Dax, who has suffered immense loss. "But, son, I fear you've lost the most out of all of us."

"Sir, it's collateral damage that I would gladly endure again if it led me back to your daughter." I glance up at Echo, who stands with tears streaming down her face. I jump up and stand right in front of her. "What's wrong, Echo?" I begin wiping away the tears.

"It's just Dylan. So much has happened. Y'all have lost so much time." She shakes her head.

"Hey, hey, hey," I say, cupping her beautiful face in my hand. She looks up at me and more than anything I want to press my lips to hers and kiss all her worries away. I know it would work. It did in the past. But I don't. Instead, I smile as I push the loose hair back behind her ear my hand trails down her jawline, resting at her chin. I swipe my finger lightly across her bottom lip. Her breath hitches and my heart pumps faster, loving I have this effect on her. "Do you trust me?"

"More than life itself." Her lip quivers as she reaches for me, running her hand along the side of my face. The urge to toss this woman over my shoulder and rush out of here flashes through my mind. Keeping my resolve with her is proving to be difficult. I'm just hoping I don't have to keep it up too much longer. But I know I'd do so for the rest of my life if that's what she needed.

"Then let me go take care of our son while you figure stuff out here."

Slightly uncertain, she looks down. She's been his sole provider his entire life. How hard it must be to relinquish some of that responsibility to someone else. I lift her face back to mine.

"Echo, please. I need this," I whisper, pleading.

"He's right." Her dad stands, placing a hand on both of our shoulders. "Dylan needs this, too. It's time."

She nods and I pull her into my embrace. So many emotions and all I want to do is ease her mind—to reassure her. "I love you more than anything in the world, Echo. I know you know that." She nods against my chest, and I rub her back and cradle her head against me as she cries. "The last thing I want to do is leave you alone to deal with all of this." My voice shakes as tears begin to stream down my face. "But I know you and I know it's what you need." I pull back enough to rest my forehead against hers. "Thank you for trusting me."

Echo's hands move to my hips, and she lets out a heavy breath. "Thank you for loving me."

"I'll never stop."

Chapter Forty-Eight

ECHO

"Have you ever done something you're so incredibly ashamed of that dying sounds better than having to face those you love, knowing you hurt them? I did." His voice begins to crack, and I wonder how I'm going to make it out of this room without crying. "I know everyone in this room knows what happened, but you haven't heard it from me."

Listening to Brian recount everything is painful. He goes back to being overseas and piecing together who Dustin was and how it triggered something in him he never knew was there—insecurity. The injury, feeling useless, fear of no longer having his career, fear that I would leave him, coupled with the pain pills that helped drown out the noise turned him into someone he didn't recognize and couldn't escape.

"I think a lot of my anger stems from when I lost my dad. I became so enraged with God and how he could let such a man of faith die. He had the power to heal him, and he didn't. Why?"

"Because it was never about your dad. Your dad's faith never swayed. But you, you lost your way. And so did I," I say with tear-filled eyes.

"I think sometimes God tests us to see if we're going to lean on him through the hard times, or crack under pressure. I believe we all failed the test," my dad says. "But as long as we're all still alive and breathing, there's time to make it right."

Tears fall down Brian's face. "I have to make this right." He sobs. Through my own tears, I watch the boy I've loved my whole life break down. Brian begins wiping away at his face, trying to hide the evidence of his sorrow. "I know what I have to do," he says through shaky breaths.

"I need to go." I stand abruptly, pushing my chair back as I do. It screeches across the linoleum, causing everyone's attention to shift my way. I rush to the door, desperate for fresh air. This room is suffocating me.

"Echo," Brian says, stopping me right as I grab the metal handle. I don't look back. "I'll be by for my stuff as soon as I'm released." He doesn't say anything else, nor does he need to. He knew we were over once he laid his hands on me.

Chapter Forty-Nine

DUSTIN

I knew walking out of the hospital and leaving Echo behind was going to be hard, but it was damn near impossible. Thankfully, I had Dax with me.

"Hey, can we make a detour before we head back?" Dax asks.

I don't know what his detour entails, but I welcome the distraction. I'm about to ask him what wild goose chase he has us going on, but then the water comes into view and a lump fills my throat.

"This is where it happened?" I ask, already knowing the answer. I put my Blazer in park right in front of a bench and sculpture that seems to be a replica of the one Dax presented at the award ceremony. Guilt instantly sweeps over me as I come to the realization that we haven't had a real conversation about him losing his friend. I've been so caught up in my problems that I forgot about him losing someone who was like a brother to him.

Dax gets out and I stay seated, giving him time alone. He walks to the statue and places his hand on it, dropping his head. I imagine him saying a prayer and I close my eyes and do the same. I haven't said a real prayer since I was eighteen, but right now, prayer feels like the most logical thing to do.

I pray for my brother, who experienced a loss I can't begin to comprehend.

I pray for Echo and for her to have the strength she needs to face her situation.

I pray for myself, to be able to truly forgive and move on from the past. I pray that I can be whatever Echo needs and a good father to our son.

And I pray for Brian…because I truly want him to get better.

I open my eyes and see Dax at the waterline. He bends over, grabs a rock, and flings his arm from the side of his body, skipping the rock across the top of the water. I hop out and make my way to where he stands and do the same. We silently fling rocks for what feels like an eternity before he begins to speak.

"You know, I loved Lynsie since the day Lincoln introduced me to her," Dax admits. "I felt like the worst best friend for having those feelings and wanting what was his." He sits down on the ground, and I join him. "It felt like a curse. I couldn't control it. I tried. I even debated on getting restationed." He laughs. "I was actually looking into it right before the accident." Dax looks over at me and I hold his stare. "It was Lincoln's last wish for me to watch over Lynsie, but I would've done so anyway."

"I'm sorry I wasn't there for you." I place my hand on his shoulder. "I got so wrapped up in my shit that I left you hanging." I look down and shake my head.

"You're here for me now. That's all that matters," Dax reassures. "I used to think my feelings for her were a curse, but after the accident, I realized they were my purpose."

His words resonate deep inside me. With everything that's happened in the past six months, I know the feeling of what seemed to be a curse shaping into a purpose. Echo being pulled from me thirteen years ago, joining the Army, getting injured, the entire situation with Brian—all of it presented itself as a curse. I literally thought I was cursed, but now I'm starting to see the bigger picture. How everything intricately weaves itself back together.

How maybe the universe doesn't hate me, after all.

"Tell me more about the Broken Wing award you received. I never got the full story behind that."

Dax laughs and shakes his head. "Two words. Suicide birds."

Chapter Fifty

ECHO

Absolute dread sets in as I pull into the driveway. It's not like I expected anything else, but the thickness of it weighs me down and has me second-guessing my decision to come here alone. But I know I need to tackle this on my own. I've kept myself together and have stayed strong for the well-being of those around me. But for what? Who's benefitted from me doing so?

Dylan.

But has it really been beneficial for him to see me fake it? To grin and bear it. What have I been teaching him in the process? Absolutely nothing. Nothing of value.

I slowly push the garage door open, scared of seeing the remnants of last night strung about. And very uncertain if I'll be able to handle the aftermath, after all. Strong Echo is starting to feel entirely too weak and fragile. The sun has set, leaving the house dim of light and life. I flip the switch right inside the doorway, turning on the dining room light. It illuminates enough light to brighten the kitchen and living room as well. Expecting to see some sort of proof of what happened last night, I find none. In fact, the house looks to be in perfect

273

condition as if my door wasn't kicked in and my husband didn't try to kill himself last night.

Fully allowing that thought to form in my mind guts me, bringing me to my knees. My body shakes as sobs rip from within. Deep, painful cries I haven't released since I was a teenage girl. I swore I'd never let myself feel this way ever again. That's why I went the safe route.

"You were supposed to be safe," I yell, slamming my fist against the carpet. "You were supposed to keep me safe." I sit kneeled in the living room—the room where he attempted to end his life—and I release all the anger I feel for him. And all the anger I've been holding onto. For the second time in the last thirteen years of my life, I pray. I pray and ask God to release me from the anger I've let consume me over the years. Once my sobs subside, I get up and head to bed.

Although this is the room it all went downhill in, I can't stomach the idea of sleeping in my own bed. I pull Dylan's comforter back and fall into his bed as if I lost all energy. Which, at this point, I have. I could easily sleep for an entire week. I welcome the idea as I begin to doze off.

THE FEELING OF tears prickling the backs of my lids awakens me, bringing me back to reality far too quickly. "Nooo," I scream into my pillow. I wanted to at least sleep a full twenty-four hours. Not wake up bright and early the next morning. I lie face down, begging for sleep to return. Maybe if I roll back and forth enough, I can lull myself back. "Fine." I accept defeat, throwing the covers off me.

I sit on the side of the bed and wonder what I'm even doing here. More importantly, wonder what I'm even doing with my life. So much chaos and confusion has settled in since Dustin showed up. So many unknowns have been in place, particularly because of my situation. But the last thing I want to do is throw me and Dylan into another unknown situation.

First things first, I sniff myself. I need a shower. I need to wash this grimy feeling of doom and gloom off me in hopes of feeling alive again. I strip off my clothes, making my way to the master bathroom. The idea of taking a long, hot bath sounds so enticing, but then the memory of Brian and me in the tub flashes through my mind and my stomach rolls at the thought. I can't just flip a switch and hate the man when I know what he's become is based on circumstances that got out of hand. Just because he crossed the line and pushed me past the point of no return doesn't mean I stop loving him. I'll just love him differently and from a distance.

Who am I kidding… I've always loved him from a distance. What I'm feeling isn't a shift in the depth of what I feel for him. No, this feeling is relief. Relief that I don't have to make a choice. Relief that I don't have to hurt someone. Relief that I don't have to continue carrying on a charade.

And relief makes me feel like a shitty person.

I step into the shower, letting my tears mix with the steaming stream of water washing over me. So much regret. So much unforgiveness. So much heaviness. I cry harder. Pray harder. And release it all, vowing to quit living in the past from this moment forward. I don't know what my future holds and I'm not in a rush to figure it out.

I turn the shower off and wrap a towel around me. I'm done crying—for now. I have to shift my focus. Right now, I just want to breathe and not think, worry, or focus on anything other than my son.

Dylan.

He's with his dad. The thought has me reaching for my phone as I walk into my bedroom, wanting to call and check in. But I slide it back on the dresser, thinking better of it. This reunion has to happen. I just thought I'd be part of it. Maybe it's better this way. It is better this way. They need to bond without me interfering and I need to figure stuff out around here while they do.

As I pull clothes out to wear, I begin pulling Brian's stuff out of the dresser, making a pile on the floor. When he gets out to come get his stuff today, I want to make it as easy and quick as possible for them to grab and go. Anything that can't fit into his vehicle for him and his mom to drive back to Oklahoma, I can mail one day.

I throw my clothes on and make my way into our walk-in closet, doing the same thing—purging Brian, refusing to cry as I do. The truth is, while I am incredibly sad about how things have gone and almost losing him for good, I'm still mad at him. And oddly enough, while I'm the victim, I feel sorry for him because I know the man I've lived with for the last six months is not the man I've loved for the last thirteen years. And it infuriates me that he let all his thoughts win him over and change him from the inside out.

But then again, *relief.* The war on his mind caused this ripple effect. What would be my life had it not? Pretending to be a happy, doting wife, longing for my past lover? I'll never know because that wasn't the hand I was dealt. Instead, I was dealt a hand to my face by the man who vowed to always keep me safe, then ripping that safety net before my very eyes.

I gather his fatigues and uniforms, lay them on the bed, and pull out the garment bag we have. He might not find value in them at the moment, but I hope his love for what they represent returns once he's healed. I keep all his military items separate from his civilian. I'm not packing up his stuff to be heartless. If that were the case, I'd be hella dramatic and toss it all on the front lawn. Glancing around at the piles before me, I realize I need some boxes. And coffee since I'm running on fumes and it's only a matter of time before exhaustion catches up with me once again.

Making my way through the house, I examine my surroundings. The light illuminating through all the windows makes some of the destruction I didn't notice last night noticeable. Holes line the walls down the hallway, leading to the living room. A splatter of something catches my eye on the far wall and I walk closer to inspect it. Remnants of dark brown flake off as I glide my hand across it, feeling a dent in the wall as I do. I look at the ground for clues of what it could be and see nothing. Then I notice my plant I had close to the window is missing.

I try to picture it all as Dustin recounted it to me. It had to have looked like a crime scene. That's what I expected to walk into. So why doesn't it? To anyone else, the house looks well kept and not like a self-destructive bomb went off two nights ago. I walk into the kitchen and stop at the dining room table. A phone and a note sit atop. I recognize the phone as Brian's. I push the button, bringing it to life. A million missed calls and text alerts flash on the screen, but the background is the three of us—a once happy-ish family.

Then I pick up the note and I can't help but smile.

Much faster than snail mail.

972-431-5800

D.

Chapter Fifty-One

DUSTIN

I pick up the takeout cups left over from our last meal together and lift the lid of the trashcan. My breath catches as I see the aftermath of what took place here filling the bag and I know exactly who took the time to do it so I wouldn't have to witness it. Dustin thinks of every little detail. His mind works like no other. I'm not sure I'll ever get used to it. But it's reassuring, especially where Dylan is concerned.

I STACK THE last box in the living room next to his camo duffle bag and drape the garment bag over the top. Nerves run rampant as a knock on the door breaks the silence. I'm unsure of why I'm nervous since we've said our peace. Maybe I wanted to avoid close contact again this soon. Maybe I'm even a bit fearful of how he might react on his own, alone with me. What if everything in the hospital was all for show? I mean, he pulled that Dr. Jekyll / Mr. Hyde move on his mom with me. He could've been pulling the wool this entire time.

I go to unlock the doorknob, realizing it wasn't locked, but the

278

deadbolt is. The door creaks as I open it, and I can see the splintered wood pieces that are left in the doorframe.

Brian stands in front of me, a shell of the man he once was like the life has been sucked out of him. It practically was. "I just came to get my stuff," he says, looking down.

"Where's your mom?" I ask, looking past him, not seeing any evidence of how he arrived.

"I had the Uber drop her off at the hotel before bringing me here. I figured I was safe to drive my truck back the couple miles away it is." That makes sense. I'm sure his poor mother needs rest after flying here and being at the hospital with him. I just hope she's up for the return drive to Oklahoma.

"Okay. Well, I packed your clothes. Everything else, I can ship to you."

"I appreciate you doing that." He finally looks up and my heart cracks a little at the shame filling his features. "Sorry for the mess you had to clean up." Brian inspects his surroundings and then stops on his pile of belongings. His hand becomes shaky, trying to keep his cane from wobbling beneath him.

"Umm, actually, I didn't have to clean anything up."

His eyes finally reach mine and well up with tears. "But I know I left this place in shambles. I wasn't that out of it."

"I have a strong feeling Dustin made sure to clean it up," I admit.

He snorts. "Sounds about right. He's always cleaning up my messes."

I want to smile at the admission, but I'm not sure how he's meaning it.

"How about I take this stuff to your truck, and you run to the back and grab your boots I forgot." I grab his keys that are hanging on the wall and head out the door with a couple of his bags. A few trips later, I'm back inside and he still hasn't made it back with his boots. I begin to walk to the master bedroom, but the sobs at the end of the hall stop me in my tracks. Before, I would've run back there without hesitation. Now I question if that's still my responsibility.

I pace back and forth, searching for the answer. It's so hard for me to leave people hanging when they need it the most. I decide to step in, but from a distance. I peek in the cracked door, seeing him sit on the edge of the bed. I slowly open it and ease my way in, then lean against the entrance. This is me loving him from a distance.

"I just hope you can forgive me one day." He sniffles.

"I do forgive you, Brian." I cross my arms, refusing to comfort him. "Now you need to forgive yourself."

"I'm not sure about that one. How can I forgive myself for being a horrible person?" He huffs.

I don't downplay the situation. I don't try to make him feel better about himself. I don't counter him by saying he's not a horrible person. What he did was pretty horrible and if I attempt to lessen the impact of it all, it won't bring justice to what I endured, nor will it bring restoration to Brian. Neither of us wins if I try to lessen the blow.

"You forgive yourself when you realize you won't heal properly without doing so." I lean my head back and close my eyes, thinking about forgiveness and how freeing it can be. "You forgive yourself because you're choosing to put yourself first and find who you are and what your new purpose in life is."

"But what if I no longer have a purpose?"

"I believe those who suffer the most have the greatest purpose of all. They just have to be willing to serve it." I want to tell him that this situation restored my relationship with my father and seemed to have done the same between Dustin and my dad. But I don't think Brian would find comfort in that, so I keep it to myself.

"Yeah, I suppose you're right." He wipes his face, grabs his boots with one hand, and then wraps his other around his cane, pushing himself off the bed. I watch him as he walks toward me and take in how frail he appears. All the pills and drinking have not only wreaked havoc on his mind, but also his body and overall health. Brian stops right beside me as he's passing through the doorway. He stands still and quiet momentarily, collecting his words. "I'm going to make you proud." His dark brown eyes find mine and hold them, begging me to believe him. I do.

"I know you will, Brian." I smile. It's weak and he doesn't deserve it, but I hope he knows it's sincere. Sometimes knowing that the people we love believe in us gives us enough confidence to believe in ourselves. And I refuse to rob him of that when he could be holding on by threads as is.

"Goodbye, Echo." He walks away without another word. I stand like a statue until I hear the front door close behind him, then slide down the wall and let the sorrow of my newfound loss take over.

Chapter Fifty-Two

DUSTIN

I walk in through Dax and Lynsie's back door and make way to where I hear the commotion. I stop in the doorway to the kitchen and lean against the frame. A Braves game is on, and Dylan is fully immersed in it as he eats his cereal. Dax is just standing off to the side, watching my boy.

My boy.

Holy shit, I'm a dad.

Dylan begins yelling at the ump for a shitty call as the batter walks to first. I just snicker from behind, and Dax begins shaking his head in utter disbelief.

Dax walks toward me, and his expressionless face amuses me. It's something I don't think I've ever witnessed. Dax, being such an animated guy, completely blank.

"Duuuude." He throws his hands on my shoulders. "That kid right there. He is so you. So you, in fact, I feel like I'm back in our childhood again. Twilight zone, man."

"I'm sure it's not that bad." I laugh at Dax, and then more so at Dylan, who is up in arms at the baseball game.

"I give you five seconds." I cock a brow, and he further explains. "Five seconds to see he's your clone."

I shake my head and pat his back as I walk past. I grab a bowl from the counter and a spoon from the drawer and take a seat next to Dylan. Without taking his eyes off the game, he slides the Fruit Loops my way. It's not Fruity Pebbles, but beggars can't be choosers. After I fill my bowl, he scoots the milk over too. I feel like I should say thanks, but then again, this seems to be some sort of silent bond we're sharing, and I'd rather not jack that up.

I take a bite, then glance over. Take a bite, then glance over. Take a bite, check out the game, then glance over. I'm trying not to stare. I'm trying not to sit here and be overcome with emotions when it's all I want to do. I try to focus on the game, to let it take over this overwhelming and unfamiliar sensation that's settled in. With each bite I take, the less I look over at my son, and the more I start to focus on the game. Soon I'm shouting at the TV just like he is.

"What are you, blind?"

"The ball was clearly in his glove. It didn't hit the ground first."

"That pitch was far too low to be a strike."

"Who rigged this game?"

"Who's winning?" Lynsie asks, making her way to the coffee.

"Braves." I glance back and smile.

"Yeah, Aunt Lyns. The Braves. Best team ever. Salazar is smoking crack if he thinks his Indians are going to win." I love hearing how easy it is for him to refer to Lynsie as his aunt. I can only wonder what he'll call me. I don't want to force him into anything. It has to be of his own accord.

"Hey, bud, you wanna go grab some real breakfast?" I look over at my boy and just can't believe how blessed I am to call him mine. I want to grab him and pull him onto my lap, give him the biggest bear hug. But I also want the kid to like me.

"Sure. Under one condition." He looks me straight in the face, then cocks a brow to his hairline. I have to do everything in my power to keep a straight face. "Don't call me bud ever again."

I half laugh, half choke, unsure how I should react.

"Told ya, dude," Dax says from the kitchen, shaking his head.

"Then what do you want me to call you?" I stand and we make our way to the front door.

"Dylan's fine. Or son," he says matter-of-factly before he bends over to slide his sneakers on, then runs outside.

"Yours," Dax whispers from behind like some creeper. He's finding this far too amusing.

I jump the short distance off the porch and watch Dylan circle around my Blazer.

"This is badass, Dad," he says with such adoration.

I want to laugh and scold him all at once, realizing the conundrum of being a parent.

Then it hits me...

He called me *dad*. And I don't know if now is the proper time for that bear hug or to cry. Instead, I decide not to make a big deal over it even though it means everything to me.

We pull into Tootie Fruitie's and I'm thankful the parking lot is empty.

"Oh, this is the place Mom and Grandma brought me to the first time we came here." He yanks the front door open. Not a shy bone in his body.

"Did you like it?" I ask.

"Well, I wasn't very hungry, so Ma ordered me your specialty." He scrunches his nose. I want to ask him what it was, but I'm too stuck on the fact he refers to Echo as Ma.

As we wait for our food, I use the time for us to figure some things out. I don't want to make any decisions without his input.

"There seems to be a lot going on right now. How are you holding up?"

He shrugs, coloring a picture with his kid's menu crayons. "I'm pretty resilient. I just want my mom to be happy." His admission pulls at my heartstrings. That's my selfless kid. "But I think she'd be happy here around all the people who love her. It's basically just been me and her."

"And you're okay if that changes?" I ask, intently watching him.

He finally glances up. "Yeah. I want a real family."

I smile. I want a real family, too.

"How do you feel about meeting your other grandparents? Or is it too soon?" I regret the idea as soon as I mention it. If I haven't scared the boy away, my mother might.

"I'd really like that." He enthusiastically nods, then lifts up the picture he's been drawing. It's my Blazer with a sunset in the back. But it's the three figures standing in front of it, holding hands, that really undo something within me. He wants this just as badly as I do. And he also wants my Blazer. Little does he know it's already his.

MY MOTHER LOOKS at Dylan, who is beside me. I revel in the fact that he feels safe near me. I believe I have Echo to thank for that. She never kept me a secret from him. She told him anything and everything he had wanted to know, even sharing pictures. I wasn't something she wanted to keep hidden like I didn't exist. In return, our son has bonded with a man he's never known personally but has gotten to experience every other way possible.

"Oh my Lord," my mom says, walking up to Dylan. She looks back and forth between the two of us, doing a double take. "You cannot deny it. Not that you'd ever want to. He is a spitting image of you."

"That's exactly what I said!" Dax exclaims, coming in the front door. I just shake my head and laugh.

My mother crouches down in front of Dylan, becoming eye level with him. "Well, hello, Dylan. I'm your grandma, Jill. It's so very good to meet you."

We hang out at my parents' house for a while since my son can talk circles around all of us. I bet he could even talk them around Dax.

"All right. I wish this could last longer, but Dylan has to get back home tomorrow for school."

"When do we get to see him again?" my mom asks, her voice shaky.

Dylan stands beside me, and I put my arm around his shoulder and pull him into me. "There're still many unknowns that we are going to have to figure out."

My mom goes to say something but thinks better of it. Such a small gesture that speaks volumes. Maybe she is learning, after all.

We begin our five-hour drive and Dylan starts asking me all sorts of questions about the Army and war, which led to my injury.

"Did it hurt?"

"Yes, initially. But I don't remember much of the incident."

"If you could go back and change something that day to keep from losing your hand, would you?" Man, this kid is deep.

I stare out the windshield and really think about his question. I used to question fate. I believed it wasn't fate that was responsible for things happening to people, but that it was luck. They had just gotten lucky, and I'd be the guy who'd never get to experience the high. But now I'm a firm believer that things happen for a reason. Every choice leads you to where you're destined to be. If I still had my hand, I wouldn't be here.

I glance over, surprised Dylan is watching me intently. I shake my head. "No, I wouldn't. You and your mom are a far more valuable appendage than my hand was. There's just no comparison." Dylan and Echo are my heart. I can survive without a hand. But no one can survive without a heart.

"Okay," Dylan replies. "So a fake hand...do you ever want one?"

I laugh. "A prosthetic? I think I'm good without one."

The closer we get, the more dread and happiness sink in. Dread that I'm going to have to say bye to my son that I just met. And happiness that I get to see Echo, but just long enough to make sure she's okay and drop Dylan off.

"Dad"—he pauses, and I don't think I could ever get tired of being called by that—"do you want Mom back?"

Without an ounce of hesitation, I reply, "More than anything in the world."

"Then you have to win her back." He shifts his little body my way.

"I know, son. That's what I've been trying to do. You have any ideas?"

"I might have a few tricks up my sleeve," he says in a devious tone, rubbing his hands together.

I would say boy am I in trouble, but I believe it's safer to say boy is Echo in trouble to have two of me.

Chapter Fifty-Three

ECHO

March 2015

Things have finally gotten back into a groove with me and Dylan. I'm still trying to figure out things long term, but I know for the interim this is where we belong. I refuse to move Dylan from his school and ball team mid-school year. I hated always being on the move and then having to make good impressions to make teams because I never had the stability of one team to grow with. I promised him once the school year and ball finishes, we can discuss other options. This is a team decision. I won't be deciding anything that he doesn't approve of.

I stand at the fence on the other side of the dugout so I can be front and center watching my third baseman. I try not to yell at the umps. I try really hard. But sometimes I do wonder if they were dropped on their heads multiple times as babies.

"Are you frickin blind?"

"Oh my gosh. His foot was on the base."

"Do I need to come do your job?"

"I can't even watch."

I turn around in disgust, looking at the ground, and run into a body. "I'm so sor—" I stop as soon as my eyes meet his. Dustin stands in front of me, wearing our boy's team shirt and a backward hat that's holding down his grown-out hair. His beard is longer and fuller, and I have the strong urge to give it a tug. His shit-eating grin tells me everything I need to know. I just gave him the reaction he was hoping for.

"What are you doing here?"

"I'm here to watch our son." He looks away, waves at Dylan, then his eyes meet mine again.

"Well, the umpires suck." I yell the last part, and he laughs.

"Sweet, let's holler at them together. Maybe we can both get ejected and make Dylan really proud."

I raise my brow. "I'm not sure if you're being for real or a smart-ass, but let's." I loop my arm through his, and we walk to the bleachers.

We spend the remainder of the game cheering Dylan on and yelling 'Pitcher has a big butt' at the other team. I was sure our son was going to be embarrassed to even acknowledge us after, but to my surprise, he came running and threw his arms around both of us. All I can do is look at Dustin and try real hard to hold back tears. This is it. This is what we've been missing out on. This is what we've all been missing out on. This is what Dylan wants and deserves.

"You did so good," Dustin says, ruffling Dylan's hair.

"Thanks, Dad! Are you coming to my next game?"

"I will be at every single game," Dustin promises and I know I'm about to start seeing a lot more of him. I can't help the excitement that ignites within me. He grabs all Dylan's ball equipment and walks us to my car. Opening our son's door first, Dustin kneels in front of him, telling him how well he did, ending it with 'I love you, son,' before they give each other a big, long hug. He then makes it to my side.

"I hope it's okay that I showed up unannounced."

"Yeah."

"The last time I saw him, he had asked me if I'd come. I couldn't let him down."

"You should be here. I just know it's a far drive."

"I will make the drive as many times as I have to until the day there isn't distance between us."

"Dustin," I start, but he hushes me by wrapping his arms around me, pulling me in.

"I know. There are unknowns. But what is known is that I love you, Echo."

I nod against his chest, wanting to acknowledge his words. He pulls away and gives me the biggest smile as he walks off backward.

"See you next week."

And for the next two months, Dustin shows up at every game, walks us to our car, and tells me he loves me before making the five-hour drive back home. And each time it's become harder and harder to watch him leave, and I count down the days until I get to see him again.

Chapter Fifty-Four

ECHO

May 2015

Today is our championship tournament and I'm one nervous mom. I pull into the parking lot early, hoping to get us good seats as people come and go during the games. I see Dustin's Blazer and it surprises me that he's beat me here. I send Dylan off with his glove to find his team, and I grab his ball bag out of the back. I stand at the bottom of the stands, trying to determine which dugout our boys will be in so I can sit his bag down.

"Echo."

"Echo."

"Echo."

"Echo."

"Echo."

"Echo."

"Echo."

Different voices say my name at different octaves like they are in fact trying to mimic the sound of an echo. I swirl around and search the stands. Taking up the entire row at the very top sits Dustin, Dax, Lynsie, Dustin's parents, and my parents. They're all wearing the same shirt that I can only imagine Dustin's mom made. My heart is so happy it could burst. I run up the stairs two at a time, making my way to Dustin first. I throw my arms around his neck, and he quickly wraps his around my waist.

"I know this is for our son. But you don't realize how much it means to me and how much it's going to mean to him."

"I would move the ends of the earth to make you both happy. I hope you know how much you mean to me." His voice shakes. I lean back just enough to look deep into the green eyes I've loved my entire life.

"How'd I get so damn lucky?" I say before crashing my lips into his. All I want to do is deepen the kiss and weld myself to this man. That's why I've held back for as long as I could because I knew one kiss would never be enough.

"I'm the lucky one," he says, pulling away, and I'm thankful he had the strength to do so.

"Finally," Dax says, dragging each syllable out. We all laugh because yes, fin-a-lly.

Lynsie smacks his arm. "Like you're one to talk."

"Hey, Ma!" Dylan hollers from near the dugout.

"What?" me and Jill say in unison. We look at one another and laugh. Something I never thought we'd do. In fact, us all being here together is something I never thought would happen. Then my gaze returns back to the man who put it all together. And as if my heart wasn't filled with enough love for him, it grows even more.

"Why are you looking at me like that?" His hand grips my waist, holding me tighter.

"Because I'm ridiculously in love with you, Dustin Ryan Adams." I smile brightly at him, unable to deny or hide my feelings any longer.

"You did it, Dad!" Dylan hollers as they wait to take the field.

"Whatdya do?" I ask.

"I won ya back."

"I've always been yours," I admit.

"I know." He leans down and kisses me once more. "There's much more where that came from, but right now, it's time to cheer on our son."

AS WE'RE HUGGING everyone bye, Dax whispers in my ear, "Before I go, I need your input."

When we're far enough from the others, he begins pacing back and forth before stopping in front of me. "Will Lynsie hate me if I never propose?"

His question shocks me.

"Umm, is this a trick question?"

"Okay, let me reword that. I know Lynsie wants to marry me, so with that being a known fact, can I just skip the proposal part and go straight for the tying the knot part?"

"Oh." I let out a sigh of relief. "You had me worried. So, like, instead of a surprise proposal, have more of a surprise wedding?"

A slow smile spreads across his face, showcasing a few of the similarities he and his brother share, such as the sharp jawlines. Though Dax doesn't have the dimples and it's a real injustice. "You are brilliant, Echo." He bear hugs me, lifting me off my feet.

"You two have some explaining to do." I hear as Dustin makes his way over. I giggle, peering over Dax's shoulder.

Dustin approaches, wearing a humorous expression, and crosses his arms as he leans back against my car. "Enlighten me to what I just stumbled upon."

"Well, big brother." Dax strides up to Dustin and places his hand on his shoulder. "We have a wedding to plan. Will you be my best man?"

"Well, duh. But when did you even get engaged?"

"That's exactly why Dax showed up," I explain. "He wants to skip that part."

"You must be pretty damn confident, bro."

"Well, duh," Dax shoots back. "I wouldn't be building a life with her if I wasn't. That'd be a waste."

"Then why the rush?" Dustin asks.

"Because my girl is ready to make it official, and I'm in the business of making her happy," Dax says matter-of-factly.

"Okay, so what all do you want and how long do I have to get this together?"

"We," Dustin corrects me, and I look over, raising a brow. "How long do we have to get this together, Dax?"

"I'm thinking next month." Dax hugs me again and gives me a spin. His giddiness apparent. "You're the best."

"Ahem." Dustin fake coughs behind me.

"Oh, hush and just stay back there looking pretty. We both know who's going to be doing the work." Dax's words make me giggle.

"I'll show you pretty," Dustin mumbles.

Dax walks off and Dustin pushes himself off my car and walks over to me.

"What's wrong?" he asks, tipping my chin up, forcing me to look at him.

I let out a breath. "I got—"

"We," he corrects.

I smile and roll my eyes. "We've got two weeks to pull this off." I bite my lip with worry. "What did I just commit to? What if I can't get everyone there?"

"I think this just means you and Dylan need to come home now. You know, so we can plan this wedding." He winks.

"Is that the only reason?" I raise a brow, urging him.

"No." He pushes my hair behind my ear then glides his thumb

across my cheek. His eyes hold mine with such an intense desire, freezing me in this moment. "I'm ready to have my life within arm's length at all times."

"Wow, that sounds very clingy-ish, Dustin." I tease, gripping his hips with both hands, pulling him closer to me.

He smiles and what a glorious site it is showcasing my favorite dimple in the world.

"Honey, arm's length is the PG version of my clingy-ness. If it was up to me, I'd be conjoined to you for the rest of eternity, but since we have a son to raise that's not an option."

"Speaking of Dylan." I look around the parking lot, seeing the last of the cars pull out.

"He went with your parents. I hope you don't mind. I just wanted to have you to myself for the night."

"Oh," I say, feeling a bit shy suddenly. Or maybe it's the butterflies fluttering that have me speechless.

"Yes." He wraps his arms around me, pulling me flush against him. His mouth hovers so close I can feel his breath teasing my lips. "I want to be clingy with you tonight." He admits, before his lips lightly press against mine. It's not needy and rushed. The kisses are slow and deliberate as we etch the feeling to our memory. But they've never left. No matter how hard either of us tried, we've never been able to escape the memories of each other.

The last of the field lights shuts off and Dustin pulls away. His eyes are wide with excitement as a big grin covers his bearded face, reminding me I still need to give it a good tug. "I have a surprise for you." He can barely contain himself as he grabs my hand, pulling me behind him.

Once we are away from the parking lot, the only thing lighting our path is the big full moon above us. It's like it's a beacon, beckoning us. I don't ask where he's leading me because I'd follow him blindly anywhere. We are almost to outfield when I notice the pallet of blankets on the grass. I throw my hand over my mouth. He didn't do what I think he did.

"Dustin." I say in awe.

"You haven't even seen the best part." He hunches down in front of me. "Giddy up, pretty lady."

"I mean, you on the ground in front of me is a nice view." I jump on his back and hold onto him.

"I'm about to give you a nice view." He glances back and winks.

I rest my head on his shoulder and take in the closeness of being wrapped around his body. We come to a stop and I take it as my cue to slowly slide down. I stand at his side and intertwine my hand in his. I look up and lean against him. The most beautiful canvas hangs above us with all the stars scattered about.

"Ahem." He interrupts me.

I finally look out in front of us. I take a few steps and drop to my knees. "This isn't—I touch the telescope and look it over—this can't be the same one."

"I told you you're present would always come with me in tow."

I jump to my feet and spin around to face him. I step up to Dustin, wrapping my hands around his biceps as I hold his stare. My eyes start to gloss over from the overwhelming emotion I'm unable to control and I'm incapable of forming words. I begin shaking my head and he grabs my chin, tilting my face up to his. He leans his forehead against mine and we just stand like this momentarily...no words needed.

"I know." He says before kissing my forehead. "Now go find our constellation."

I bounce up and down a few times before turning away from him. I stare out into space for what feels like eternity. I could never get tired of God's majesty that surrounds us.

"It's gorgeous. Wanna look?" I peel my eye away and look over at Dustin who is sitting on the pallet of blankets, watching me intently.

"I've been staring at the night sky the last thirteen years to feel closer to you. Now that you're here with me there's nothing more beautiful I'd rather stare at."

I walk the short distance to where he sits and straddle him. He groans from the pressure and tightly wraps his arms around me. I let my fingers trace the side of his face, pushing back his loose hair.

"I want to kiss every scar." I lightly press my lips to his temple and trail kisses down to where they disappear beneath his beard.

"That's a lot of kisses." He shivers and pulls me in tighter. The motion causes me to gasp. "Echo." His voice is raspy with need. "I'm not going to be able to control myself with you sitting on me like this."

"I want you to lose control." I whisper in his ear.

"Say no more," He lays us down, rolling on top of me. I look up and I'm not sure I've ever seen a more beautiful view in my life. Dustin's face looking down at me with such love and adoration with the sky above encasing it.

Chapter Fifty-Five
DUSTIN

June 2015

The plan is for Echo to keep Lynsie in her studio until we cue the music. We convinced her that we need family pictures and should have their pond as the backdrop. It wasn't a lie. There will be plenty of family pictures taken. We tried coming up with better ways to set this all up without her knowing, but this idea seemed like the safest to execute. We had far too much to keep secret to risk her figuring out anything. Just like getting her parents into town. Family pictures are a logical excuse.

Everyone is quiet. Stealthy, ninja-like quiet as we quickly get the chairs in place. We all get into our positions. I stand near the dock next to Dax, taking my place as his best man. Lynsie's dad stands near the door of her studio, ready to escort his daughter down the make-shift aisle. The sun begins to kiss the water behind us, giving the most beautiful backdrop.

The music begins and I watch as the door opens. Lynsie smiles big and hugs her dad, unaware of what's taking place. Echo's dad meets her halfway and escorts her the rest of the way down. She stands across from me, and I can't help but fantasize about our day.

Mr. Price takes his place, and we all watch in anticipation as Lynsie finally begins looking around, taking in her surroundings. The only thing lighting the backyard is the sunset. Dylan plugs in the lights and switches the song. The dangling lights in the trees shimmer around us as Lynsie covers her mouth in shock. She looks at all of us, and then over at the man whose arm she's holding.

She looks around with awe, catching every little detail. Amazement fills her eyes as she stares at Dax and tears begin to follow. Sweet Lynsie is a crier. My sweet, sensitive sister-in-law covers her mouth as she chokes back a sob.

She regains her composure and gives her soon-to-be husband a devious smile. "You sneaky boy," she whispers and then looks back and forth between me and Echo and wags her finger.

Dax grabs her hands into his, intertwining their fingers.

Echo's dad begins the speech, cutting a lot of the fluff out.

Dax pulls out a piece of worn paper and unfolds it. Lynsie instantly tears up, bringing a hand to her mouth. Then he clears his throat, "Ahem.

Lynsie, my love, I want you for life.
   The only thing left is to make you my wife.
   I'm usually good with words,
   But when it comes to you, I'm at a loss.
   Nothing I say could ever be good enough.
   So let's cut to the chase, and go against the grain.
   Let's skip the engagement and jump in the fast lane.
   We aren't promised tomorrow, and I want no regrets.
   Become Mrs. Adams, and make it a day we never forget."

• • •

"I do!" she yells, jumping into his arms and wrapping her legs around his hips. We all begin to clap and cheer for the now happily married couple.

I watch Echo as she wipes away tears of joy. She's so happy for her best friend. She's so happy for them being happy. Now I have to come up with my own way to make her feel just as

special as Dax did Lynsie. My brother isn't the only sly Adams boy. It's time for me to look around in my hat full of tricks. Or maybe ask my son since he seems to have a hat, as well.

Chapter Fifty-Six

ECHO

This feels weird. Almost surreal. My dad and I back in the last backyard we ever practiced in. The yard where I finally perfected my pitch. I haven't even attempted to do what he's asking in over thirteen years. I left my sport behind when I had to leave the other thing I loved behind.

"Dad, I haven't done this in years," I say, causing his face to drop momentarily. The fact that I gave up that dream that he instilled into me as a young girl makes him sad. Hell, it made me sad knowing that I had to give up the colleges that wanted to give me full rides. But I'd never regret the reason why I did. It's not like they would have accepted a pregnant player.

"Just one pitch, please." His eyes light up. "You were such a natural. You only think you've lost it because you haven't wanted to do it." He walks up to me with a smile, and I smile back.

Him and my mom were only supposed to swing by on their way out of town to grab Dylan for a few days. But now I feel it was just a plow to get me to play catch. I know he's trying to rekindle the main thing we use to bond over. But then he holds out a glove in one hand

301

and a softball in the other. I gasp as I grab the glove. I trail my finger along the discolored bottom part of my old glove. I pull the opening back and see where my name is still barely visible. After all these years, he held onto it. I thought he surely trashed all my belongings—especially the ones we bonded over.

"Thank you," I say as a tear slides down my cheek. I quickly wipe it away.

I hold my empty hand out for the softball he's still holding. "Got your glove?" I ask with a smirk, sliding my hand into the old, worn leather. It's just as soft as I remember and still fits perfectly.

He starts walking backward, reaching behind with one hand. "Right here," he says with a wink, holding up his glove he had tucked in the back of his pants.

I roll the ball in my hand, getting reacquainted with the seams and finding that perfect placement of where I want my fingers to grip. I drag my foot into the dirt, lining out my pitcher's mound. I place the toes of my right foot on the line, and with my gloved hand, I cup my right hand with the ball, swing my arms forward, drop them, lean into my right leg, and rotate my right arm almost full circle behind me as I do. Once my arm is pointing toward the sky, I push off with my right foot, swinging my arm around as my left leg shoots out in front of me. My right foot begins sliding up from behind as soon as my left one connects with the ground. All while my pitching arm rotates full circle once before my hand releases midway near my hip during the second rotation.

I hear the sound of the ball smacking into my dad's leather glove and satisfaction washes over me. I can't even control the huge grin breaking out across my face. That felt so good. Yeah, I've played catch with my son here and there when he was younger, or before he was "too cool" for me. But I always kept myself from seeing if I still had it when I'd question myself. I didn't want to chance the memories it'd drag out. I wanted to keep all things relating to

Dustin, and even my father, buried. It kept the guilt at bay—temporarily.

Dylan was a daily reminder that I would never be able to hide away. Not that I'd ever want to. I'd choke down the pain and memories for that boy of mine. Out of all the things I've done in life, right or wrong, he's been the one thing I'd never change, no matter the consequences.

"Whew." My dad stands from his crouching position and shakes his gloved hand. "You sure you haven't been practicing that?"

"I swear." I laugh, amazed that I do, in fact, still have it. I hold my gloved hand up, signaling him to toss me back the ball. I want to do it again.

He tosses it back. "This time don't go easy on me."

"Okay, old man," I tease, rolling the ball in my hand. I dig my toes into my makeshift mound and push in a little deeper, drawing my line out even more. He crouches back down and I take my stance. I do everything the same again.

Just faster.

I push into the ground even harder with my right foot, giving me more height as my left foot flies in front of me. Left foot lands. Arm swings around once. Right foot slides up from behind. Arm swings around halfway. Hand releases ball. Ball instantly slams into Dad's glove, knocking him on his ass.

"Holy shit, Mom," I hear from behind. "You are badass."

"Dylan," I say with a laugh.

"Sorry. I'm just referencing what Dad said." Dylan shrugs like that gets him off the hook.

And sadly, it does.

I look back at Dustin, who walks up to our son and places his hand on his shoulder from behind.

"Sorry." He shrugs, just like his son had. "But you are badass, Striker."

I just shake my head. I'm so in trouble with these two. But I wouldn't have it any other way. I get lost in staring at the boys in my life. Dylan is a replica of his father—in every way. It amazes me how alike they are when they spent over a decade apart.

Apparently, genetics go beyond looks.

And these handsome, stubborn, goofy, blond-haired, blue-eyed babes are all mine.

"Dustin," my dad says, walking up to my boys. He extends his hand out. Dustin has his arms draped over Dylan, and sticks his right hand out, shaking my dad's.

"By chance you were a pitcher as well when you played ball?" my dad asks sincerely, wanting to know. Baseball has always been his thing. That's why I was pushed into it at such a young age. I knew that he and Dustin could bond over the love they shared for the sport back when we were in high school, but that was only if my dad could get over his stubbornness.

But it took that long for me as well.

Guess it's one of those genetic things.

"No, sir. Third base."

"Ahh. Just like good ole Chipper Jones."

"Yes, sir. He was my idol." Dustin smiled, gripping Dylan's shoulder with his hand. I love how close the two of them are already. It's like this long-lost, instant connection.

"I happen to have tickets for the game next week. I'd love for us all to go. But understand if—"

Dustin stops him. "Sir," he says as he playfully wraps his arm around Dylan's neck in a chokehold and rubs his forearm across the top of his head, messing his hair all up. "I believe you had us at 'tickets.'"

I laugh and walk over to my boys, standing next to them with my arm around Dustin.

"There's only one condition," my dad says, tossing the ball up in the air. Dylan breaks free of his father's hold to catch it. "No more calling me sir."

Dustin grins then. "I'll try, but no guarantees."

Dylan yells, "Hey, Dad! Watch this!" And Dustin stops and does just that, giving our son his full attention. "I bet you can't do this," he says as he begins juggling the softball and what looks to be a tennis ball.

"You got me there, son." Dustin laughs, holding up his handless arm. I giggle at the lightheartedness. Dustin has come a long way in such a short time. I know it's because I was right. He might be missing his hand, but that wasn't the problem. It was his wounded heart that was the issue. It just needed to be mended.

All of ours did.

Dustin continues watching our son with such pride and adoration. I know he would have been the most amazing dad from the beginning. I hate that we were robbed of that. I plan to give him that experience one day. It's one I know he'd truly cherish.

My dad holds out his hand, and Dustin places his in it. As they shake hands, my dad puts his other one on top, fully enclosing Dustin's. "Thank you for serving our country. You truly are a hero in and out of the uniform. We are blessed to have you as part of our family."

"Thank you, sir," Dustin replies stoically. He usually waves off being called a hero. I'm so proud that he didn't this time. My father cocks a brow at Dustin's use of sir again, and I giggle to myself. "Mr. Price."

"Just call me Eric," my dad clarifies.

"Well, Eric. It's been really good catching up with you," Dustin says. "But as you know, I have some business to tend to." He winks.

My dad pats Dustin's shoulder as he heads for the gate. I watch as he retreats, and Dylan continues juggling the balls. Luckily, the porch light gives him enough illumination to catch the balls with his hands and not his face. I glance upward, watching as the stars begin to blink down on us.

"Hey, babe," Dustin says, and I swirl around in his direction. "Catch." He tosses a yellow softball. I look down, read the black letters written on it, and gasp.

D+E 4-EVER

BE MY WIFE

ONE YEAR LATER

Chapter Fifty-Seven

DUSTIN

July 2016

I open my eyes, catching the last glow of the Orion's Belt on the ceiling above as the sun begins to spill in, filling our room. I roll to my side and snuggle up against Echo's back, nuzzling my face into the crook of her neck as she lightly snores. My hand roams back and forth against her stomach, beckoning our sweet baby girl to move for Daddy. Echo's hand finds mine and leads it farther down. She stops and applies slight pressure. The movement beneath our hands causes my emotions to stir. I'm not sure I'll ever get used to the overwhelming feeling of happiness I've felt since this woman came back into my life.

"Thank you for sharing," I whisper, placing a kiss below her ear.

"I wish I could share more so I could get some sleep," she mumbles.

I smile and rub her extended belly one more time. Being a father to Dylan has completely changed my life in the best way possible. But getting to experience this from the beginning has turned me into a complete sap. I believe the overall journey is to blame. It's made me appreciate life more. It's made me love more. It's made me a better man so I can be a better husband, father, brother, and son. It's made me an all-around better human.

I kiss the love of my life, the mother of my children, my reason for breathing...my wife one last time before rolling out of bed. It's time to get a start on those early morning practices I promised Dylan we could do before freshman year begins.

Freshman year. I have a high schooler.

I yank my shirt over my head as I round the hallway. My boy stands propped against the wall, tossing a ball. I swear he's grown a foot since last summer and will be taller than me in no time.

"Mornin', Coach." He smirks and I feel like I'm looking in a mirror at my younger, carefree self.

"Hey, it's still Dad at home." I wrap my arm around him, pulling him in for a hug. "Leave Coach for the field."

"Deal."

"Did you eat breakfast?" I ask, making my way to the kitchen.

"Yep, had my Wheaties," he replies as he plops down on the couch.

"Well, I'm going to make myself some coffee and something to eat before we head out."

"Maybe I should call you old man," Dylan teases.

"Hey, I heard that. So I must not be that old."

"You're my old man," Echo says, wrapping her arms around me from behind.

I twist my body in her grip so I'm facing her and drape my arms over her shoulders. Her hair sits on top of her head and although she looks so tired, she glows in the most magnificent way.

"I'm whatever you want me to be." I bend down and kiss her forehead. Her stomach growls and we both laugh. "Got it. Chef it is."

"Anything but eggs," she says with a shiver. "The smell does something to me." Echo pulls a stool out and sits at the kitchen island. "What's this?"

I glance over and she's holding up an envelope. "Probably junk mail." I shrug.

"Well, it looks important."

She holds it out, and the idea of trashing it crosses my mind, but I decide to open it to appease her curiosity. I begin reading and instantly regret opening it. This must be some sort of sick joke or a scam. I read it again closely, analyzing all the details, credentials, signatures, and embellishments that make it appear to be official.

"Well?" Echo stands up and makes her way to me.

"Umm." I swallow. "I've been nominated," I say with disbelief.

"Nominated for what?"

I look up, my eyes meeting hers. "A Purple Heart award."

"HEAR YE, HEAR ye," Dax's friend and former copilot, Peterson, says, walking up with a solo cup in hand as we all sit around the bonfire in Dax and Lynsie's backyard.

I shake my head and laugh. We all do. Even Zack laughs a bit at himself, knowing he's a clown. I can only imagine the type of hell he stirred up when he was a youngster. As he stands, I remember the story Dax told me about the suicide birds that almost took them out. He said how Peterson isn't everyone's cup of tea, but the more you fight to not like him, the more likely he'll win you over. Dax also mentioned how Peterson doesn't really have any family, so he made it his mission to take him in. And because of that, I'm willing to do the same.

"All right, guys. Simmer down." He motions with his hands. His face turns somber as we all sit around the bonfire and quiet down. All of our parents are here: mine and Dax's, Lincoln's, Lynsie's, and Echo's. It's such a surreal feeling to be able to have us all together. It's a feeling I never knew existed. I had always thought that if Echo and I were to ever exist as one, we'd be on our own little planet together. But here we are, the center of our own personal universe.

And I wouldn't have it any other way.

I wrap my arm around my girl and pull her into me. Then I place my right hand on her belly. "Have you thought of a name for our princess yet, momma?"

The moment I laid eyes on this woman, I never thought it'd be possible for her to look more beautiful, but then she told me she loved me for the first time. Then she told me she was still in love with me after thirteen years apart. Then she agreed to be my wife. But now, she's carrying our daughter, and I couldn't imagine a more beautiful sight to see. She just keeps proving me wrong.

She looks over and nods, biting her lip to contain her grin. "Yes. I'm really liking Desa Rose." I thought nothing would compare to the way she looked as she walked up to home plate to become my wife, and then this little bundle of joy happened. And the bigger and bigger she grows, the more beautiful she becomes.

She doesn't agree. But it's not up for debate.

"Then Desa Rose it is." I grab her hand and bring it to my lips, loving that she wants to keep with the D R initials.

"Three years ago, we lost an amazing man. Lincoln was truly a mentor, and he put up with my ass. It might not seem like it, but that day forever changed my life. Not to mention the second time when Dax saved my ass." Peterson continues, "I don't have much in terms of family, and I've never been good at making friends." He pauses.

I want to yell out something smartass-ish, but he's actually being serious, and I don't want to ruin the mood. Tonight is about Lincoln, and even though I didn't know him as well as I should have, everyone here loved him, and knowing the hearts that these people I'm surrounded by have, tells me how great he was.

"I just want to thank you guys for always welcoming me with open arms. It truly means a lot." Peterson takes a seat next to Dax, who wraps his arm around him and pulls him in for a side hug.

Dax hands his cup over to Lynsie before standing and runs his hands down the front of his shorts before reaching into his pocket to pull out a piece of folded paper. "I kind of feel like this is my memorial to him. I know I can talk to him wherever I am, and he'll hear me. I know he'd love us all being gathered around in his memory. He'd probably think we were crazy and say we should find something better to do, but deep down he'd love the idea of all his loved ones being together, and knowing he was the one to unite us is what would make him happy." He sniffles and wipes at his face.

I do the same.

"I wrote another poem for my best friend. And instead of only sharing it with him, I want to share it with him and his loved ones."

He clears his throat and then begins.

"Lincoln, man, it's been three years.
So much has happened since, but there will always be tears.

They're happy ones now, remembering what we all had.
I will always be the best I can be to make you proud.
But when it comes to being the best, I can only hope it's at being a dad.

Blu Skye's a beauty, that's a given.
She's the best sissy ever to her baby brother, always so loving.

. . .

Jett Fox is what we named him, bringing your stuffed airplane to existence.

    The things we come up with to keep your memory consistent.

I wish you could see us; I gathered the whole crew.

    Who am I kidding, man, you've got the best view.

Let me end this by giving credit where credit is due.

    I'm living this life that was never intended for me because of you.

I have my brother back in my life with his new wife by his side.

    She has the most adorable belly now, showing what she can no longer hide.

He briefly pauses, looks up at us, and smiles brightly with pride before continuing.

Both of our families are growing. That's more than obvious.

    I can only hope and pray that you'll continue watching over us.

I've said it once, I'll say it again, and I'll forever keep sayin' it.

    We love you, Wings. Don't you ever forget it."

Epilogue

BRIAN

November 2016

I haven't worn this suit since I attended the award ceremony for Dax three years ago. How fitting that I'm now suiting up for his brother's. Except this suit isn't fitting like it used to. In fact, it's snugger than I remember. I button the blue jacket and hug myself, making sure there's enough give in the fabric before grabbing my cane.

"My handsome boy," my mom says with such pride.

"You're just saying that because you're obligated to."

She walks up and places a fragile hand on my freshly shaven cheek. "You're not an obligation. You're my son. And you're handsome...just like your dad." She turns her gaze, glancing out the window, and I see the longing for what was. To a time when he was alive and the life they lived. Knowing I left her alone to deal with the aftermath of his cancer diagnosis and death has been the hardest thing to forgive myself for. What I put Echo through ranking second.

"Thanks, Mom." Her face turns back to mine, and I smile, bringing her back to the now.

"I think we have somewhere to be," she says, adjusting my tie.

My mom has been essential to my healing journey this past year. When I decided on this trip down memory lane, I knew she would be pivotal to include. I wouldn't be where I am today or doing what I'm about to do if it weren't for her.

It took me a while to get this planned. It had to be coordinated around the return of our platoon from overseas. That in itself is worth celebrating. But tonight, we're celebrating one person.

WE ALL STAND to the side of the stage where we can't be seen, and I watch the table Dustin and Echo sit at. She looks beautiful as ever. The jealousy I expected to feel is replaced with happiness and it surprises me. It solidifies my healing journey.

First Sergeant Mills takes the stage, and I watch Dustin's demeanor change. He straightens his back, sitting taller. His composure is stoic, but I feel it's taken him everything within to keep it that way. He always tried to act hard and impenetrable. But it was just a façade. That's evident now. We all walk around fragmented by what life has thrown our way, but we have the choice to continue a life in brokenness or decide to mend our hearts.

"Good evening," Mills addresses the crowd. "We are here tonight to honor a man I've had the privilege of being around most of his tenure in the military. Let me start by saying Sergeant Adams wasn't a delightful person to be around." Everyone laughs, and Dustin even nods in acknowledgment and shrugs. "He came into the Army with a chip on his shoulder, and boy was it visible. You see, we all have different forces driving us. Some simply join because they want to protect their country. Others do so because they can't afford college, and they want the opportunity for a better future. Some want to see the world and travel. And some, like Adams, do so because they are running with no clear destination in sight. But no matter how tough and impersonable he tried to be, protecting those around him was always his top priority. He might kick your ass, but he'd also be the one saving it in the line of duty. Which brings us to why we are here. Adams wasn't the only one running from his past. And when his past and present collided, his protectiveness didn't falter. In fact, it took over. I was recently made aware of the entirety of a situation and the self-sacrifice Adams did to protect the man who nominated him for a Purple Heart, Lieutenant Brian Williams."

I take my cue and make my way to the two steps that lead up the stage. I made sure to practice beforehand, so I don't accidentally lose my footing and fall on my face in front of everyone. Thankfully, railing lines the steps, so I have something to hold on to. Once I'm on the stage, I pause and look at the crowd. Echo throws her hand over her mouth, Dustin smiles, shaking his head, and Dax elbows him and points. Then unexpectedly and unwarranted, Dustin pushes his chair back, stands, and begins clapping as I make my way to the oak podium. Everyone else in the building follows his lead.

"Thank you, but this isn't about me. Well, that's a lie." I let out a nervous laugh, resting my cane against the podium. Everyone takes their seats, and I continue. "Truth is, I wouldn't be alive today if it weren't for Sergeant Adams. In fact, he saved my life twice and the second time is what I want to take this time to focus on." I grip my fingers around the wooden sides, balancing myself and taking a deep breath. "PTSD." I pause. "Shhh, I know. It's not something we're supposed to talk about. If we acknowledge it's real, then we're guilty of its outcomes, right? While enlisted, we not only have a duty to serve and protect our country, but we also have a duty to protect our fellow soldiers. No soldier left behind. As if being in a war isn't damaging enough, some of us return wounded but stripped of our identity and self-worth. PTSD: post-traumatic stress disorder. It was something I didn't fully believe in until it almost took me out."

I look down and shake my head, remembering how low I was in

that moment. I slowly glance up into the crowd, stopping at the table in front of me. Echo and Dustin give me a nod of encouragement. My eyes travel around the table, passing by Dax and Lynsie, then stopping at Echo's parents. They both smile and nod, urging me to continue. I feel the stage slightly shift before hands are placed on me from behind. I don't need to turn around to know. Dustin's face says it all. The rest of our unit is now on stage with me. This wasn't the plan, but the support gives me the strength to continue.

"You see, when I returned home, I was lost. I was injured, no longer had a career, and feared losing my wife. These things accompanied by pain pills and alcohol turned me into a monster I no longer recognized. The day I lost control and hit my wife was the day." I suck in a deep breath and pause to gain my composure. "The day I hit my wife was the day I tried to end it all. I was so ashamed of what I had done...of what I had become. You see, six months prior, Sergeant Adams saved my life during one of our missions. And that night, lying on the floor, overdosing on prescription pills, he saved my life again. I know he was coming there with the intention of kicking my ass, not saving it. But I think the urgency behind him doing so was because he knew." Looking down, I let the tears fall. "He knew," I whisper. The men behind me crowd closer around me and speak words of encouragement.

"So I want to end by saying it's easy for us to regret our past and wish things had never happened. But while I'm not proud of mine, I'm thankful for it because now that I've lived it, I can help others. Let's not forget that the war in our mind is more dangerous than any other war and we are losing far too many veterans to it. I'm alive because of you." I point out to Dustin.

And in unison, our entire platoon yells, "Sergeant Adams, come receive your Purple Heart."

Acknowledgments

Nine years ago, I wrote Brokenness, and it was a dumpster fire of a story. Life happened and I just threw it to the world hoping it'd stick but knowing I didn't give the characters the story they deserved. Then I went on an 8-year writing hiatus with this book haunting me the entire time. It was as if I couldn't find my way back until I rightfully tackled this book and gave it the story it was intended.

NINE YEARS LATER, I found my way back to this story and the love I first had for it. My passion to write returned and I know I only have God to thank for that. He's the one who instilled this passion within me in the first place. I told myself to just start from the beginning by reading through it and change things as I go. The past section was pretty easy as I didn't alter much of it, but I debated if I should include it and had taken it out. But the present section...IT KILLED ME. Let me just say it's much easier to write a book from scratch than it is to go back and completely rewire the story. But man do I love how it turned out.

NINE YEARS LATER, and I have completely given this story an upgrade—new name, Mended Hearts. New cover (isn't it stunning). And a whole new story for readers to fall in love with. The story that Echo and Dustin deserved nine years ago but I wasn't in a place to deliver it. I'm a firm believer in timing working out when it's supposed to and that's exactly why I was able to do a 10th Anniversary Edition for Broken Wings in hopes of it bringing more awareness to Mended

Hearts so I'm not just throwing this story back into the world with no safety net.

So, I want to thank the readers – the ones who've been with me since the beginning. Thank you for sticking by me during the duration of writing this book. You've stayed by my side, pushing and encouraging me to keep going. This book wouldn't be here today, without your support.

I want to thank the new readers for giving Broken Wings a chance after it's been out for 10 years, and I come across as a newbie / unknown author. It means more than you ever know when you give an indie author a chance in a world filled with so many amazing authors and stories.

This book has been in the making for a solid 10 years. I won't remember everyone who's had an impact on it, and that really sucks. I just really hope each and every one of you who reads D + E's story falls in love with it just as much as I did writing it this time around. And I hope you guys continue to stick around because I have so much more to share with y'all!

A special thanks goes out to Brian Pool – yes, he's also a character in the book. Without your insight into being deployed and helping me shape the scenery to a more accurate account, I would have been lost. Google will never compare to someone who has lived it. I will forever appreciate your time and help, and hope I did what y'all experience as much justice as my fictional self could. Thank you for your service to our country!

Finally, I'd be remise if I didn't thank and acknowledge my kids. I began writing when they were barely in school, and now they're all almost adults. I pray they see the passion, grit, and determination it takes to follow your dreams and to never give up. Everything I do is for them.

About the Author

ERIKA ASHBY GREW up an Army Brat, spending most of her childhood in Oklahoma, where she finally put down roots in 2003. She currently lives in Edmond, OK where she faithfully attends NORTH.CHURCH with her kids. She's a blessed mom of four who loves Jesus and serving others. Her hobbies include attending dirt track races, concerts, reading, DIY, and making red dirt shirts. Erika is an advocate of 'it's never too late to go after a dream'. After all, it wasn't until the ripe age of twenty-seven when she realized she had a hidden passion for reading. Up until that point in her life, she claimed to have hated it. Six months later, she was hit with another revelation: the desire to tell stories. Knowing she had failed all writing assignments in school, she set out on this journey mainly to prove to herself she could do it. So here she is today, claiming she's an author. Erika wants to encourage anyone with a dream to go for it. "We are our biggest obstacle, and only regret the chances we don't take."

Facebook: @authorEAshby
TikTok: @authorerikaashby
Instagram: @authorerikaashby
Website: Authorerikaashby.com